CW00517892

We Are Unknown

How much do we really know about those we
are closest to?

Janet Jones lives and writes in Somerset. She
has written several prize-winning short stories and
this is her first novel.

We Are Unknown

Janet Jones

Watersmeet publications

This book is dedicated to Mum & Dad, who often took us to the West Country and who encouraged our love of books and stories, and also to Peter, without whose support and encouragement this book would never have been completed.

PROLOGUE

The cobbler works on, after his shop has closed for the day. He is surrounded by a small mountain – a scarp slope one might say – of shoes. Elegant block dancing shoes, worn down by waltzing, rough working boots ridged with the soil and dust of a thousand days' work; stout men's day shoes shaped by miles walked, backwards and forwards to the train station or the bus; ladies sensible brogues, made for trips to the butcher and the baker, baby-walking and blustery days.

Slowly he works his way through the pile which has built up since his son has left the business, gone in search of greater riches in the city, riches which come from the brain not from the hand, which can be garnered in a suit not a brown overall, with clean hands not blackened nails.

As he puts the last tack in Mr Evans' boots he glances up at the shelf. A pair of ladies' court shoes, size 5, have sat there for weeks, he realises. He puts Mr Evans' boots to one side with their ticket, ready for collection, and reaches up for the court shoes. They are navy blue, well-polished, but well worn. He has made a good job of re-soling and re-healing them he thinks, and he wonders why they are still here with him, and not on the woman's feet. They are the sort of shoe worn every day, the sort of shoe that lends itself to many an outfit, so that they

1

might become a lady's favourite. He looks for the ticket which accompanies their stay with him and realises they have been sitting on the shelf far longer than he thought – they have been with him for half a year – six months with no owner clamouring to take them back. He checks the name on the ticket; he remembers the woman well – a pretty girl with a head full of natural blonde curls nestled into the nape of her neck; but a pretty girl with a worry on her brow and space in her purse where more coins should have been.

Now he thinks about it, he hasn't seen her for some while. How long? Who knows – he hasn't seen many people – not properly – over this hillock of shoes, not for some time. But he can't help wondering why she hasn't returned, why her everyday shoes, brushed and buffed, are still sitting on his shelf after six months.

A rap on the door – and as he peers round the dusty blind he sees in the foreground, looming large, Mr Evans desperate for his boots, and in the background a woman walking briskly to the telephone kiosk. The cobbler replaces the polished blue shoes on his shelf, still wondering why summer has passed through to dwindling leaves and falling sleet and still the woman has gone without her favourite shoes.

CHAPTER ONE

July 1952

The wireless was still playing as she walked back into the house – but there was no sign of Teddy.

She turned the dial and switched off the dance band, but the silence was immediately too much; she flicked it back on and waited for it to spark into life again, all the time still churning Teddy's words over in her head. They had crept up on her and begun strangling her, the minute they had left Teddy's lips. She knew it was running away – and she had promised herself that she wouldn't run away – but she needed to breathe, and so she had gone anyway, walking silently from his sight.

•

Children had been still playing in the park in the late evening sun, creeping up on each other in an animated game of Grandma's Footsteps, shrieking at each moment when they were almost caught. A solitary child worked the creaking swing, pushing it higher and higher until it was almost parallel with the ground; Alice turned away – the screech of the unoiled metal scratching at her already-raw nerve endings. As she stumbled on the uncut grass something had caught her eye, something on the ground.

3

It wasn't the sight of the magpie, lying still, which had halted her breath though. A clan of the black and white birds were circling on the ground in funeral procession. As they slowed, one hopped up and began to peck gently at the corpse; others followed suit. Unable to look away, Alice watched as the bird snatched up blades of grass in its beak and then laid them gently at the side of its dead companion; a parade of others did the same, and Alice was shocked to realise that tears were streaming down her cheeks – but whether for the mourned bird or for Teddy she had no idea.

●

As the music burst forth once more and danced around her head she slipped into a seat at the dining room table. The crockery sat where she had left it – with cold carrots and congealed Shepherd's pie decorating the plates. She picked at the crust on the serving dish, feeling like the pathetic woman in the Dickens novel, and spent a pointless minute trying to recall her name, when really she should have been trying to make some sense of the mess.

She shivered, rubbing a hand over the goose pimples on her arms as she began gathering the dishes together.

'It doesn't matter.' She wasn't sure if she had spoken the words aloud, but she stopped in her tracks. 'No – it doesn't matter, Teddy Hathaway, if it's "only for a few days", it really doesn't....'

The words – his words – weren't just the flippant announcement he had made them out to be. They had opened the door on the thoughts which had been jumping around and creeping up on her, like the game in the park, for weeks now; and his announcement had brought them to her shoulder and shaken her.

CHAPTER TWO

'I'm going away ... just for a few days.' The words had eventually tumbled out, too quickly and too quietly. He had gulped from the water tumbler in front of him, then clamped his fingers to his mouth, as if to stop more words escaping.

Teddy had been avoiding her eye for many a week, avoiding her presence, avoiding any time together. She had watched him playing with the food on his plate for the best part of ten minutes, then, fork abandoned, staring blindly out of the window, a flood of thoughts appearing to come and go. As she had glanced from the corner of her eye, Teddy had reached over and switched off the wireless – the Home Service – which they'd had on as much to fill the silence as for the announcements of the evening news. Britain's equestrian team had won a gold medal at the Olympic Games in Helsinki – news which would usually have put Teddy in excellent spirits, but today it seemed to pass him by.

Alice had said nothing. Expected or not, his words had caught in her throat like the food she had been attempting to swallow. It was far too hot for the mince and potatoes she had cooked, and the food had stuck to her lips.

'It's a work thing – got to go down to the West Country,' he had continued, looking at the picture on the wall above Alice's head.

She looked up in surprise. This she hadn't expected, that he would announce that work was involved. His job at the Ministry had always seemed an endless stream of tedious routine as far as she could gather. He rarely talked about it in any detail, but it had never appeared to be the sort of thing which would require anything more taxing than a stroll to the neighbouring office. She continued to eat, churning each forkful round in her mouth.

'Old Prendergast – you remember him?' Teddy fidgeted in the clock-ticking quietness of the room.

Alice vaguely recollected an older man in an ill-fitting linen suit and dinner-stained tie at a works cricket do last summer, but she gave no sign of acknowledgement.

'Well, anyway …' Teddy seemed anxious to fill the silence. '…Prendergast has broken his leg, old fool – trying for an extra run at the charity match at Little Buxton of all places …'

Alice glanced up at the overly cheerful voice, the attempt at levity, her eyebrow raised, waiting for the rest of the improbable story.

'Anyway, the long and the short of it is,' Teddy rattled on, 'Prendergast was due to carry out some fieldwork … but obviously he can't go gallivanting around the country with a gammy leg, so Atkinson has asked me to go instead.' Teddy gabbled, seemingly eager to get his story out before Alice could interrupt his practised words with an awkward question. 'Quite a coup, old girl – they could have chosen anyone, but it's me who's been given the job. A bit more money in the offing as well, which obviously won't go amiss. Good news all round, eh?'

Teddy finally looked over at Alice for approval, like a boy who had scored his first rugby try with his father watching critically from the sidelines; and to give him his due, she thought, this was a more intricately embroidered story than he would usually have come up with. And so she wondered if there might be the smallest element of truth in it; it was worth testing at least, she thought.

'So what exactly is this fieldwork you've been asked to do?' she said, placing her knife and fork at "half past six" on her finished plate.

'Ah, well, that's the thing,' Teddy had jumped straight in. 'Atkinson has sworn me to complete secrecy.'

Alice shook her head.

'No, no really – he made it very clear – he said specifically that I'm not to discuss it with anyone – not at work, not even you. He's practically threatened me with treason ...' Teddy laughed too heartily at his attempted joke, but as he saw the expression on Alice's face his voice faded away.

She had started to clear the plates and dishes from the table. Teddy's plate was still half-full, and she scraped the tepid food into the vegetable dish. He tensed. She knew he hated her cleaning the plates at the table, something his mother would never have countenanced. She continued to scrape and stack.

'Look,' Teddy started again. 'I know this whole thing probably sounds a bit of a cock and bull story … but really, this is exactly how it is.'

Alice stood, arms folded, allowing the silence to hang in the air like a summer fog.

'All I can tell you is that this work …well, it could affect the whole country –other countries as well, if it all comes off …'

Even for Teddy, this was a story too far. Alice let go of the stack of china and the bundle of cutlery so that they clattered noisily to the table as she slumped onto a chair.

'So who else is going?'

Teddy glanced up, and for the first time during the whole conversation he looked her directly in the eye.

'Oh, it's just me – definitely a one-man job.'

His eyes were unblinking, and Alice was unsure whether that was a sign of the truth or just flat-out blatant lying. With Teddy it could so easily have been either.

'So, you mean they're entrusting a matter of national importance - just to you?'

For a moment Teddy looked as surprised as Alice at the significance of her words, as if, until that point he had given no thought to the implications of what he was describing. She watched as he began chewing the skin at the side of his thumbnail – something she hadn't seen him do in months. She hesitated, wanting to apply more pressure on him – to squeeze him like a boil and force the truth out; but as she'd looked at him the significance of what he was saying screwed all her arguments into an angry ball so that she couldn't separate one thought from

9

another. Walking out of the door had seemed the only option.

CHAPTER THREE

She didn't hear Teddy return that night; he must have hunkered down in the box room because there was no sign of him when she woke. He'd left breakfast dishes on the table, and as she pushed them into the sink, emptying the kettle of boiling water over the congealed food, she churned over what Teddy had told her. A torrent of questions was building in her head, and the more she thought about them, the more the lack of opportunity to direct them anywhere felt like a gag, tied tightly around her mouth.

She rampaged about the house, trying to channel her anger, haphazardly hanging Teddy's clothes back in the wardrobe, scrubbing at toothpaste drips on the bathroom floor – but nothing stopped her mind from constantly charging back to the idea that Teddy was having an affair. Eventually Alice could contain herself no longer; the walls of every room had begun to close in on her as she tried to unravel her knotted thoughts and she snatched her coat and hat from the hall stand, with no more thought in her head than to get away from the house.

She pulled her bicycle from its usual place, propped against the garage, and rammed her shopping bag into

11

the front pannier. As soon as she reached the end of the road she started to pedal like fury until she reached Sixpenny Hill, where even her anger wouldn't get her to the top without stopping. She pushed the bike the last few yards, allowing the breeze to cool the perspiration on her skin before she jumped back on and freewheeled towards the town. The gentle wind calmed her spirit a little, and by the time she was parking her bike by the bandstand Alice felt a little more positive.

She made her way to Woolworth's, running through her shopping list in her head. Although she only needed a couple of items from the haberdashery department, Alice took her time wandering around the high counters, looking at the choices of stationery and make up and sets of china. She had no spare money – the housekeeping Teddy gave her seemed to be more stretched every week, barely covering their food – but it didn't stop her planning what the house would look like when she could afford to buy a few extra bits and pieces to make it her own. When she could stretch out her daydreaming no longer, she went and purchased the two reels of cotton – one yellow, one blue - and the yard of elastic, then checked the coins left in her purse. She had just about enough left for a quarter of corned beef for their dinner, and was about to head for the International Stores; but the image of Teddy sitting smugly at the table suddenly came back to her. 'Bugger it,' she muttered and strode back to the make-up counter. She picked out a scarlet lipstick and handed over the change from her purse before any sense could return to her.

The thrill of the purchase began to wear off as she drifted aimlessly around the meagre-looking stalls of the

Tuesday market, reluctant to make her way back home. There were piles of empty wooden crates, others half-filled with what seemed to Alice mainly wilted leaves and mud.

The stall holders were doing their best with the limited produce they had gathered, singing out their sales patter to entice customers, holding out their wares in the scoop from the scales, keen to sell everything before the end of the day.

In her rush to leave the house Alice had forgone her lunch, and the nibbling in her stomach made her regret her impulsive buy. A banana was what she really fancied – or a still unattainable orange - something that would ooze down your chin and make you lick your lips. Visions of a Carmen Miranda-type fruit bowl with pineapples and melons and cherries, unseen for so long, swam in her head, and she was so caught up in the image that she jumped in shock when someone tapped her on the shoulder.

'Josie!' Alice had gasped. 'How wonderful to see you. It's been an age!'

'I've been calling out to you for at least five minutes,' Josie giggled, and the two women hugged and gabbled and laughed like only old friends can, until Josie took Alice's arm and steered her towards the café in the middle of the square. 'Tea and a bun - come on, my treat,' Josie said, pushing open the door before Alice could object.

The thin young waitress, uncomfortable in her black dress and starched apron, fidgeted from one foot to the other as she waited for a break in their conversation.

They ordered quickly, sniggering at the girl's silent reprimand as they resumed their flood of chatter.

'So what's it like then – this married woman lark?' Josie asked.

'Oh, don't even ask,' Alice moaned, as the waitress sniffed and plonked down a brown teapot, spilling a little on the white tablecloth.

'Oh come on Alice, you're so lucky – you have a lovely house by the sounds of it, and a wonderful husband and …'

'And? And what? That's just it Josie. I have the washing and the polishing, and the cleaning and the ironing … Do you know what the highlight of my day is?' Alice went on before Josie could answer. 'Unpicking an old jumper so that I can knit myself a new one – or maybe I'll find some antimacassar to embroider that I've seen in Good Housekeeping.' Alice's animated face became more serious; she put down the bun she had been holding and not eating. 'At least you still have a job, Josie. I had to give mine up when I married Teddy.'

'A lot of people would …' Josie tried to interject.

'It's just not like our days in the WAAF,' Alice went on, hardly taking a breath. 'I know we moaned about the routines and the uniform and all the rest of it, but it was fun wasn't it? We were always out and about, driving some big wig to his meetings, and we got into such scrapes didn't we? Do you remember when I rescued the Wing Commander's dog from that rabbit hole?' Alice smiled, thinking about the moment, then looked dejectedly at Josie. 'But now – oh, I don't know … it's just ….'

14

Josie hesitated. 'Some people might envy you, you know,' she said, pouring more tea. They were silent for a moment, both lost in their own thoughts. 'And anyway,' Josie perked up, 'I'm sure it won't be long before there are tiny feet running round the house.'

Alice was silent. It felt like admitting defeat, to share what she was thinking.

'Something wrong?' Josie asked, her cup suspended between saucer and mouth.

Alice looked down at her half eaten bun.

'Oh, I'm sorry.' Josie looked crestfallen. 'None of my business. Shouldn't ask.'

'No, no – it's okay.' Alice smiled weakly at her old friend. 'It's just that – well – since the honeymoon – Teddy just doesn't seem that bothered about me.' Alice turned her head towards the window. 'Well, not in that way, if you know what I mean.' Despite their old friendship, something stopped her from mentioning the trip which Teddy was about to embark on.

Josie looked up. 'Well, I'm probably not the one who should be giving advice am I? – twenty nine and still no husband. But maybe he's just overworked – tired, perhaps?'

'Well, that's what I thought - at first – I made all sorts of excuses for him. But…well … I think there's more to it than that.' She still couldn't bring herself to say it. 'He's always out on the town – just not with me.'

The church bells chimed the hour.

'Oh Golly, is that the time?' Alice jumped up. 'I must fly. No potatoes ready yet, and Teddy hates it when dinner's late.' Alice clutched her right wrist and then her left. 'Damn,' she muttered.

15

'What's the matter?'

'Forgotten my watch – that's all.' She smiled weakly at Josie, reaching down for her shopping bag. 'I must have put it down somewhere.' She smiled again, more genuinely this time. 'This has been wonderful Josie – we must do it again – when we've both got a bit more time.'

'Look, I'll check my rota for next week – or the week after – see when I've got an afternoon free.' Josie rummaged in her handbag and pulled out a battered notebook and a pencil. 'Here - scribble down your address and I'll drop you a line as soon as I can.'

Alice's heart sank. An image of their house came into her head, and it was probably not the picture which Josie had conjured up in hers. She knew she was being ridiculous, but she couldn't bring herself to invite Josie, or even give her the address; a spur-of-the-moment visit would be even worse.

'Look, it'll be much better if you telephone me,' Alice said quickly. 'That way we can make arrangements straight away, without having to wait for letters to go back and forth ...'

'Oh ... okay.' The smile had disappeared from Josie's face. 'It'll mean me going to the kiosk at the end of the road that's all, and it's not always free, so I don't know how quickly ...'

Alice took the notebook and scribbled down her number. 'Don't worry – whenever you can manage will be great. I'll look forward to it.'

Josie thrust her notebook back into her bag and pecked Alice on the cheek as she pushed her towards the door. 'Off you go then – Mrs Perfect Housewife – back to that man of yours!'

As Alice walked back to the bandstand to collect her bicycle she questioned what she was doing. She was so much in the habit of preparing dinner on the dot that she'd reacted to the chimes like a performing monkey. She'd abandoned Josie to the prospect of her miserable little bedsitting room, only to rush back for someone who was probably in the throes of being unfaithful to her.

But it was too late to return to Josie, and so she wheeled the bike as far as the town bridge. The river looked wonderful – two teams were rowing along the calm water, and despite her hurry, Alice was for a moment mesmerised by the regularity of their movements, pulling and dipping their oars in perfect harmony. A swan was leading her family of cygnets towards the bank where a woman was holding out a handful of bread. As she freewheeled away and headed off down the side roads towards Thursday Lane Alice's thoughts returned to Teddy and how she was going to manage the stifled conversation they would probably be sitting through again this evening.

•

As she bustled through the front door the telephone was already ringing. Alice dropped her bags and rushed to pick it up.

'Alice. I thought you were never going to answer.'

'Oh "hello and how are you, too" Alice thought as she braced herself for an onslaught from her mother-in-law. Just as she was about to make some feeble excuse, she heard Teddy's key in the lock. 'Oh, you're just in time Isobel, Teddy's just coming through the door.'

To her surprise, her mother-in-law, faltered. 'No, no – it's fine. It's you I wanted, but I'll call you again tomorrow. I expect you're busy now getting Edward's dinner...' The last words faded into the click of the call being ended, and Alice was left looking at a silent receiver.

'Who was that dear?' Teddy asked, throwing his trilby at the hat stand. 'Another of your admirers?'

'No – actually it was your mother,' Alice snapped, wondering what had got into the woman who would normally grab at the chance to talk to her beloved son rather than her daughter-in-law. 'She said she'd call back tomorrow.'

Teddy seemed hardly to have heard. 'What time's dinner? I need to be out by seven.'

CHAPTER FOUR

Alice hadn't quite forgotten about the call, but she was still surprised when the telephone rang just as she was clearing away the breakfast things.

'Alice. I need you to find something for me.'

Her mother-in-law's lack of social chit chat raised her hackles as it always did.

'Oh, what's that?' Her voice was terse.

'Edward's birth certificate. I don't seem to have it.'

'Do you need it for something specific?' Alice found a ridiculous pleasure in not bowing down at the first time of asking.

'Oh – oh it's far too complicated dear,' her mother-in-law dismissed her. 'Could you just go and look and tell me if it's there, dear. It's probably in his bedside drawer.'

Alice was tempted to slam the telephone down. How dare this woman presume to know her husband's habits better than she did? Instead she was silent.

'Are you still there my dear?'

Alice had never known anyone who could make innocent words so acerbic.

'I'll go and look. I'll call you back.' she put down the phone before she said something which Teddy would regret on her behalf. 'Bloody woman,' she muttered, as she stomped up the stairs.

She pulled open the drawer and ran her hand over the clutter – men's clutter - a small screwdriver, a bolt with a washer hanging loosely from the thread, a couple of neatly folded handkerchiefs, a handful of pennies and threepenny bits. She swept the debris from side to side, making little effort to find what she was supposed to be looking for; in fact willing the birth certificate not to be there at all, so that she could tell Isobel she had been entirely wrong.

Alice allowed her fingers to move to the back of the drawer, rummaging there without even bothering to look at what might be present. There was no paper, envelopes, documents of any kind beneath her fingertips, and she was about to give up, but as she made one final sweep of the drawer she touched on a small rigid rectangle.

Her first thought was that it was one of those slim boxes in which a jeweller might set a necklace or a bracelet, that there was ribbon holding the lid on the delicate trinket inside; the second thought, following rapidly in succession, was that she had got Teddy all wrong – that he had hidden here a surprise for her, a surprise he was saving for some appropriate time. She pushed it once more to the back of the drawer, reluctant to spoil Teddy's grand moment when he might hand over his specially chosen gift. It brought a sudden lightness to her – the thought that things might not be as hopeless as she had begun to see them - and an unexpected prickle of excitement at this surprise to come.

But then, just as she was pushing the drawer home again, it came to her that the box was not in fact a box – that it was too shallow, that her fingers had run down ridges on the sides; that the narrow band around it was far too stiff and coarse to be ribbon.

She pulled on the small handle once more, this time yanking the drawer until it hung almost out of its runners, and reached in.

What she pulled out was not a box but a small book, bound in red leather, gilt edges to the pages, held firmly in place by an elasticated strap.

She sat on the edge of the bed, turning the diary over and over. She had never so much as opened a single letter of Teddy's – not by mistake, and certainly not deliberately. She'd known plenty of women who regularly held their husband's mail up to the steam of the kettle so that they could peel back the flap and take in every word of the contents before resealing; but it wasn't her style.

She thrust the book back where she had found it, into the shadows at the back of the drawer and shut it with a bang. No, she wouldn't stoop so low. 'I'm going to sort out the garden,' she announced irritably to no-one except her mirror-reflection, and pulled her old gardening clothes from her wardrobe.

CHAPTER FIVE

Alice had never been much of a gardener; her mother had given her a square of thick clay soil for her own when she was eight years old, but after the initial novelty of watering it and slopping around the gloopy mud and pushing in twigs which never grew into plants, she had pretty much given up on it. One year she had managed a reasonable display of marigolds, simply by sprinkling as many seeds as she could over the patch, and throwing a jug of water over them whenever she remembered, but school and exams and friends had taken over after that, and the square had remained barren and deserted. When they'd moved to this house, Teddy had had big ideas about what he would do with the garden –colour-themed flower borders and prize vegetables – but none of it had made the transition from paper to soil, and it had fallen to her to keep the garden in some sort of order. The rationing, which seemed to be dragging on forever, had prompted Alice to try her hand at vegetables, and, when he'd poked his head over the fence and seen her pathetic attempts, Mr Pearson, their elderly neighbour, had started to coach her, directing what to plant, and when.

She pulled a fork from the garden shed and began attacking the potato patch with an excess of energy.

Normally she enjoyed the magic of the small white flashes appearing amongst the dark loamy soil, bending and unearthing handfuls of fresh potatoes, planning what she would make with them, and where the surplus would be stored. But today the fork stabbed through more vegetables than it scooped out, and she was irritated by the less than perfect harvest she was making. The image of the diary kept returning to her, and her concentration was anywhere but on the task in hand. As she brushed the soil from the last few potatoes, she had reached the point of thinking that a little knowledge might actually be a good thing – that breaking her own code and looking inside the diary might give her some insight into this man who, even after two years, was steadily becoming more of an enigma to her.

Overtaken by a sudden decisiveness, she left the basket of vegetables on the path and strode back into the house, abandoning her gardening gloves on the kitchen table. She ran up the stairs and pulled open the drawer of Teddy's bedside table once more. Without giving herself time to reconsider she snatched out the diary and flicked back the elastic strap; but then it came to her – that by holding another person's diary in one's hand you might be cradling a handful of their secrets or an insight into their most intimate thoughts. While the book stays closed the balance is maintained; but as soon as you look, as soon as even one page has revealed its contents, you have crossed a line. The other person's feelings and words have been transferred into your head, and you can never un-know them again.

She closed her eyes, and let the book fall open at a random page – as if putting the decision of what she might read into the hands of the gods. She took a breath and glanced down – but to her disappointment saw only blanks leaves. She allowed her fingers to turn just one page, and then several. Emptiness continued to stare back at her. Thinking that the diary might be another impulsive idea of her husband's which had never come to fruition Alice hurriedly fanned the pages, allowing them to flick through her fingers; a flash of blue-black ink jumped out, and then another and another. Now she just had to find those pages again.

Eventually, amongst the emptiness, she found an entry – Monday, 16th June – but there were no heart-rending thoughts, no confessions, just two initials. She flicked pages again, and the same two letters appeared twice more.

As Alice turned the pages she saw the same letters regularly appearing "J.F. 7.30pm"; "J.F. 7 o'clock". She cast her mind round all their friends; there weren't many, but certainly no "JF". She thought about the dates on which the notes fell, trying to think what she had been doing or, more to the point, what Teddy had told her *he* had been doing – but nothing rang any bells. She moved forward a few more weeks – still random entries at various intervals, some with "JF", some just times – but never any places. She could no longer stop herself; now that she had broken the seal on this private world she had to look for the date when Teddy had told her he was going away for work.

There, for two weeks on Wednesday, she saw in Teddy's neat copperplate hand simply the words:

"Rushcombe, North Devon – 3 days?"

Nothing more. No names or initials or any clue that this was anything other than the work event, he had outlined to her.

The lack of evidence, of any misdeeds, should have reassured her, but instead it left her more dissatisfied. Alice had convinced herself that there must now be more – that so far she had seen only a brief glimpse of the story. She needed to check the whole book, she thought, go through the days more methodically to find what she had obviously missed. And so she turned back to the front cover, skipping past the tables of pints and quarts, rods poles and perches; past the bank holidays and the international times compared to Greenwich Mean Time. But though she searched from January to December, there was nothing which gave any further clue to what appeared to be going on in Teddy's life.

CHAPTER SIX

'What's that old girl?' Teddy had been immersed in the book on his lap, only half-heartedly listening to Alice.

The atmosphere between them had been tense over dinner – too much "Pass the salt" and too little "How are you" - none of which was helped by the doubts which were beginning to creep into Alice's head. What if Teddy *was* telling the truth, she kept thinking as she blindly turned the pages of the newspaper. What if he really *had* been asked to go on this jaunt by his superior – and, to be honest, there was no evidence that it was any other way - then she might be making both their lives impossible over nothing.

The uncomfortable silences were just as much her doing as his, and now she needed to talk. She opened her mouth to tell him about the bizarre incident with the magpies in the park, wanting to share that disturbing image which kept recurring in her dreams, but she stopped herself. It was too peculiar, and she couldn't bear it if Teddy simply ridiculed her over it. No, if she were going to make a step towards reconciliation it had to be something neutral.

Alice flipped the newspaper pages back and forth, choosing the first article that caught her eye. 'Princess

26

Elizabeth ... well, I suppose I should say *Queen* Elizabeth now, shouldn't I - She's been opening a new housing estate – one of those new towns they've been building for people to move out of London after the war damage.'

Teddy's head was still down, concentrating on the pages of his book.

'All that smiling and being gracious when all the time she must want to cry for what's happened.' Alice turned the page, trying to make the story more interesting. 'I see she's stopped wearing black, but quite honestly she looks as though she'd be more comfortable if she could still be in mourning instead of that lovely summer outfit. ' Alice realised that she was boring even herself, and that Teddy was miles away, and she stopped, staring at the pictures of the young woman who was actually two years younger than Alice, and yet who seemed already to be making great strides in a world she'd been thrust into before she was fully ready.

'Any chance of a coffee, old thing?' Teddy interrupted Alice's thoughts, slamming shut his book. 'Think I'll go for a stroll round the estate,' he said, indicating their garden. 'Bring it out there would you, there's a dear.'

And there it was. Teddy was out of the door before Alice could even answer, and the gateway to reconciliation had been closed. He was carrying on exactly as if nothing had happened ...and for him, Alice thought, as she took the cups from the cupboard, life *was* exactly as it had been last week or the week before that. She didn't know how to act with him any more – what she really wanted was to rage and shout and get some reaction from him. But if she did that, she thought, as she started to make the coffee, then she would have to explain herself – to confess to reading his diary. And what if he then said 'Well, there's the door …' what would she do? After all, it was his family house; it had belonged to his grandfather and had apparently stood empty for months while the family deliberated on its future. But then Teddy's engagement to her had finally settled things – the house had been given to them as a wedding present. Well, loaned to them in actual fact, as Alice had come to realise later. Their names had not been put on the deeds –her mother-in-law was far too canny for that. 'But we can live in it as our own,' Teddy had told her excitedly immediately after his parents had made their announcement.

'But what if we ever want to move?' she remembered having asked him.

'But why would we want to do that, my little worrier?' he'd said. 'We've got everything we could possibly want here.'

So effectively, Teddy could do what he liked. She knew – well she thought she knew – that he wouldn't, that for the time being anyway, their current arrangement was just as convenient for him as it was for her, but she couldn't forget that he would always have the upper hand. And so for the moment, she would continue to provide dinner and coffee and a clean house, and go along with his ridiculous stories.

As she put the coffee pot on a tray, Alice glanced again at the royal pictures in the newspaper. There was something inspiring about that woman, Alice thought, something which made you realise that anyone had the strength to deal with adversity if they dug deep enough inside themselves. She closed the cutlery drawer with a slam and made up her mind. Whatever Teddy was up to, she was going to find out.

CHAPTER SEVEN

And so, on Tuesday morning, when she would normally have been luxuriating in that half an hour before she had to get up, letting thoughts drift around in that "otherworld" that existed only in her head - about what she might do if she came into money, what job she might excel at, or what names she might give her children, Alice was waiting only to hear the front door closing.

She pulled back the faded curtain an inch to check that Teddy was indeed on his way to the station, watching as he stopped to talk to Mr Baxter at number 49, then catching up with Mr Wilsden at the corner before turning out of sight. She didn't dawdle over her wash, smeared only the merest hint of face cream on her cheeks, and pulled on her oldest clothes.

She didn't give a thought to breakfast. She went immediately to the bedside drawer where she had found the barely-hidden diary yesterday. Alice pulled the drawer wider and searched amongst the contents she had only briefly handled the day before. Amongst the assortment of loose change was a French franc note, and it occurred to Alice that Teddy had never mentioned travelling to France. As she put the note down her hand fell on a small package, which she immediately started to unwrap; but then she realised that it was what the WAAF girls had referred to as "French letters", and quickly shoved it to the back of the drawer . A business card from a hotel in York caught Alice's eye, but she saw that it was dated 1947 and put it back in its place. There was nothing else of any significance, and Alice closed the drawer with a slam. She looked around the bedroom, then dragged the chair from the dressing table over to Teddy's wardrobe. She ran her hand blindly along the top but there was nothing but fluff and dust. She searched the bottom of the cupboard and the larger drawers, but there was naught but neatly stacked shirts and underwear, and a regimental row of highly polished shoes.

Alice flounced on the bed, perspiring and discouraged. Where else to look? The obvious move was to progress to Teddy's study, but something niggled at her, a voice in her head making her hesitate. When they had first moved into the house Teddy had immediately dropped his box of books on the floor of the small downstairs room overlooking the garden, staking his claim. 'This will do me nicely,' he had said, looking around, presumably already seeing himself sitting at a grand oak desk with leather-bound blotter, earnest books lining the shelves and a tumbler of whisky in his hand. In reality they had found a rather battered old desk in a second –hand shop, and the books were donated by Teddy's parents who probably couldn't wait to be rid of them, but the whisky bottle was as present in reality as it had been in Teddy's vision.

Alice stopped herself from tiptoeing as she went back down the stairs; she told herself that she was a grown woman and if she couldn't use all the rooms in her own house then really what was the point in anything. She strode down the bare wooden staircase and up to the door of Teddy's study. It was forever closed – even to any attempts to clean - and despite her reprimands to herself, Alice's hand still hesitated on the door knob.

•

She hadn't seen the room properly since Teddy had taken it over; it was surprisingly dull. There was an ingrained smell of stale smoke and Alice suspected that every book would give off a similar unused odour if they were opened. The desk was a messy sort of tidy. There were heaps of papers and files, but each was a distinct pile, one with a neatly folded newspaper sitting on the top. There was a notepad on the blotter, with Teddy's favourite fountain pen sitting atop a page filled with his beautifully neat handwriting in blue-black ink.

Alice craned her neck over the writing pad, trying desperately to resist the temptation to pick it up. She tilted her head from side to side, straining to read the words around the pen – words which, she realised, contradicted the beauty of the writing. The neat even rows of copperplate flowing across the page were graceful enough to be the framework of a love letter, but the words themselves spoke not of love but of presumptions, of theories and harsh technical terms.

They were, presumably, some notes Teddy which had been making as part of his work, something which he had put together after reading the papers which sat anonymously in their buff-coloured folders, each awaiting further attention. The words meant little to her – disappointed her, when she realised that no stranger was involved, no secrets were revealed - and her eyes moved from the notepad to the front of the desk and the array of drawers. It wouldn't have surprised her to find them all locked, but each one slid open as smoothly as the battered old timber would allow. She pulled first the middle drawer and then the right hand one, randomly casting her eyes over the contents, dismissing them almost before she had really looked.

Everything was too tidy, too organised. As she looked at the ranks of pencils lined up militarily in the centre drawer, the twelve inch ruler and a set square; notepaper squared up, unblemished and smooth, Alice supposed that there would be nothing here which would be of any use to her – nothing which would reveal even a hint of Teddy's secrets.

'Well, that's it.' She sighed loudly, glancing out at the garden which was comfortably sunning itself, flaunting its own productiveness and cocking a snook at her own fruitless efforts.

Reluctantly she pushed back the worn captain's chair, but as she stood, the newspaper on top of the stack of manila files caught her attention. She'd ignored it previously, looking for more personal items, but the bold Gothic lettering was different to any of their usual newspapers. The folded front page revealed a broken header "...derley Advertiser", and as she looked more closely she noticed that the paper wasn't a recent one. It dated back to April, which, given that Teddy would often be putting their own newspapers into the fire basket even before she'd had chance to open them, made the whole thing quite bizarre. If Teddy found something useful in a paper he would normally cut the article out and file it;

it was most unlike him to keep a complete newspaper which was nearly four months old.

Alice's hand hovered over the folded paper for only a moment before she picked it up and shook it out to its full size. As she turned to the front page, the complete extent of the Gothic lettering announced "The Alderley Edge and Wilmslow Advertiser".

'Wilmslow … Wilmslow?' Alice turned the name over in her head. It was a place she had come across before, she was sure of that. The name tickled at the back of her mind. Was it somewhere she had driven to in her WAAF days perhaps? She cast round again. Cheshire – yes, that was it, Wilmslow, Cheshire – she vaguely recalled a long drive through abysmal rain and low cloud. It had been miles away and had taken them half the day to get there.

Alice lay the broadsheet on the desk, and opened it gingerly, careful not crease or tear the thin paper, to leave any tell-tale evidence of her presence. Just as she bent forward to peer at the miniscule typeface, the telephone rang.

•

'Hello' she murmured, anxiety evident in her breathless voice.

'I thought it was customary to give your number when answering the telephone,' the distinctive tones of her mother-in-law enunciated rather too loudly in her ear.

'Good morning Mrs Hathaway … Isobel.' Alice spoke as though someone were pinching the skin on the back of her arm.

'Well it might be if you had bothered to return my call.' There was a pause, as if more contempt were being brewed. 'One does expect that when someone promises to do something that they will actually fulfil that promise.'

'Sorry Mrs Hathaway. It's been a bit hectic.' Alice rattled on before her mother-in-law could ask what exactly was so frantic in her suburban little life. 'Anyway, I've checked Teddy's bedside drawer - as you suggested – and there's no sign of his birth certificate.'

'Are you sure?'

'Absolutely Mrs Hathaway.' Alice was aware that she sounded like an over-eager Girl Guide, but nevertheless she continued. 'I could check his study if you like,' – the thought suddenly occurring to her that this would give legitimacy to her presence in Teddy's private world.

'Certainly not. A man's study is his own preserve. One wouldn't dream of interfering. I'll speak to Edward myself.' With that the line went dead and Alice was once more dismissed.

'Well why didn't you do that in the first place, you stupid woman,' Alice yelled at the disconnected line. The agitation however had given her a charge of determination. She marched back into the study, pulled out the chair and made herself at home at the desk.

CHAPTER EIGHT

'Oh, for goodness sake. It's like the telephone exchange in this house lately. I can't believe how many times that woman is going to call me.'

Alice had been looking through the pages of the Alderley Edge and Wilmslow Gazette, convinced by its presence that it must have some relevance to Teddy, but despite her efforts she had so far found nothing. The newspaper refused to move neatly back into its folds, and the more Alice tried to persuade it the more unresponsive it became. The continued ringing of the telephone increased her agitation, but eventually she managed to replace the paper on the desk. She dashed into the hallway, muttering about Isobel under her breath.

'Yes?' she blurted, breathlessly.

'It's Josie.' The voice at the other end of the line sounded somewhat put out.

'Oh – sorry,' Alice sighed. 'Sorry – I didn't mean to snap. I thought you were the dreaded Isobel again.'

'Mother-in-law you mean? Not your favourite person at the moment then?'

'Oh – I don't even want to start on that subject.' Alice pushed her unwashed hair back out of her eyes.

She caught sight of herself in the hall mirror and realised, as she listened to her friend, that she probably needed a long soak in the bath.

'Well, I was just calling to arrange to meet up again...'

'Oh Josie – that would be wonderful – just what the doctor ordered. I ...'

'Is there something wrong? ' Josie interrupted. 'Are you ill?'

'No, no – it's nothing that a good old natter won't sort out,' Alice hesitated '...And I have got a few things to tell you.'

'That sounds intriguing. How about Thursday afternoon?'

Alice replaced the receiver absentmindedly, and drifted back to the study. As she slipped into the captain's chair, her thoughts meandered between Josie and Teddy. She desperately wanted to talk to someone about what seemed to be happening, but the more she thought about it, the more she realised she didn't yet have any concrete evidence of anything actually going on at all. The newspaper again caught her eye; she pulled it towards her and began scanning through the main articles. A farmer's tractor had been stolen and the Council were concerned about the ongoing costs of repairing bomb-damaged public buildings. But what any of this had to do with Teddy she really didn't know; none of it made any sense to her.

She put it to one side and swivelled a little on the chair, looking across the landscape of the desk. There were two thick manila files, untitled and unlabelled, on one side, and to the other, a pile of what appeared to be random papers, stacked haphazardly.

Presumably contained within them all was the information which Atkinson had insisted that Teddy read before his field trip. She hesitated. Sneaking a look at a newspaper was one thing – it was public knowledge from the second it was out on the streets – but work files..? As her fingers reached for the top folder she heard Teddy's words "…he's sworn me to secrecy … can't discuss … not even with you …"

'Oh bunkum,' Alice spoke aloud. She flicked back the cover of the top file and began to read.

•

A key turning in the front door jolted Alice.

Goodness knows how much time had drifted past while she sat reading at the desk, she thought. In a panic, she realised that she was too late to leave Teddy's study by way of the hall. She could already hear him blustering about, dropping a heavy briefcase on the floor. She closed the file, hastily pushing pages back inside; she glanced across the desk, checking that everything was in its original place. For a moment she couldn't remember which of the files had been at the top of the pile or whether they had all been stacked together. She took the top one and left it in the middle of the desk.

'Alice. Alice – I'm home.'

She kept absolutely still.

'Alice – where are you? I'm home.'

She looked again at the file, deciding that it had, after all, been on the pile, and quickly moved it.

She pushed the handle of the French door, trying to manoeuvre it as quietly as she could. It creaked, but she managed to slip through the narrowest of gaps and pressed it shut again.

Her trug and secateurs were on the garden table, and she picked them up as she walked round to the kitchen door.

'Ahh – there you are.' Teddy stared at her, gin bottle in hand. 'I thought for a minute you'd run away from home –left me to fend for myself.' Despite his jocular tone his eyes continued to search her face.

'Just finishing off a bit of gardening – deadheading the roses,' Alice said, putting her basket down at the kitchen door, hoping Teddy wouldn't register the lack of dead flowers. 'Garden's a bit non-stop at this time of year,' she said, busying herself opening cupboards, finding tumblers. 'But the beans are doing well thanks to Mr Pearson.' She looked up at Teddy, glad to have moved the conversation to safer ground.

'Mr Pearson?' Teddy threw her a suspicious glance.

'Old man next door – you remember, he gave us all those plants, got our veg patch sorted …'

Teddy nodded, appearing bored already with gardening talk, as she knew he would be.

'Good day at the office?' she asked, feeling ridiculously like an actress in an American film. She opened the pantry door, looking to see if there might be a sliver of lemon left for their drinks – anything but give Teddy the chance to peer at her face and grill her with questions.

'Oh – the usual,' he said, sighing heavily. He wandered out of the kitchen and through to the sitting room, glass in hand. Alice followed, keen to head him off from the study for as long as possible.

'Any more news on the field trip?' It was her turn to study his face.

'No definite plans yet,' Teddy said, swilling his drink around in the glass, avoiding her eyes. He fidgeted in his chair, fiddling with his tie, running his hand through his hair. Still she said nothing, waiting for him to come up with more words, true or false.

'When's dinner?' he said eventually. 'I need to pop out later – but I'll just get on with a bit of work while I'm waiting.'

Alice held her breath as the study door closed. She waited for a shout, a call, an outburst of expletives at the disrupted desk, but the house was silent except for the ticking of the mantel clock, ten minutes fast.

CHAPTER NINE

Teddy

His eyes scanned the room. Something was different. He looked at the shelves, the desk, the chair – nothing he could immediately put his finger on, but something was not as he'd left it. He moved over to the desk, touching nothing, just allowing his eyes to wander across the surface. Folders neatly piled, his notepad and pen just where he had left them, in the middle of the blotter. A shiver fingered its way down his spine; he had no idea why – the sun was still blazing outside, the room was stuffy. He walked over to the French window ready to let in fresh air …. and there he saw that the key was on the floor. He picked it up, absentmindedly slipping it into his pocket, and returned to the desk. This time he picked up the batch of manila files and shuffled through them; they had been in order when he left them – reference numbers from 011 to 023; now 022 was at the top, 014 next. He didn't bother to look further, pulling the newspaper towards him as he replaced the files. At first glance it was still folded with the same square uppermost, but as he picked it up he was aware that the folds weren't quite as crisp as they had been, there was a bulkiness to the paper which hadn't been there before.

He turned to the window.

She knew something now, that was for sure – but *what* did she know? He wasn't so worried about the files – anyone in their right mind would be bored to death with the graphs and the statistics long before they got to anything of any importance … but the newspaper? For all her naivety, Alice could sometimes be quite astute. Had she put two and two together – or was she so hung up on the idea that he was going away for an illicit few days with some floozy that she hadn't thought beyond that?

'Teddy – dinner will be five minutes.' The call came from across the hallway, but he didn't answer; he sat drumming his fingers on the desk as he considered what his next move might be.

CHAPTER TEN

'So come on then, tell all.' Josie gabbled, intrigued no doubt by the conversation they had had on the telephone.

The two women had found a table in the corner of the tearoom, away from the thin assortment of other customers. Four other tables were occupied, and all seemed to be full of bobbing heads bent in whispers, linked by shocked glances.

Alice could feel Josie's gaze, her eagerness for a good story; but as she wound her fingers anxiously through her blonde curls her friend's impatience clutched at her, like a hand over her mouth, and all she could do was to stare straight into space and shake her head.

'Oh Alice – I'm so sorry. Here you are, in the depths of despair, and all I can do is make the whole thing into a second-rate drama …'

'No, no, it's alright …'

'No – it's not alright. I'm being thoughtless and selfish.' Josie paused, and they both sat looking at their teacups, unsure how to ease themselves back into their normal easy conversation.

'He told me on Tuesday.' Alice said eventually, having to force the words out.

'Told you what?' Josie looked up, her wide eyes showing off the incredible blue of her irises.

'He's going away …' Alice began, and then hesitated, uncertain how to continue. Two pieces of cake sat untouched on their plates.

'What – for good?'

'No – no, it's not as bad as that,' Alice almost smiled. 'Well, at least I presume it isn't. He's just off gallivanting – I think.' At last she took a sip of her tea, on which a skin had begun to form.

'What – just like that? Going away – without any explanation? Do you think …?'

'Well – he *says* it's for work,' Alice interrupted, not sure that she wanted to hear her own suspicions spoken out loud by a third party.

Josie raised her eyebrows. 'And what do you say?'

Alice looked down at the cotton tablecloth, running her finger along the freshly-pressed creases. She rubbed her forehead, trying to push away the headache she realised had been hanging over her for days.

'Oh Josie – I don't know. I questioned him – tried to see if I could catch him out, but …'

'But….?'

'But he didn't falter. To be honest, his story was so outlandish that I doubt Teddy would have been ingenious enough just to make it up. But …'

Josie put down her cup and turned to Alice. 'So there obviously *is* a "but"?'

Alice nodded. 'I think there's someone else…' She looked back down at the table. She pushed away the slice of Victoria sponge which Josie had ordered for her, her appetite now completely disappeared.

'But what makes you so sure?' Josie poured more tea into both their cups, and topped up the pot with hot water.

'It's probably nothing ...'

'Well, it's obviously something. Teddy tells you he's going away for work and you immediately think that he's having an affair ...' Josie's voice rose.

'Sshh!' Alice put a hand on her friend's arm and looked around, but if any of the women sitting nearby had heard, they were doing a good job of concealing it.

'Sorry,' Josie whispered, 'but you're obviously not telling me the full story.'

Both women sat in silence, Josie playing with the sugar in the bowl, Alice watching the movements of the young waitress. She realised with a sudden clarity that all of this had become a web of facts in her own head, based on only the thinnest sliver of evidence, and she wasn't sure that she wanted to present what now seemed a pathetic story to her friend. Eventually she looked over, to find Josie staring back at her.

'Well – you're not, are you?' Josie said, 'Being honest?'

'I found a diary,' Alice began eventually.

Josie raised her eyebrows but remained silent.

'It had some initials .... They came up time after time ...'

'But they could be ...' Josie interrupted.

'JF,' Alice continued calmly. 'I've gone through everyone I know – we know – and there is no-one with those initials. And if it were work,' she carried on before Josie could interrupt again, 'If it were work – then why would it be in his personal diary, and why would it always be in the evenings and weekends?'

Josie closed her mouth, as if all her possible answers had been stolen away. 'Where has he told you he's going?' she asked quietly.

Alice sighed, turning back to the window. A child was having a temper tantrum on the pavement, refusing to get back into its pushchair after being allowed to totter around on its reins. She watched as she tried to decide.

'Derbyshire,' she said suddenly, with no idea why she was lying. 'The Peak District – some field work that's needed apparently, and the usual chap who does this sort of thing has broken his leg.'

Alice looked across at Josie, who was deep in thought.

'So – the diary and the trip away … Don't you think, well, that maybe you're putting two and two together …?

'And making five? I could easily be – I mean, when you say it out loud it does seem a bit thin, but when you put it together with how Teddy's been – you know, like I told you before –not really that bothered about me – well it does seem …'

'A bit of a co-incidence?'

'Oh, I don't know Josie – I'm not sure of anything at the moment.' She paused, trying to get her thoughts straight. 'But what I do know is that something just isn't right – and I don't think I'm going to be able to rest until I know what it is.' The strength of Alice's words made her friend sit back, stunned by what she was hearing.

'What are you going to do?' Josie murmured eventually, absentmindedly breaking the remains of her cake into crumbs.

'I haven't got the slightest idea,' Alice whispered, shaking her head. 'The whole thing is such – oh, I don't know, I don't understand any of it,' she said, biting her lip to hold back the tears. But immediately she had spoken the words Alice realised that she had known all along what she wanted to do – what might actually bring her some peace of mind or some truth – and that was to follow Teddy on this trip to the West Country.

CHAPTER ELEVEN

Did Mother telephone you?' Teddy asked tetchily as he waited for Alice to pour coffee.

'Umm – yes – she called this morning.' Alice was unsure how much she should be saying.

'Well, I hope you didn't give her whatever it was she was asking for.'

It was unlike Teddy to be so het up about his mother. Normally he would be singing her praises, even when she had said or done something totally indefensible.

'She's poking her nose in where she has no right to,' Teddy continued. 'Really, one would think I was twelve years old when you consider the way she tries to take over my life sometimes.'

Alice bit her tongue. It was too tempting to suggest that, occasionally he could be more like a twelve year old than he might care to realise, where his mother was concerned; sometimes he reminded Alice of a boy wheedling for toffees or sixpence extra pocket money.

'She seems to have got some ridiculous idea into her head …'

'What sort of idea?' Alice was keen to know what it was that had shaken Teddy from his normally carefree state.

'Oh, don't ask me. It doesn't even bear repeating,' Teddy sighed, shaking his head despairingly. But he hesitated, as if wanting to continue.

'Is there anything I can do?' This seemed to Alice rather more than the birth certificate issue which Isobel had spoken to her about, and Alice was intrigued, if not slightly apprehensive, to find out more.

'No, no, definitely not. I've told her – we've had a falling out actually – I've told her in no uncertain terms to mind her own bloody business.'

Alice looked around her. She had no issue about anyone putting Isobel in her place - it was about time someone stood up to her – but that conversation with Teddy – the one about the house, their home, came back to her immediately. She felt as if she were balancing on a narrow ledge, where only the slightest tap would push her into the unknown.

'Was that a good idea Teddy? I mean the house …'

'Look, I can't let that woman rule the whole of our lives. If she really wanted to help, she should be handing over the money, not stuffing it into some stupid investment …'

For a moment Alice was distracted by the "our" in Teddy's rant; he was normally very much an "I and me" person, and she was surprised at how touched she felt to be included in his world for once. But the whole question of money, and more importantly, getting on the wrong side of Isobel, was beginning to make her anxious. She knew that money would continue to run through Teddy's fingers like sand regardless of how full his fists might start out, but she also knew that Isobel would do exactly as she pleased, whatever anyone else might say or think.

'Perhaps if you asked them to lunch...?' Alice immediately saw the look on Teddy's face. 'I'm not bowing down to her Teddy – you know I wouldn't do that. But perhaps we can smooth things over a bit …?'

She realised she was gripping the arm of the chair as she regarded her surroundings, not wanting to be parted from any of them – and definitely not by some silly disagreement between two inordinately stubborn people. She turned away to wipe an unexpected tear from the corner of her eye, coughing to dispel the alarm she could feel building in her chest.

When she looked back, she saw that Teddy had been watching her; his face had softened.

'Bit of an over-reaction on my part, d'you think?' he said, forcing a smile.

'Look – you know I'd be the first in the queue if there was an opportunity to put your mother in her place, but however it is that she's upset you, I'm sure she was only trying to help.' Alice didn't believe a word of what was coming out of her own mouth; she might as well have been reading a Grimms Fairy Tale, but for the moment she had too many other things on her mind without getting into a battle with her mother-in-law, when everyone knew there would only ever be one winner in that conflict.

'If we must then,' Teddy sighed again. 'I suppose you're right. Ask them to lunch on Sunday and we'll do our best to be nice to the old dragon. You never know, she might change her mind.'

Alice smiled, but inside she still felt the churnings of anxiety. For her own part, she had no problem with Isobel's plan; but it seemed that Teddy's desire for money was increasing and Alice could only speculate on the reasons why.

•

'I wanted it to be a surprise – for Edward.' Isobel had followed Alice into the kitchen. 'I just thought life insurance might be useful.'

Alice could think of no polite answer, her mind still focused on getting through the day without any hiccups. She had been mildly pleased with her efforts at Sunday lunch. The potatoes were crispy and the beef tender, rather than the other way round as it often was; and at least nothing had burned, as it had been on the previous two occasions when her in-laws had been invited. She had even been able to cope with being ignored as Isobel talked incessantly about people who Alice had never heard of. Douglas had given her an occasional wink, and topped her glass up whenever Isobel and Teddy weren't looking. She'd escaped to the kitchen as soon as she could after they'd finished the apple crumble, but her heart had sunk when Isobel's head appeared round the kitchen door.

Isobel picked up a tea towel, looked at it vaguely, and put it down again. 'I didn't want to call you again, in case *he* answered the telephone,' she said, indicating her son in the other room with a nod of her head. 'He got so very cross with me the other day.' She stood watching intently as Alice sorted dishes, piling them on the draining board, scrubbing at a few more, soap suds plastering her forearms and dropping to the floor in frothing hillocks. 'But I really do need that birth certificate.'

'I have looked…' Alice grabbed the tea towel to dry some pans so that she could make room for more. As she moved across the kitchen to put them away she slipped on the soapy linoleum, just managing to grab the table before her legs went completely from under her.

'Careful dear,' Isobel muttered eventually. 'We don't want any accidents, do we?'

Isobel's laugh sounded to Alice as though there was nothing her mother-in-law would have liked better than to have a widowed son for everyone to fawn over.

'I'd really appreciate it if you could have a more careful look my dear.'

'I'll have another look – tomorrow,' Alice said pointedly, 'When I'm a little less busy,' and carried on with her chores in silence.

Isobel must have seen the annoyance pass across Alice's face. 'Oh, silly me – I'm distracting you – I'll leave you to make the coffee shall I?' Isobel turned, with a smile that didn't reach her eyes, and made her way back to the men.

Alice threw the tea towel across the room and eased herself down onto the kitchen stool. A muscle in her groin had twanged when she slipped, and the pain was making her feel slightly sick.

She was suddenly struck by the idea that Isobel was being extraordinarily pushy about something relatively unimportant. Was she really trying to buy life insurance, or was there more to this than Isobel was letting on? Alice scolded herself. She was seeing puzzles and secrets wherever she looked just lately. Isobel was probably the last person to be involved in any sort of intrigue; she was unnervingly matter-of-fact about most things, although Alice had often suspected that Teddy's deviousness came directly from his mother's milk.

As she continued her battle against the dishes, Alice convinced herself that this whole exercise was just Isobel's attempt to prove a point, to maintain her control over her precious "Edward", and to ensure that her daughter-in-law was kept in her place – in the dark and in the kitchen.

'Is that coffee nearly ready old girl?' Teddy was calling out from the sitting room. 'We're almost dying of thirst in here.'

She continued to massage the inside of her leg as she hobbled around, reaching to the back of the cupboard for a matching sugar bowl and milk jug, loading a tray with the best china.

Teddy's father was doing his best to keep the discussion more general as they sipped their coffee – too slowly for Alice's liking – but the conversation was as arid and artificial as a dried egg.

'I see that they are going ahead with introducing charges for prescriptions under the National Health Service,' Alice said after yet another awkward silence.

Isobel raised an eyebrow, at what she presumably considered an unsuitable topic of conversation for a woman.

'Don't you think that undermines the whole purpose of the Health Service?' Alice continued, when the room remained silent.

'You make a good point dear.' Isobel eventually replied. Her apparent compliment had all the subtlety of an army truck in attempting to close down the conversation.

'I also think that charges for dental treatment will simply mean that poor families will stop attending the dentist,' Alice continued, determined not to let Isobel dictate the direction of events.

Teddy looked unsure where all this was going, and tried vainly to change the subject; his father though encouraged Alice, 'I couldn't agree more – one pound for the average working man is far too much in my opinion and …'

'Anyway – it's time we were going, Douglas.' Isobel interrupted her husband mid-sentence, already standing, putting her spectacles back into her handbag. 'Thank you for lunch,' she said, kissing her son's cheek.

Alice went ahead of them all into the hall, lifting Douglas's hat from the coat stand and holding it ready for him.

The old man winked at her again as he took it. 'Lovely lunch my dear. Best apple crumble I've had in ages - and definitely the most interesting discussion,' he added, looking slyly at Isobel, and chuckling as he went out.

Teddy followed his father but Alice was conscious of Isobel holding back, fiddling unnecessarily with the clasp of her handbag.

'What we spoke about earlier dear,' she said with a sidelong glance through the open front door. 'It occurs to me that I might also be able to do a little something for you – if you could let me have your birth certificate as well.' The older woman bustled out, leaving Alice with a question on her lips, but Isobel was already shouting 'Door, Douglas, door,' waiting for her husband to perform the necessary courtesies to usher her into the vehicle.

As they stood on the doorstep waving at the receding car, Alice looked at Teddy and wondered if any of them really had any idea at all what was going on in their lives.

CHAPTER TWELVE

Alice tugged at the lid of the tin. It had always been snug, but with years of little use it had become even tighter, budging only after Alice had gone to the kitchen and found a butter knife with which to attack it.

As had happened many times before when she opened the box, the contents presented themselves at the same time both familiar and new. She recognised the old photographs – of a tiny her perched on a dilapidated deckchair, broken doll on the grass beside her, ribbon falling out of her generous blonde curls. Another of her sitting by a Christmas tree in her dressing gown, next to a small doll's house. She remembered yearning for that house for weeks and months after she had seen it in a shop window, and how her mother had alternated between "we'll see" and "Father Christmas has to buy for lots of children you know; he might not be able to afford it this year." And then, on Christmas morning, it was there. The scent of pine needles came back to her, the tangerine at the end of her stocking, the tempting scent of the rare roast dinner tickling her nostrils, the feeling that she almost dare not touch the doll's house in case someone came and said 'No, no that's not yours … you play with the ball instead.'

Alice put down the sheaf of photographs, collecting up those which had escaped the pile and slithered to the floor. She put aside notebooks and diaries belonging to a distant grandfather, and paperwork about her mother's grave and the cost of the plot and the date her mother's stay there would need to be reviewed. At the bottom of the tin were several brown envelopes, but she knew exactly the one she was looking for. There was only one with her mother's handwriting, crookedly stating that this was her daughter's certificate.

She had no idea how many times she might have taken it out and looked at it. On the first occasion she had been just a child; it had been a strange experience, with her feeling then as though she had existed forever in this world and then seeing the document stating that she had only been here since 1924. It made her feel insignificant, like the tiny pinprick she always felt herself to be when she looked up at the galaxy on a clear night – when it was densely dark but the more she concentrated the more stars seemed to appear, until there seemed not a single patch of sky without a star; patterns and swirls and images, travelling on into infinity above her head, making her shrink to the minutest speck in the significance of all things.

The small square of cream paper, printed in red, stated brashly just her name and her date of birth – nothing more significant, bland enough to send Isobel into a rage of frustration. But of course Alice had seen the fuller version; she remembered how shocked she had been when she had first come across it.

She had been pootling around in her mother's bedroom as she often did when her mother left her on her own for a while. 'Don't open the door to anyone,' she would shout out as she always did before slamming the front door. Alice had loved that moment of silence when the wireless had been switched off and her mother's chattering had gone with her out of the garden gate. Alice had pulled open her mother's dressing table drawer and opened the small boxes inside, but on that day the flowered brooch and the sparkling necklace which she had always wanted to believe was diamonds and which, even at that age, she knew were not, didn't hold their usual fascination. She had seen them once too often and they were no longer secret treasure. She pulled open another drawer and then another; scarves, handkerchiefs, nothing of any excitement. She picked up a lipstick, which unusually her mother had left by the mirror; but she knew, if she used it, that the colour would linger, that however hard she tried to rub it away there would be a tell-tale streak of red left behind in some crevice of her mouth. She had replaced the gold tube and looked around for some other amusement. That was the first time she had found the tin. As she wobbled on the old chair, peering around the top shelf of her mother's wardrobe she had spotted the corner of the box behind two hats. She had stretched as far as she could, but only the very tips of her fingers reached the tin; gradually, gradually she had fingered it forward until she could manoeuvre it to the front of the shelf. It was too heavy for her small arms and she had been afraid that the whole thing might crash to the floor. So she had forced up the lid and pulled things out above her head, like a conjuror. The envelope must have been nearer the top then because she had found it quickly – the same familiar writing on the envelope, but that certificate, the one she had pulled out then - although it was the same cream paper and the same red print - told a very different story. There she was Margaret Alice, not the Alice Margaret of today. There she was the daughter of Elizabeth Moore and "father unknown", not the daughter of Charles "killed in action" in the battles for independence in Ireland. There she was born in Kentish Town in London, rather than the quiet of the Hertfordshire suburbs she now gave as her birthplace.

Alice had asked her mother over and over, her need to know more about herself overwhelming any possible punishment for snooping in cupboards and things which shouldn't concern her. Up until that point her mother had told her time and again of how she had heard the news of her husband's death – the look on the poor telegram boy's face; but she had confessed years later that the troubles in Ireland had ended long before Alice was even thought of, and although the boy and his terrible delivery were true, it had happened not to her, but to her neighbour right in front of her as they had stood talking at the front gate. She had adopted the story when she found herself alone with a child, and retold it so many times that it had become the truth.

The "father unknown" – the line drawn through the "Name and Surname of Father" section - had preyed on Alice. She couldn't forget about it, wanting to know who he was, where he was, could she meet him, why didn't he care about her – why didn't he visit and bring them money? Her mother had only tipped her head in a small insignificant shake and spoken no words. There had been nothing vindictive or sly in Alice creating a new life, a new history for herself; it had started as a way of filling the gaps which her mother had refused to plug. But just as her mother's story had become fact, her own had begun to take shape and absorb details until, when she joined the WAAF, she had emerged as Alice Margaret, an educated young woman with two parents, both deceased. Her upbringing and her education had in reality been down to no-one but Alice. She had read every book she could lay her hands on and got herself a scholarship, had copied the manners and the voices and the vocabulary of the well-healed girls at the grammar school. She knew her illegitimacy might not mean that much to anyone else, but to her, covering it up had been life-changing; in her own mind she had gone from being insignificant and somehow worthless, to having a life which was meaningful. Alice had blossomed in the WAAF, able at last to be the person she had wanted to be; her new life had built and grown. Meeting Teddy had been an unbelievable step, and she had had to pinch herself every time he asked her out. Marriage had felt like the doll's house all over again – she knew that it was really hers but she was so afraid that someone would come and take it away. And now they might do just that – whether it was Isobel and her meddling into what she would see as Alice's unacceptable past, or Teddy and his gallivanting, she didn't know, but between them Alice was sure that someone was going to snatch away her happiness.

Nevertheless, she put the short-form certificate back in its envelope and slipped it into her apron pocket, still debating in her mind when – or whether – she would give it to Isobel.

CHAPTER THIRTEEN

By Monday morning, Alice was agitated, and generally out of sorts. The time spent with Isobel, and the whole question of the birth certificates had taken her mind away from Teddy and what he was up to, but she had woken up in the middle of the night and had begun turning things over in her head. Sleep had evaded her from that moment on, and now she was not only irritable from lack of sleep, but she was also desperate to find out more.

She was up before Teddy, and having made herself a glass of Epsom Salts to try to settle her stomach, she sat playing with her Cornflakes at the kitchen table and stirring her tea so vigorously that Teddy had had to ask her to stop. As she had stood on the doorstep, uncharacteristically waving him off, she could see confusion on his face as he looked back over his shoulder on the way to the station, but she wanted to check that he had definitely gone before she started ferreting around again.

As soon as she had closed the front door, Alice headed straight for Teddy's study. The newspaper had been moved to one side, and the pile of loose papers seemed to have disappeared, but the heap of buff folders seemed to have grown. She splayed them out, hoping to see one that might be different from the others – one that wasn't work-based and which might contain a hint of what was going on in his life. They all looked distinctly unpromising, the same uniform dull and completely uninspiring. But she had nothing else to go on – nowhere else to look, and so she took the top one and made herself comfortable in Teddy's captain's chair and began leafing through the contents.

•

Something made her glance up at the clock; she couldn't believe that an hour had passed, and all she had unearthed was table after table of figures, comparisons of weather conditions across the British Isles for the past twelve months. Temperatures, wind speeds, rainfall; then comparisons with previous years, plus or minus. It was warm at the desk with the morning sun streaming through the window, and the heat penetrated through to her bones. Initially Alice soaked it up, feeling her body relax for the first time in ages. But as she worked through more pages, still unaccountably convinced that amongst all the work material there would be a hint of something more devious, the figures began to ebb and flow in front of her and her eyes began to close. She fidgeted in the chair, trying to concentrate her efforts, but no matter how many times she went back over the words and statistics she found nothing of any significance. She closed the file with a sigh. 'I'll try again tomorrow, when I'm feeling fresher,' she thought, putting everything back in its place.

Casting an eye over the desk, to make sure everything was as she had found it, Alice aimlessly picked up the newspaper again. It had revealed nothing to her before, but she was still intrigued by its presence. Shaking it open once more Alice began to scan the columns more systematically; it seemed to her that the more important and interesting an article was, the less space it had been allocated, but there was nothing ringed or highlighted in any way which might indicate why the broadsheet was of interest. It hadn't come in the post for Teddy, she knew that, so presumably someone had passed it on to him. And if they had wanted him to look at something in particular, wouldn't they have indicated in some way what it was, or at least which page to look at?

'Oh, it's beyond me,' she said aloud, beginning to fold the paper once more. But as she pushed it back into its original creases she noticed a feint pencil note, almost invisible on the fold at the top of the front page. It stated simply "No.8". Presumably a note for the paperboy, she thought, but then, as she looked again at the scribble, a thought occurred to her. She flipped through the newspaper once more until she reached page eight.

"Cleggs of Wilmslow Easter Fashion Suggestions" dominated the page. Dresses at nearly £6 and twin sets at £3/12/8, in angora and wool, pink, powder blue or cherry. No-one could fail to notice that Gilberts were holding a Special Hosiery Week, and that Maison Sydney Hairdressers was offering its very best services. Everything was there for the wealthy women of Wilmslow to throw their money at, but there was nothing that had any bearing – at least as far as Alice could see – to Teddy or his work.

As she scanned the page again, there, squeezed into a thin column between the Rotary Club Arts Festival and the Rex Theatre programme, was an article headed "University Reader Put on Probation". Alice's heart quickened as she noticed the faintest pencil arrow pointing to the heading. She read rapidly through the details of what was obviously a court report, of a hearing at Cheshire Quarter Sessions. Two men had pleaded guilty to charges of gross indecency. She knew the term of course, but now, seeing it in print, Alice admitted to herself that her knowledge of what it *actually* meant was really quite vague. It was one of those phrases about which there seemed to be an "understanding"; something about which everyone made assumptions, but which no-one ever discussed. Alice squirmed at her ignorance, but it was her very lack of knowledge which made her read on, drinking in the details as you might when you saw a deer lying dead in the woods. You didn't want to see the pecked eyes and the torn skin, or the white bone unnaturally exposed, but nothing could stop you glancing back, and then looking again to take in every savage detail.

The image which the words had at first conjured was of inadequate men rather pathetically exposing gross naked flesh to others who had never asked to see it; but as she read on it became apparent that there was more to this than two deviant men in a park. The younger man had been invited to the house of the other – a man who according to witness accounts was highly educated, and exceptionally honest. Perhaps too honest it would seem, as he had eventually gone of his own accord to a police station to report the disappearance of some money. It appeared that it was this which had started the unravelling of the whole episode and was the thing which had brought the indecency to the attention of the police. The bald notes of the case implied that the young man had been led astray, but he had stolen and begged money from his companion, and Alice wasn't sure who was more to blame.

So engrossed was she in the story of these two men's lives that it took a while for her to come back to the present - and to the reasons why someone had decided to send the article to Teddy in the first place. It referred to the older man being involved in important work for the nation, and the words were so close to those which Teddy had used when he had first told her he was going away, that she began to think that this must be the link – that this man must be involved in the same sort of work. But as she slowly re-read, she saw that he was in fact a mathematician – an eminent brain in that subject; surely that would have no direct relationship with weather conditions, regardless of the acres of statistics which had appeared in Teddy's files.

So why had Teddy seen fit to keep the article for all these months? Were these men known to him? Could one be an old friend who had found himself on the wrong side of the law? Alice shuddered at what appeared to have happened. Such things had been furtively sniggered at when she was in the WAAF, but she had always shied away from the detail of it, preferring to imagine that it existed only as innuendo in comedy programmes on the wireless.

For some reason she didn't understand, it was an activity she associated with boys at boarding school or officers in military training. And if this were the case then it was more than possible that Teddy would have come across someone like these men. She knew that he had attended both types of establishment, and perhaps a fellow "old boy" or former trainee had wanted to point the finger … "Look where old Turing ended up – didn't we always say he would come to a sticky end?"

So maybe it was just schoolboy bullying, with the safety of a twenty year gap?

'Oh, who knows?' Alice decided that she had more important things to think about at the moment, but just as she got up from the desk another thought occurred to her.

At the very top of the piece, the men's names had been given. She realised she was holding her breath as she checked to see if those familiar initials from Teddy's diary might be present … but Mr A Murray and Mr A Turing were the men concerned. She even checked the names of the solicitors representing them, but there were no initials corresponding to "JF".

Alice threw the paper down. 'Just more questions,' she sighed. 'I go looking for answers, and all I find are more questions. Things I don't even want to think about.' She got up, resigned to putting the whole thing to the back of her mind for the afternoon at least. As she turned to go she checked the desk, bending absentmindedly to pick up a paperclip from beneath the chair. She reached for the drawer to put it with the others when it occurred to her that nothing she had handled had had papers clipped together; and she was certain the paperclip hadn't been there when she had first come in. A clip meant a loose piece of paper and she didn't want to leave anything lying about which would tell tales of her presence.

She re-checked everything – and there it was, between the bottom two files, ones her boredom had prevented her from getting to. She could see the clip mark on the cardboard, where the note had been presumably attached to the inside cover. But now it was sitting between her fingers and she was able to read the details of the memo.

CHAPTER FOURTEEN

As she rubbed the lard into the flour, making pastry for a corned beef pie, the words from the slip of paper, bold and blunt, continued to jump around in Alice's head.

> *I have managed to book 3 Nights at*
>
> *Riversmead Hotel, Rushcombe -*
>
> *12th to 15th August.*
>
> *Booking is in the name of Hathaway; only twin rooms available.*

So there it was. She had found the information she had been looking for, but now, what was she going to do with it? Despite everything she knew that she didn't want to challenge Teddy – partly because he would come up with some cock and bull story which would sound just convincing enough that she couldn't challenge it, but also because if he didn't – if he held his hands up and said "You're right Alice, I've been cheating on you old thing, because this marriage just isn't working for me" – if he said that, what would she do? This life – and her marriage - might not always be how she had imagined it, but could she really just walk away from it? She had no real money of her own, no job; where would she go? She thought of Josie. When they had left the WAAF she remembered Josie finding the tiniest flat; it had no bath and hot water only once a day and a single gas ring to cook her lonely soup on. Alice slumped down at the table, trying not to picture herself in the same situation – or worse.

And of course, this still didn't mean anything more than Teddy had already told her, she realised as she mulled it all over. Nothing on that piece of paper said that he was having an affair, that the work story was just a cover, that he was taking the opportunity to have a few days away with this dreadful woman. But her gut told her that that was exactly what was happening. Her gut screamed at her that other women's husbands didn't just peck them on the cheek, night after night, only occasionally taking them into their arms when they'd had one too many whiskies.

And so, as she pulled herself up and began pummelling the pastry dough, she made up her mind. Following Teddy would tell her once and for all what was going on, and then she would at least be able to make a decision based on facts. And having come to that conclusion – just any conclusion - actually made her feel better. As she manoeuvred the dough onto the pie plate and trimmed the edges she began to think more positively, more constructively, even made some pastry leaves for the top as plans began to take shape in her head.

She already had the "when" and the "where" of Teddy's jaunt – his diary had given that from the very beginning. And Teddy had mentioned - several times now - that the powers that be were expecting him to travel to Devon by train. He had related the fact sulkily, as if this were completely beneath someone of his newly acquired importance, but this hadn't stopped him regaling her with details of the changes of train, and the number of stations, and how difficult the whole thing would be. Alice had been only half listening, nodding whenever there was a lull in his ramblings, but now it occurred to her that, if this *were* to be the case, then their ancient little Vauxhall 10 would still be sitting in the garage after Teddy had departed, and so would be available for *her* to use.

He had never said it outright, but she knew that Teddy hated her driving the car. He would always find some reason for her not to, and would certainly have baulked at the idea of her driving it to the other end of the country – but this defiant thought made Alice smile as she realised that, for once, he wouldn't be around to override her decision.

'And at least petrol's come off rationing,' she thought, as she envisaged herself once more in the driver's seat, sailing through the English countryside as she had done as a WAAF, sun blazing through the windscreen and fresh air thundering in at the open windows. The idea of a journey cheered Alice up – to be free for a while of Teddy and Isobel and the housekeeping, with only her own opinions and decisions to worry about. But as Alice followed her thoughts through to their conclusion and she saw herself arriving in the unfamiliar town with no real plans, and with the only measure of her success being the sight of her husband with another woman, the whole thing began to turn sour in her mouth.

She was tempted to slide the whole thing to the back of her mind, wash up the mixing bowl and spoons and close the door on any further thought of journeys and affairs. But she realised that this might mean drifting through the next thirty years with her eyes closed and her mind switched to neutral, pretending that nothing was happening and that life was good. Did she really want to spend her days watching everyone else having a life while she stood on the sidelines with her hands over her ears? She had known someone like that – many years ago now - a small colourless woman, who had enthused over the minutiae of life, and endlessly boasted of her husband's kindness and generosity when everyone else knew that he changed his mistress as often as they changed their bedsheets.

'Dear Lord - save me from that,' Alice groaned. 'I'm not going to be her, whatever happens. I'd rather be penniless in Josie's bedsit than that.' And those words, once spoken aloud, seemed to shift something in her head; her fixation with not losing the house, and the way this had begun to shackle her thoughts… well maybe there would be something else out there for her? After all, she had managed before she met Teddy. 'And if not,' she thought, 'At least I'll go down fighting.'

And so she had taken the map from Teddy's bookshelf – a Bartholomew's British Isles Contour Motoring Map. Alice was shocked to see that Teddy had paid seven and sixpence for it – money she would rather have used to buy an extra piece of fish or some of the tinned fruit which was now off rationing. Or at least something more exciting than that dreadful brawn which she detested making, but which did at least stretch the housekeeping a little further.

Nevertheless she needed the map, so she unfolded the stiff linen-backed paper and spread it out on the kitchen table so that she could see both Cotford and the little town of Rushcombe on the north Devon coast. She pulled her largest cookery book from the shelf and lined up the spine up between the two places, trying to find the shortest route. The resulting course skirted her into the sea, but with a bit of manoeuvring around the Bristol Channel she managed to come up with a more or less direct journey. The places almost lined themselves up, and it wasn't long before she was reciting the list in her head. Buckingham to Bicester, Bicester to Woodstock, then Woodstock to Burford; that would certainly get her started. She rummaged around in the drawer and found a piece of butcher's twine and, by winding it carefully along the roads, she estimated how many miles she would need to drive, and converted this into minutes and hours.

'Possibly 73 miles,' she mused, 'and an average speed of what? – 30 miles an hour?' She did the calculation quickly. 'Say – two and a half, three hours?' Three hours seemed quite reasonable – she could do that in a morning, stop and have a cup of tea, maybe a sandwich - and be back on the road again by half past one. 'And where would another three hours take me to?' she wondered. 'Wouldn't it be good if I could do the whole journey in one day,' she thought, peering up and down the map, 'Then I wouldn't have to pay for a room on the way.'

The thought of money and paying for what might end up as a wild goose chase sent a spasm of panic through Alice. Before she did anything else she knew she ought to check her savings book and pull out the emergency money which she had salted away in an old Oxo tin, pushed to the back of the shelf, whenever she had a few coins spare from her housekeeping.

She was tempted to do it immediately - to find the tin and the book and start totting up figures, but she knew Teddy would be walking back through the door in about twenty minutes.

'I'll definitely do that tomorrow,' she said firmly to herself. '… check my book and maybe even go to the post office and take out all the cash; but I'd better sort this lot out before Teddy comes home.' And so she returned to the map with her length of string, winding and calculating her way down the straggle of roads leading to the south west.

Over 140 miles,' she sighed. Nowhere near as good as the first leg. At 30 miles an hour that would take her nearly five hours, even if she didn't make a stop. And that meant that she wouldn't arrive until late evening… and the thought of arriving in a strange place - at night with no familiar faces and nowhere to stay - did little to dispel her panic.

'Damn – that means I *will* have to find somewhere to stop overnight.' She threw the string and pencil down on the table, sinking her chin into her hands. 'Oh well,' she sighed. 'No point in worrying about any of this I suppose until I see how much money I can pull together.' She tugged the map towards her, realising as she folded it expertly back into its precise creases that insufficient money could mean no trip at all. 'Oh, let's just see what tomorrow brings,' she said resignedly as she took the map and replaced it carefully on Teddy's bookshelf.

CHAPTER FIFTEEN

She could tell by Isobel's face. It was set like aspic in a colourless rigidity; there was no eye contact, just a permanent gaze which scanned the room, fixing occasionally on her beloved son, or on her husband, but never on Alice. No comments, no niceties; it was as though she were determined to conjure Alice to another place by the concentrated disregarding of her. As if, by turning her back on the eyesore in the landscape, she could pretend that the prettiness in the opposite direction was the only view which existed.

Isobel and Douglas had appeared at half past two on Saturday afternoon. Alice had no idea why they were at the house – they hadn't come with armfuls of anything or news or gossip - but Teddy seemed unsurprised to see them at the door, beaming and almost bouncing as he invited them inside. The four of them sat on the edges of their worn armchairs, each waiting for another to introduce some topic or purpose to the visit, which they could all then get their teeth into; but as Alice looked from face to face, nothing was forthcoming. Eventually the weather surfaced as a conversation piece, followed by the latest headlines, but still Isobel avoided any direct words with Alice.

Teddy seemed not to notice, but it was all too obvious that Douglas had. He made a point of pulling Alice into the conversation – of asking her opinion, comparing notes with her, commenting on her dress – anything to counter Isobel's blatant attempts to obliterate her.

For a while Alice enjoyed being out of the usual firing line. It made a pleasant change not to be verbally poked and prodded about her choice of curtains or cookery or clothes. But even with the strongest will it is difficult to be the isolated one, and as much as Alice tried to answer Douglas's enquiries enthusiastically, she began to feel ground down by Isobel's behaviour.

Eventually Teddy stood, rather awkwardly.

'Let me show you that problem with the car,' he said pointedly to his father, as if this were some pre-arranged code. Douglas gave no indication that he knew what was going on, but nevertheless meekly followed his son out of the door.

Left to themselves, Alice was tempted to pick up her book from the table – a copy of the latest Agatha Christie - and carry on reading, leaving Isobel to stew in her dramatic sighs. But she lost her nerve, and fell back on the saviour of many a situation. 'I'll go and put the kettle on,' she announced to the window. 'I'm sure the men will be back in soon.' She scuttled out of the silent room before Isobel could say no, or ask for something she didn't have, like Earl Grey or lemon slices.

As she busied herself with cups and cake forks, Alice contemplated the reason for her in-laws' visit. It was unlike Isobel to be so reticent – she usually announced her purpose the minute she came through the front door, but today it had been all dramatic looks and raised

76

eyebrows. She knew it was only a matter of time before the subject of birth certificates was raised again, and she was almost tempted to rush back into the sitting room before the men returned and yell… 'All right – I give in. Here's the wretched piece of paper you want so badly. Just take it and do whatever you want with it. I really don't care anymore.'

She wanted the woman off her back; she had plenty of other things to think about at the moment, and she'd had just about enough of the passive bullying in which her mother-in-law seemed to specialise. But giving in wasn't just about handing over the piece of paper – it was about admitting defeat, admitting that she wasn't quite the person she appeared to be.

As she rattled around noisily in the kitchen it occurred to Alice that Teddy might be tapping his father for money – selling him some story about his impending trip and promise of promotion, but needing cash to tide him over. She could hear him saying it - "As soon as this takes off I'll be in the money Pa – pay you back threefold". And she was still immersed in this little daydream when Isobel eventually came in for the kill.

It was just as Alice was making the tea. Just as she was pulling the green tin from the shelf to cut slices of her newly-baked caraway seed cake, she heard a sound behind her. She turned to find Isobel standing too close, handbag firmly clasped in front, staring directly into her face.

'I can only presume you are being deliberately obtuse, Alice.' Isobel paused and Alice took the opportunity to turn away and cut the cake.

Alice piled the slices onto her best floral cake plate, then turned up the flame under the kettle. She kept her eyes very firmly on her tasks, and this seemed to stir Isobel's vitriol all the more. The woman continued, every word clipped and strained, every little part of her severely controlled.

'The fact that you have refused my offer leads me to believe there is something you have to hide.'

Alice spun round, ready to bat away whatever Isobel was about to throw at her. She noticed that face powder had settled into the creases on the older woman's face; that instead of hiding her lines the cosmetic was actually accentuating them; and this small imperfection gave her great satisfaction. The make-up did nothing either to conceal the older woman's look of surprise. Presumably she had expected tears and pleading; what she got was fiery and battle-ready - a side of her daughter-in-law which she hadn't seriously encountered before. Nevertheless, Isobel seemed determined to continue.

The kettle began singing as it came to the boil, but Alice didn't back down. She continued to re-arrange the cake slices and fill the milk jug. Steam started to build around the two women, until they looked like strangers waiting on a station platform.

'Alice.' The unexpected urgency in Isobel's voice made Alice jump, and she dropped the cake knife. It landed very close to her mother-in-law's foot as the woman turned to switch off the screeching kettle.

Alice bent to retrieve the knife from the linoleum floor and as she did so Isobel spoke to her bowed position.

'This situation is entirely unacceptable. Really Alice, you leave me with no alternative …' The woman's voice shook enough to tell Alice that she was wavering on what the threat might be. 'I have suspected for some time that things are not as they appear with you Alice ...'

Alice looked her mother-in-law directly in the eye. She was still holding the knife, which Isobel seemed only now to have noticed. 'You must do as you see fit Mrs Hathaway. But you might want to remember the saying about people in glass houses.' Just for that moment Alice hoped that her suspicions about Teddy and an affair might be true so that she could throw them into Isobel's supercilious face. She felt the extraordinary pounding of her heart and was sure it must be visible through the thin fabric of her blouse; She could feel the colour had risen in her cheeks and it was all that she could do to keep her voice even and low, but the doubt which crossed Isobel's face gave Alice the strength to continue.

'I may not be the only one in this family with skeletons in their cupboard, Mrs Hathaway – and mine might well be smaller than others …'

The other woman took a breath, stepping back as if readying herself for the final assault, but Alice carried on before she could lose her nerve.

'Third drawer down, under the tea towels,' she spat out the words as she lifted the tea tray and pushed past Isobel.

As she headed for the sitting room where she could hear Douglas and Teddy laughing, Alice smiled to herself. She might have relented, but it was only the short version of her birth certificate which she had handed over, and the victory still seemed hers.

It was some while before Isobel re-appeared, grey-faced and stormy-eyed, to join them. For the remainder of the visit the older woman sat in silence, responding to offers of tea and cake with small nods or shakes of her head. The blood which had boiled in Alice's veins in response to the bullying had calmed a little, but her determination not to be walked all over was as strong as ever.

CHAPTER SIXTEEN

Monday morning, and the rain was coming down so heavily Alice could barely see across the street. She had planned to go to the Post Office to get her savings book made up, and perhaps withdraw some funds for her trip, but it was obvious that she would be drenched within minutes if she went out in this downpour. She'd tuned in hopefully to the weather forecast on the Home Service but they had said that it wouldn't brighten until late afternoon and so Alice was at a loose end now that her plans were on hold.

She knew that she could be washing – although where would she put sopping sheets and dripping dresses? And there was the pantry to clean out and brass to polish, but none of those activities in any way satisfied her need to be *doing* something. In the end she was drawn irresistibly back to Teddy's study, but it was chilly in there with the rain beating against the windows, and so she grabbed a file and took it back to the kitchen table, where at least there was a bit of heat still left from the oven.

As she sipped at the remains of her tea, Alice realised she had read the initial sections already. She flicked through to the later pages, scanning them to see if they would reveal anything more interesting. There were fewer tables and figures here, and more text, less mentions of wind-speed and temperature and more of precipitation. She was intrigued by two things which kept jumping out at her - the title "Operation Cumulus" cropped up several times, as did the phrase "the use of Silver Iodide". Alice put the file down, absentmindedly stirring her tea, trying hard to recall science lessons from what seemed an eternity ago. Chemicals and their actions and reactions had been even more alien to her world than most other school subjects, and nothing she had been taught had sparked even the smallest glow of interest or appeared to have any relevance to what she might do once her school days were finished. She could clearly remember copying out formulae and recording the experiments which the teacher had long-windedly described, but apart from H2O being water, and Sodium Chloride being table salt, the rest had faded along with her school uniform. She was pretty certain though that she had never come across Silver Iodide.

She pulled the small dictionary from the shelf where she kept her cookery books, the one she occasionally used for her coffee time crosswords, and flicked to "S"; but it was obviously too-specialised a term to be in the small reference volume, and she closed the book thoughtfully. Was there something more comprehensive on the shelves in Teddy's study, she wondered, drifting back in that direction.

She knelt and scanned the lower shelves to the bookcase, certain that she had seen a large volume sitting there when she had glanced at the titles before. She bypassed an atlas of the world, several art books relating to artists she had only vaguely heard of, a history of the Roman Empire, but there were no books of general knowledge – and definitely nothing more science-based.

Reluctantly Alice went back to the kitchen. It was as though everything was conspiring against her, she thought – the rain was still hammering against the windows, barring her outing in to town; she seemed to be unearthing nothing but more questions to which she could find no answers and the housework was nagging at her to be done. Eventually she made herself an early lunch then forced herself upstairs to give the bathroom the scrub which it had needed for days.

Typically the weather only began to brighten when it was too late for her to go out. Dinner needed to be prepared so that Teddy wouldn't start nit-picking the minute he was home from work.

As she half-heartedly went through the basket, dithering over which vegetables to prepare for their evening meal, her thoughts began to wander again, mulling over where she might find out about the words and phrases she had read in Teddy's file. It was only as she turned to put the saucepan onto the stove that she noticed the file still on the kitchen table.

Alice swept it up, shuffling papers back into place. She dashed from the kitchen to the study, quickly replacing it on the desk. Just as she picked up the paring knife again, ready to finish the carrots, she heard a key in the front door.

●

Later, when she was clearing away after their meal, she heard Teddy calling irritably from the hallway.

'Alice – Alice?'

She hated it when he insisted on dragging her to *his* conversation rather than coming to find her; but nevertheless she put down the Brillo pad with which she had been trying desperately to remove burnt potato from the bottom of the saucepan, wiped the soap suds from her arms and went into the hall, tea towel still in hand.

'What is it Teddy? I'm trying to get the washing up finished so that we can both sit down with a coffee and listen to Variety Fanfare on the wireless.'

He looked surprised at her sharp words. He stopped for a moment, mouth open, then barked out his question as if her words had inflamed his own.

'My study Alice…?'

'Yes – is there something the matter?' Alice made a conscious effort to drop the strong words, returning to her usual conciliatory manner. She was anxious about what might be coming next.

'Has anyone been in my study?' The muscles in his neck strained as he spoke.

'Well, there's only you and me here Teddy …'

'Yes, I'm well aware of that …'

Despite his irritability, Alice forced her own tone to be gentler. 'I don't understand my dear. What makes you think that someone's been in there?'

'I don't *think* someone's been in there -- I *know* someone has – and presumably it was you.' He glared at her, his face growing redder. 'I told you that my work was highly confidential, that it was to be shared with no-one, but you've seen fit to completely ignore what I've said - to sneak into my study as soon as I'm out of the house, and start snooping around, looking into things which are none of your business, which you have no right to be looking at …'

Teddy rarely lost his temper; that was one of his redeeming features, that he took everything in his stride. His placidness could even by quite annoying sometimes, but this made his puce face and this uncharacteristic explosion of words all the more alarming.

'Is there a problem?' Alice stalled, unsure whether to confess or to brazen it out. 'Has something gone missing?'

'It doesn't bloody matter whether something's missing or not – you've been in my study, that's the point – my study which has always been out of bounds …' His breathing had begun to quicken as he worked himself into a stew. 'And what is totally outrageous, completely bloody unacceptable … is that you've obviously been going through my papers –papers which I've specifically told you are completely confidential …'

Alice was desperate to find the right words to say, but her mind had emptied itself of even a single idea. Before she could come up with anything at all, Teddy had turned his back on her and walked away. He slammed the study door, but just as Alice let out a breath of relief the door opened again.

'Don't let me ever find that you have been in my study,' he poked his finger violently into the air, '– or near any of my things – ever EVER again,' he yelled.

And it was the shouting – the previously unheard raising of his voice - which shocked Alice the most.

She went back to the kitchen and closed the door, standing with her back against it. She breathed out deeply, realising that she was trembling. She slipped into a chair, hand over her mouth, trying to calm herself.

Eventually she got up, still shaking, and filled the kettle, putting it carefully on the stove. She trawled through her mind, trying to think what it might be that had alerted Teddy's suspicions, what she had left in the wrong place, or put back too tidily, or … She suddenly panicked that she had left something behind. She'd forbidden herself a notepad and pencil from the start; anything new coming into the study was far too much of a risk, and she'd done well, keeping everything she'd seen in her head. 'No, I definitely didn't leave anything,' she whispered to herself, forgetting to put the coffee into the pot before she poured in the water. But she knew that it was easy enough to drop something. Only yesterday she had spotted a hairgrip, camouflaged by the patterned rug, just as she'd been about to leave the room.

She dare not open the study door, so left a small tray of coffee outside. She took her own cup through to the lounge, hoping against hope that Teddy wouldn't join her there, while she gave some thought to how she might retrieve the situation.

CHAPTER SEVENTEEN

Her hand trembled as she brushed her hair. Alice concentrated on every stroke, trying not to think about what she was about to do. She studied her face in the mirror, hoping to see the strong person that she needed to be to go ahead with her plan. Maybe there was a more serious glint in her eyes, less doe-like, more steely, or perhaps it was just the embarrassed pink of her cheeks which was altering the look of her features.

She reached for the perfume bottle and squeezed the atomiser, allowing a small spray of her precious "Evening in Paris" to meet her neck. She knew it would make little difference to Teddy, but to her it added to the part she was trying to play, a piece of her costume. The silky nightdress had helped too. She had bought it for their honeymoon, but had previously felt too self-conscious, ridiculous even, putting it on; it had been too obvious, too showy - but tonight it felt right. She propped herself up on the clean white pillows and waited for Teddy. Last night he had slept amongst the clutter in the box bedroom, and she could only hope that things would return to normal this evening if her plan were to work.

She listened as Teddy banged the bathroom door, noisily lifting the lavatory seat. How different life had become in such a short space of time, she thought. Only a week ago – two at the most – she had lay in bed, longing for Teddy to take hold of her, to do whatever he wished with her, anything rather than him climbing into bed and turning his back, falling almost immediately into a deep, snore-filled sleep. Now she was orchestrating things, taking matters into her own hands – even if it was only in desperation, to distract his anger at her prying. A shiver went down her back and she was unsure whether it was the feel of the silk against her skin or the tingle of anticipation mixed with fear at what was about to happen.

He looked over at her as he came back from the bathroom; looked again, his eyes picking up something which he didn't appear to recognise. He looked wrong-footed, unsure of himself, hesitated as if he had been trapped in a cul-de-sac. 'You look nice,' he muttered, then seemed surprised that the words had come out of his own mouth.

Teddy pulled off his clothes, piled them on the wicker chair, unfolded. He looked weary, irritated in his tiredness, his pyjamas hanging loosely, making him for a moment look much older than his years.

'Perhaps I'll wait 'til tomorrow,' Alice thought, already beginning to slide under the sheets. But then she knew she would lose her nerve completely if she had to set all this up again. Casually she put her book down on the bedside cabinet and smiled at Teddy.

'Long day dear?' she whispered. 'Here, come and let me rub your back.'

He peeled back the covers, bundling up the eiderdown and stared at her. She knew that her curves were emphasised by the soft shiny fabric of her gown, was for once proud of her full breasts.

'Hmm,' he murmured, but it was possibly a murmur of approval and Alice knelt up as he slid himself between the sheets.

She tried to stroke his skin through the thickness of the pyjamas, but it was having little effect and she worried that the moment would be gone before she had the chance to take advantage of it.

'Here – let me take this off,' she said, pulling at the striped fabric, grasping for the buttons. She thought for a minute that Teddy was about to refuse, to claim abject tiredness and need for sleep, but he seemed after a moment to relax, resigned to her ministrations. Alice removed the pyjama jacket and began to run her fingers lightly over his shoulders. He grunted then turned, so that she was able to manipulate his back, finding the knots in his muscles, kneading then soothing, gradually allowing her fingers to fall further and further until they were slipping beneath the waistband of his pyjama bottoms.

It was as if she had pushed a button. The contented sighs stopped and he grappled his way up to sitting, pulling her towards him, grasping her arms, breathing hotly on her neck.

He pushed her down, running his hand over her thighs, over the silky fabric at first, and then sliding his eager fingers under the lacy edging and further up her body.

She pulled at the gown, wanting to remove it, wanting to feel his skin against hers, but he moved her hands, holding her wrists as he slid up and down her body.

He flipped her over, caressing her back, her buttocks, slipping his hand between her legs, moving them apart.

'Please Teddy,' Alice murmured, trying unsuccessfully to turn herself onto her back. He had taken her like that before and she had most definitely not enjoyed it. He grunted, but she could feel his urgency, his desire and he turned her back, quickly manoeuvring her into position.

He heaved and grunted, eyes tightly shut as he gave a final thrust and collapsed, sated, on top of her.

Alice lay for what seemed like hours, eyes wide open, listening to his breathing gradually calm. She was overwhelmed by the fire and urgency of it all, something which hadn't happened between her and Teddy before; she was uncomfortable with the weight of his body still on top of her, but she felt, in her own way, triumphant. Her intention had only ever been to try to distract him from the whole study thing and her meddling in his business, but now it felt as though maybe they had turned a corner, that something somewhere had changed between them and that perhaps he would begin to look at her as a woman, and his wife, again

CHAPTER EIGHTEEN

Teddy had slipped silently from their bed. She was aware of nothing until she turned over, putting out a hand to pull the eiderdown back to her side, to find only cool sheets and an empty pillow. It was still only half past seven and Alice drifted in and out of sleep for a few moments longer until the events of the previous night filtered through to her consciousness. She hesitated to remember it as a reality, convinced that she must have dreamed the whole thing, until she moved her hand over her body and was stirred by the tenderness beneath her fingers.

Despite the fact that all the hot water would be gone for the day, Alice ran herself a bath and lowered herself slowly into the welcoming warmth. She lay there, moving only occasionally, until the water began to grow cold. Then she wrapped herself in a towel and sat on the side of the bath, dabbing her skin gently until it was dry.

She wanted nothing to eat, but brewed herself a pot of tea, sitting at the kitchen table to drink it, pushing herself to think of the tasks which needed doing, rather than hoping too hard that things for her and Teddy might be able to change. But it took very little for her thoughts to snowball – to visions of a normal family life, of children … and there Alice had to pull herself up. It might matter little what was going on in their own bed if there was another woman enticing Teddy into hers. And then there was all this other stuff about Teddy's work, which seemed to be growing its own set of secrets.

Alice sighed. 'I don't know that I've got the energy for all of this,' she thought. 'Why am I worrying about what he's getting himself into – it's not going to change anything, is it?' She pulled yesterday's newspaper towards her, looked at the remaining gaps in the crossword, trying to take her mind off Teddy for a few minutes at least. She inked in a few words that she had only guessed at yesterday, then moved on to five across - "Home for a bibliophile?", seven letters. She must have missed that one before – it was easy enough, she thought, as she began to write in the answer.

'Library - Why in God's name didn't you think of that earlier?' Alice muttered to herself, flinging the newspaper to one side.

Whatever her thoughts about Teddy, her curiosity had been peeked about Operation Cumulus and Silver Iodide, and the phrases would not go away, in the same way as an annoying crossword clue needed to be solved. She was unlikely to unearth the details of Cumulus, but she could at least try to find out about the chemical, and the library might just provide her with some answers. 'And while I'm in town I can call in and deal with my Post Office book as well,' she thought.

Pleased to have at least some sort of a plan, Alice left the teapot and cup unwashed on the draining board, and threw her purse into her shopping basket along with her savings book and her finished library book. She could, she thought, have been doing something useful over the past few days instead of reading this ridiculous Agatha Christie nonsense. She pulled the front door shut and looked at her bicycle lying at the side of the garage where she had abandoned it amongst the overgrown ivy after her last outing. The tyres looked distinctly flabby and she decided instead to walk.

Inside the hushed interior of the 1920s building Alice returned her book to the counter, collected her ticket and wandered off amongst the library shelves. The building smelled of polish and dust, silence and isolation. She bypassed the comfortable familiarity of the fiction shelves, acutely aware of the tapping of her footsteps on the hushed parquet floor as she ventured across the large open room. She'd been ignoring the fact that her favourite navy shoes needed re-heeling, waiting until she had spare money in her housekeeping purse, but the insistent clunking of her worn heels told her that she couldn't put off a trip to the cobbler for much longer.

Alice made her way to the non-fiction area, and looked at the headings above each section, unsure really where to begin her search. The science shelves, when she found them were full of closely packed books mainly without dust jackets, stern in their uniform blues and browns. She strained to read the titles metallically embossed on the spines, until the muscles in her neck began to ache with the constant need to tilt her head. After ten minutes she had found nothing that looked even remotely like the sort of book that might help. A librarian with an armful of books paused and glared over the top of horn-rimmed spectacles, as if Alice had just wandered in from the streets and might be about to pocket a precious tome.

'Can I help you?'

'Well actually yes, you can. I'm looking for books about ...' Alice's nerve instantly left her. To say she wanted – or expected there to be – a whole book about Silver Iodide would show her ignorance, but what was it that she really needed? 'Um - do you have any books about the weather please?' she blurted out, for want of anything more sensible to say.

Alice felt herself being examined, as if it were on the tip of the librarian's tongue to suggest that she might be much happier amongst the latest Romances; Alice, though, continued with her best Sunday school smile, and the woman's professional standing seemed eventually to get the better of her. 'Follow me,' she said, her words as clipped and blunt as her movements, as she disappeared around the bookshelves without waiting to see if Alice was following.

Alice came to, and trotted along in the direction the librarian had taken. The woman was waiting for her, lips pursed, sighing heavily as she pointed to another forbidding shelf of tightly stacked books.

'This *may* be what you are looking for?' she announced doubtfully, and marched off before Alice could ask further questions.

Alice glanced despondently at shelf after shelf of more dreary brown covers. She pulled out a thin volume, hoping, at the very least, that it would be less wordy than its stout companions. But the pages of solidly packed text did little to inspire her even to begin reading; a smile came momentarily to her lips as she remembered her namesake's words - "And what is the use of a book ... without pictures or conversation?" 'Quite right Alice,' she thought, as she returned the book to its place. As she did so the librarian popped her head around the bookshelves again.

'Of course you might find what you need in the Children's Section,' she said abruptly, turning on her heal before Alice could react.

'Damned cheek,' Alice muttered, and defiantly removed two of the largest volumes from the shelves.

As she struggled back to the desk with the weighty tomes, a different librarian was filing away tickets. She had a warm smile which matched the string of pearls round her slender neck.

'Did you find what you needed?' she whispered in a Welsh lilt, looking over her shoulder towards her less than helpful colleague. 'You could always try the Britannica,' she said as she stamped the books vigorously. 'Encyclopaedia Britannica - that usually has enough information for most people's needs.' She slipped the books back into Alice's waiting hands. 'Far corner – reference section,' she mouthed conspiratorially, smiling as Alice turned back towards the waiting shelves.

As she walked in the direction the woman had indicated, Alice wondered at her own sanity and common sense. If she'd given more than a minute's thought to what she was doing she would have headed straight for the encyclopaedias instead of all that dithering around. But the friendly librarian hadn't seemed to think any less of her, and Alice put it down to having too many things on her mind. It took her only minutes to find the right volume and to turn the heavy pages to the appropriate section. She pored over the words, jotting them down in her notebook as neatly as she could, so that they would still make sense when she got home.

Silver Iodide is an odourless bright yellow inorganic compound, formula AgI. It often contains impurities of metallic silver (giving a grey colouration) which arises because the compound is photosensitive. This light-sensitive property is used in silver-based photography – built on a technique pioneered by Frederick Scott Archer in 1851. Silver Iodide can also be used as an antiseptic.

She also scribbled down its mass and density and melting point and boiling point, knowing as the pen slid across the paper that she was highly unlikely to need such details – but you never knew.

As she wandered back out into the street she churned the words and information over. What on earth would any of this have to do with Teddy's work, she mused, lost in thought as she wandered carelessly along the road. A car pulled out suddenly from a side street and Alice had to jump back onto the pavement out of its way.

'You watch yourself Mrs H,' a voice called out to her. As Alice shook herself and focussed, she realised that Mr Atkins was on the opposite side of the road, waving something at her. 'Don't want you disappearing before you can plant out these little cabbage seedlings I've got for you.'

Alice waved back at the old man who had presumably been to his allotment. 'That's really kind – I'll pop round later and pick them up.' All thoughts of chemicals disappeared from her mind as she tried to think when she was going to find time to plant cabbages amongst everything else that was going on.

•

It wasn't until Alice had settled herself in a chair in the garden and began studying her notebook once more that she realised she had completely forgotten about the Post Office and her savings. She swore under her breath, but hadn't the energy to walk into the town again. Instead she tried to make some sense of the notes, searching for any clue about what Teddy and his cronies might be up to. She was still puzzling over it all when a head popped up at the fence.

'Ready for your cabbages, Mrs H?' Mr Atkins called.

It was really the last thing Alice needed, but her neighbour had been so kind she couldn't offend him.

'Oh, absolutely. Where's the best place for them?' she asked, thinking that she might as well get it over with straightaway.

As she raked and hoed and made dips in the soil for the tiny plants, she let her thoughts drift once more to the Silver Iodide. She could read the notes a hundred times, she realised, and still have no idea what they meant. She wished she were still in the WAAF – someone there would be bound to know what it was all about; and almost immediately her thoughts jumped to Josie. Josie still worked for the Air Ministry and, unlike Alice, she had kept in touch with some of their Forces chums. Someone somewhere out there would know the meaning of all of this, and could perhaps explain it in layman's terms.

Alice felt a bizarre sort of excitement in the pit of her stomach as she dashed to the hall and picked up the telephone. It took only a moment for her eagerness to deflate.

CHAPTER NINETEEN

Receiver in hand, Alice realised that she had no way of contacting Josie. It was only now that it occurred to her that it had always been Josie who had done the ringing – so Alice had no telephone number for her. And she had always assumed that she knew where Josie's work was based, but now that she came to think about it she wasn't entirely sure of that either.

She reluctantly replaced the receiver, and dropped down onto the bottom stair, hugging her arms, head completely empty of ideas. But oddly, as she sat there musing, the telephone started to ring. The sound of the pips and the pause as pennies were pushed into the public call box convinced Alice that it must be Josie, bizarrely summoned by her own thoughts.

'Is that the Vicarage? I'd like to arrange a funeral.' A hesitant voice spoke at the other end.

'Eh – no. I think you've …'

'It's my Ernie. He's gone at last. He was …'

'I'm very sorry to hear that,' Alice broke in quickly before the story had time to build. 'But I'm afraid this isn't the Vicarage. I think you have the wrong number.'

She tried to speak kindly to the poor woman, to reassure her, but after she had finished the call, Alice was more unsettled than ever. She was cross with herself for not taking more of an interest in Josie, and, if she was honest, feeling guilty at the proof in front of her that their relationship had been so one-sided. But she knew from experience that sitting around was only going to make her agitation worse.

She grabbed her hat and jacket, and snatching up her basket again she marched out of the house.

The sky was fresh and bright; a small breeze was blowing, but it was warm, and washed over Alice like a bath, lapping on her skin and gradually calming her. She had decided to walk again, and was glad that she had when she reached the main road and realised that her thoughts had been wandering down so many different lanes that she hadn't the slightest memory of getting to that point.

As she crossed over the bridge and into the square, her subconscious seemed to be leading her; she walked straight to the place where she had gone with Josie when they last met.

The church clock chimed the third quarter and Alice looked up. A quarter to two; there was just a chance that Josie might still be on her lunch break and have popped into town. Alice poked her head round the tearoom door. It was still busy with late lunches but there was no sign of Josie. A woman in a feathered hat looked up, tutting pointedly at the mild draft which Alice was presumably allowing in at the door. Alice closed it quietly and walked on, trying desperately to remember if Josie had made any mention of where she was now living; but no useful thoughts came into her head. A final circuit of the shops revealed nothing more, and reluctantly Alice made her way back home, with only a loaf of bread to show for her troubles. She dropped it on the kitchen table and reached absentmindedly for the kettle, her thoughts leapfrogging between finding Josie and the phrases which were infuriatingly refusing to leave her head. She had just pulled the tea caddy from the shelf when there was a knock at the front door.

'Oh Alice – at last!'

Alice was dumbstruck. The woman she had been searching for had unaccountably appeared on her doorstep.

'I saw you in town.' Josie explained breathlessly. 'I waved and called but you were in a little world of your own.'

The kettle's whistle was reaching fever pitch.

'Hadn't you better get that before it boils dry?' Josie looked anxiously at her friend.

'Oh – yes – I will.' Alice was flustered, not knowing whether to attend to her friend or the kettle or the thoughts in her head.

'Oh, I'll do it shall I? You sit down - you look dreadful.'

The kettle's whistle diminished to a sigh as Josie tipped the boiling water into the waiting pot. She transferred the tea to the kitchen table where Alice, now seated, seemed dazed and uncomfortable.

'Are you okay?' Josie asked as she poured tea into two un-matching cups she had found in the nearest cupboard.

'I'm – no – I'm fine.' Alice stared up at Josie. 'But how did you know where I lived?' she asked baldly.

'Well, after you didn't hear me calling I tried to catch up with you, but you walk pretty fast you know.' Josie took a sip of her tea. 'Anyway, I was getting closer and you'd just turned into this street but then I went over on my ankle and the damned strap broke on my shoe. I could only hobble along after that, but at least I managed to keep an eye on where you were going and well ... here I am.'

Alice stared again at Josie, without speaking.

'It's not a problem is it – me coming here?' Josie looked around as if Teddy or someone else might suddenly appear.

Alice was silent for a moment, and then she got up, beckoning Josie to follow her. She stood aside at the sitting room door so that Josie could see the two faded fraying armchairs, the coffee table propped up by books, and the wireless set sitting on the bare floor. She moved silently onto the dining room and waved her hand resignedly at a room empty except for a basic square table and four battered chairs.

'But it's lovely Alice. What's wrong?'

Alice felt the tears begin to slide down her cheeks.

'Most newlyweds don't have much furniture – particularly when they've had to rely on coupons,' Josie tried to re-assure her. 'But that's part of the fun isn't it – setting up house together, gradually building your new home ...'

'Teddy is gradually "un-building" ours,' Alice sniffed.

'What on earth do you mean?'

'We *had* furniture – we inherited it with the house. It was all Teddy's grandfather's, and we took over the whole lot when Teddy's parents let us have the house as our wedding present.' She stopped and took a large gulp of the tea. 'Gradually though it's all disappearing. Teddy covers it well of course – says what do we want with all this old-fashioned stuff, we'll get something modern and new – and off goes another bit to auction, but nothing comes back to take its place. He thinks I don't realise – about his spending money we haven't got – buying expensive clothes, entertaining … anything to keep up with people who earn twice as much as he does, or who've inherited pots of money …'. Alice angrily brushed away a tear. 'Even my watch …' the words disappeared into a muddle of sniffing and sobbing, but the hint of "pawnbroker" and "gambling" was in there somewhere.

Josie put an arm round her and steered her back to the kitchen table. 'Have you got anything stronger than tea in these cupboards?' Josie said, opening doors and drawers. Cooking sherry was the best she could lay her hand on, and she poured two decent measures.

'Alice – they're only tables and chairs; bits of wood. It doesn't matter.'

Alice pondered for a moment about telling Josie about her wristwatch, which had also disappeared – presumably to the man Teddy referred to as "Uncle", but decided she'd revealed enough for now. 'Yes – you're right - I know. It's just the …' She had been about to say "deceitfulness", the being treated as a fool, but she didn't want to go back into the mire which was hers and Teddy's life together. After a moment she looked up.

'Josie - do you know anything about Silver Nitrate?'

'What?' Josie held up her glass. 'Have you been sneaking extra glasses of this stuff while I've not been looking?' she laughed.

'No – no, I'm fine. But do you?' Alice persisted.

'Well – it vaguely rings a bell – but what's that got to do with anything? Why do you want to know?'

'Oh, it's just something I've been reading.' Alice paused. 'Could you find out for me – ask around at work d'you think?'

'Well … yes, I s'pose,' Josie looked hard at Alice, as if trying to read her face. 'You've got me intrigued now … you'll have to tell me more than that if you want me to ask the right questions.'

Alice looked at her friend. She had no idea what to tell her.

CHAPTER TWENTY

'Well, without thinking I just mentioned the subject while we were at the pub the other night – me and a few others from work.'

It was Saturday afternoon, and the tea room was busy. They had had to wait for a table, and by the time they sat down Alice was desperate to find out if Josie had any information for her. But as soon as she heard Josie's words, Alice squirmed. Her friend's tone of voice more than hinted at the sort of reception she had received to her innocent question.

'And what did they say – your friends?' Alice tried for a matter-of-fact tone; she was pretty sure she wasn't succeeding.

'Well – there was a dead silence – at first. Everyone suddenly seemed to have other things to do – you know – making patterns on the table with their beer glass, or blowing their noses, or needing to go to the lavatory.'

'Oh …'

'"Oh" you might well say,' Josie said in a loud whisper. 'Luckily old Billy Allsop saved the day – eventually.' Josie was indignant now. 'He started talking about photography and how silver iodide changes colour when exposed to light and so on.

Eventually the others joined in, throwing in their twopenneth about the best ways to develop photos and how Blenkinsop had made a complete ass of himself by letting light into the darkroom and ruining several reels of important film.' Josie paused. 'But of course I knew by that point that I'd somehow put my foot in it – that I'd asked something only a complete wet behind the ears novice would ask. I felt such a fool …'

'I'm really sorry Josie, I didn't mean to get you into trouble …'

'Look – if you want me to help you, you need to be up front with me Alice. We're old chums – surely you could have let me in on the real story, instead of leaving me to squirm?'

'Well – it's not that I didn't want to tell you,' Alice hesitated, 'It's just that it's really difficult. I'm not really supposed to know anything about any of this myself, let alone be talking to others about it …'

'So this tale about the son of a poorly friend, and his homework, is all completely fictitious – is that right?'

'Well – yes. I had to come up with something.'

'You're a brilliant liar, I'll say that for you Alice.' Josie was quiet for a moment, taking stock. 'Well, if I were you I'd tell me a lot more about what's going on, because after that pub incident one of the chaps offered to walk me home …'

'Oh, that was nice …'

'No, it wasn't. He just wanted an excuse to talk to me on his own.'

Alice felt a tingling of expectation. 'So what did he say …?'

'He said that he could give me more information – completely off the record of course – he'd be for the high jump if anyone found out – you know we all have to sign the Official Secrets Act - but he wants to know what the information is for and who wants it before he'll say another word.'

'But why would he do that? Why would he be prepared to talk about something that's obviously off-limits?' Alice looked rather shocked.

'Oh come on Alice - he's sweet on me, that's why. I've known it for a while – he sends me little notes, leaves an apple on my desk now and then, that sort of thing. He's awfully shy, not much experience with girls I'd guess.' Josie lit a cigarette and blew out the smoke in a long continuous stream. 'I've played it very cool up until now – he's okay, very kind, steady, but not exactly going to set the world on fire. Presumably he sees this as his big chance – help me out and I'll be his for ever...'

'Oh Josie. I don't know what to say.' Alice paused, a hundred questions running through her head. 'I don't want to push you into something you're not happy with …' And I don't want to dig myself deeper into this by talking about something I'm not even supposed to have seen, she thought.

'Don't worry. A girl's gotta give in sometime …. I can't stay on the shelf forever, can I?' Josie laughed quietly, but Alice couldn't help noticing the uncertain note behind her friend's words. 'All you've got to do is tell me why you need to know...'

•

'I don't know where to start.' Alice sighed, guilt, doubts and questions all vying for position in her head,

107

nothing making any sense. They had finished their lunch and couldn't take up a table in the busy café any longer. Josie had suggested a walk – some fresh air, a change of scenery - and they had wandered down to the river, arm in arm, and found a bench to watch the world from.

They sat in silence for a while, and Alice gazed at the leaves on the riverside path – still green, brought down prematurely by an unseasonable high wind. She watched the sun bouncing off the water, sending glittering cascades across the wake left by the rowing boat. For some reason the beauty it displayed brought a heaviness to her chest; she felt overwhelmed by all that seemed to be going on about her – none of which she felt she seemed to be able to get a hold on.

'Oh just start anywhere,' Josie snapped, 'But for God's sake – start.'

Once a tear had come to her eye she couldn't stop another, and then a regular trickle started up, until she was overcome, past the point of caring whether anyone heard her sobs or thought she looked a frightful sight.

And then Josie must have heard the sobs which Alice was trying so hard to muffle; she reached out and put an arm round Alice.

'I'm sorry… I didn't mean to snap. I didn't mean to …'

Alice sniffed loudly, trying desperately to stem the tears. 'It's not your fault. Someone needs to get a grip on this situation …' She wiped a hand across her cheek. 'Oh, Josie – I don't know which way to turn anymore. There's so much going on – I'm just swamped in it all and the more I find out the worse it all gets, and I feel like I'm being sucked into some sort of quicksand, and the more I try to get myself out of it, the more everything pulls me down, but the more I have to struggle to ...'

The sobs overtook her again, and Josie just sat, her hand rubbing Alice's bent back, trying to sooth and re-assure until the worst of it subsided.

'I know this sounds like the sort of thing your Auntie Maud would say ...' Josie began, when Alice seemed a little calmer.

'I don't have an Auntie Maud ...' Alice sniffed, looking up in confusion.

'Oh you nincompoop!' Josie laughed, and Alice broke into a half-laugh, half sob; but the giggle won out and they both sat laughing to themselves, watching a group of ducks trying unsuccessfully to climb the muddy bank, for a few joyful moments.

'What I was *trying* to say,' Josie said eventually, 'Was that, even though I sound like someone's spinster aunt, it probably is just best to start at the beginning and tell me the whole story.'

Alice looked up, conscious of the tears which had dried on her cheeks and which were pulling her skin taut. 'You're a good friend Josie –', she said, and, with a deep breath, began to relate the events of the past few days, or at least as much of it as was needed to put Josie in the picture.

'So – what you're saying is that – let me just try and get this right,' Josie struggled to get her thoughts in order. 'You're saying that – as well as some sort of affair –' Alice squirmed at the word, but Josie was in full flow. 'As well as that, Teddy is involved in some sort of suspicious-sounding research – and that's what he's going to be looking at when he goes to Derbyshire?'

'What I'm saying is,' Alice tried to keep the impatience out of her voice, 'Is that I don't know what any of this stuff means ... All I do know is that page after page of Teddy's files refer to Silver Iodide – and I'm certain it's nothing to do with taking photos – or developing them, or whatever else your friends were talking about.' Alice paused, catching her thoughts as well as her breath.

Josie played with a sycamore leaf which had fallen into her lap, twirling it backwards and forwards between her fingers.

'And then there's all the stuff about "Operation Cumulus", Alice went on, almost in a whisper. 'Why would you call something an "operation" if all you were doing was monitoring the weather?'

The two friends sat in contemplation, neither of them able to put forward any answers to their questions. 'When you told me how the people in the pub had reacted – well that just put the tin lid on it as far as I was concerned. It's obvious that something really serious is going on, and that Teddy's tied up right in the middle of it.' Alice looked over at her friend. 'Well it is isn't it?'

Neither of the women spoke for a few moments, but then Alice went on.

'I never meant to make things difficult for you Josie. But I didn't know who else to ask – who might have had even a clue about the whole thing.' She turned to Josie. 'I knew you'd have connections at work – people who'd be in the know, but I didn't ...' Alice stopped, and looked at her friend.

'Well – my date with Billy is definitely on – that's for sure, after all this,' Josie exclaimed. 'All I've got to do now is try and put this to him in such a way that I don't blow Teddy's position … or yours for that matter, Alice.' The two women looked at each other, uneasiness marking both their faces.

'Do you want me to come with you?' Alice looked over at Josie who seemed to be miles away, surveying the river. It took a few minutes before the words seemed to filter through.

Josie jumped round. 'Let me get this right, Mrs Alice,' she said, suddenly laughing. 'I've got my first date in months, and you want to come along and play gooseberry!'

Alice couldn't help but laugh as well. 'Well, I just thought you might need …'

'Oh, I think I can manage dear old Billy,' she smirked. 'Getting the information will be the easy bit … it'll be controlling him afterwards – when he thinks it's payback time - that might be the issue.'

CHAPTER TWENTY ONE

Alice tried hard not to look at the peeling wallpaper in Josie's bedsitting room. The war had left so many people homeless that houses like this, converted into dozens of dingy rooms, were commonplace. The walls on the stairway somehow seemed to have absorbed the smells of badly cooked vegetables and were only too keen to hand them out to any passing visitor, but they were just a passing place, somewhere to be got through. It was in here where Josie had to spend her time, looking at this once-pretty room, faded flowers shrivelled on the walls, falling forward in their death throes. She had to look at this every morning when she woke, every time she warmed a tin of soup on that pitiful electric ring, every time she looked up from the book she was reading. Alice felt an overwhelming sense of shame for the self-pity she had shown when Josie had come to visit her; a whole house at her disposal, to do with whatever she chose, a proper kitchen to bake and fry and casserole, a garden to dry her shirts and her stockings.

Josie bent and held a match to the gas fire sitting precariously in the grate. 'It'll warm up soon,' she smiled, 'I don't bother when it's just me – an extra jumper does the same.' She busied herself, taking a teapot from a tiny cupboard, a tea caddy from the shelf, everything in its neatly stacked place.

Alice started to remove her jacket.

'You might want to keep that on for a minute,' Josie laughed. 'Even in the middle of summer it's freezing in this room.'

Alice felt the damp hanging in the air; she tried to ignore it and looked around for somewhere to sit. There was only one chair, wooden, worn, at the small square of table squeezed in front of the kitchen sink.

'Plonk yourself down over there,' Josie indicated the pink eiderdowned single bed, thrust into a corner. 'It's the most comfortable place in my little empire.'

Alice had been desperate to hear what had been discussed on Josie's "date"; they had agreed to meet as soon as they could, but it was the weekend, and there was every chance of Teddy turning up unexpectedly if they met at Alice's, so they had finally agreed on Josie's place. But despite their long friendship and their normally relaxed manner with each other, Alice sensed Josie's discomfort. It wasn't just the surroundings – as soon as Josie had finished making tea and sat herself down, she began to fiddle; the cosy on the teapot was taken off and re-arranged, a small speck of fluff was brushed from the sleeve of her navy cardigan, the clip in her hair was removed and re-positioned. Eventually the words burst out from her.

'Oh, Alice. This is all so – just so bloody awful.'

Alice was stunned. Yes, she had expected whatever Josie had found out to be something significant – otherwise why would it all be so "hush hush"? But for Josie to feel so strongly about it … And now that Alice looked more closely, she could see that Josie was stunned, almost as if someone had slapped her face, and left her reeling.

'What is it, Josie? What's happened?'

'Well, I met with Billy yesterday – just as we'd planned. We went for a drink at the Rose and Crown ...' Josie stopped, looking into space as though she were watching the event replay on a distant screen.

Even if she didn't really want to hear what Josie had to say, Alice was keen to hear the worst and come to terms with it. She wriggled, trying to find a comfortable spot on the edge of the rickety bed. But the creaking of the bedsprings seemed to jolt Josie out of her reverie, and she started gabbling her story.

'Well we chatted – you know, the usual stuff – the weather, and films we'd seen and places we'd like to go –like any normal date really; but we were onto our second drink and I thought we were never going to get round to talking about it. In the end I had to push him. "You were going to tell me about Silver Iodide," I said, after I'd bought him another Mild and Bitter.' Josie looked directly at Alice. 'He was looking like he'd hoped I'd forgotten – nodding as if to say "Yes, I did say that, but now I wish I hadn't." Anyway, he gulped his beer and started rattling on, talking about the photography, and all that stuff we've heard before, and then he just launched into it ...' Josie swallowed a mouthful her tea. 'Look Alice…I don't know how to say any of this … and whatever I say isn't going to make it any more palatable…' She looked down, almost whispering. 'So I'm just going to spit it out –tell it just like Billy told it to me.'

Alice forgot the discomfort of the bedsprings and the heat which was reaching no further than her toes, and concentrated on her friend's words.

'Well - It seems that the Air Ministry has been using this Silver Iodide for something completely different from all that photography stuff.' Josie sighed loudly. 'According to Billy, the scientists have discovered that if you drop the stuff into rain clouds, it forms crystals, and these create a sort of "platform" on which water can condense ...'

Josie paused, but Alice was impatient for more. 'Well that doesn't sound so bad. Then what?'

'Well, apparently that forms water droplets – which obviously creates rain.' Josie allowed the words to tumble out at speed, as if she were relieved to have got them into the open.

'So – this "cloud seeding" that I read about ... this is what it means then – they just do something to clouds to create much more rain than there would have been otherwise?'

Josie nodded, still looking as if she had been punched in the stomach.

As strange as it all sounded, Alice didn't see what was so awful about it all. In her mind's eye she saw images of clouds, slowly puffing up like sponge cakes in the oven, and then shedding their contents onto the land below - pools of rainwater gathering in the dips of the landscape, growing into temporary ponds or at worst small lakes. Surely these fleeting alterations weren't so disastrous?

'Well, isn't that a good thing – you know – bringing water in times of drought?' she hesitated. 'Especially in places like Africa or India where their crops regularly fail? Wouldn't it be great to push some rain their way and give their produce a chance …'

'Well, yes, it would be if it worked like that,' Josie butted in, 'But there's just one problem. As Billy pointed out you have to have some clouds in the first place to be able to seed them … and in the sort of places you're talking about they might not see a cloud from one week to the next, so it really wouldn't work …'

'Well, what's the point of it all then?' Alice demanded irritably. 'What's the use of creating more rain where we've already got it, and no rain in the places that need it? The whole thing doesn't make any sense.' For a moment she had begun to see Teddy as a bit of a hero – bringing much-needed water to the driest parts of the world - but Josie had burst that bubble almost before she had had time to let it form.

'But it isn't just a shower, Alice – this is about serious amounts of rain - major cloudbursts …' Josie suddenly seemed to have found a compelling interest in the spoon in the sugar bowl. 'And then there's – well - the damned difficult bit – the bit that no-one likes talking about.'

Alice looked up. 'Well what? What is it? You can't tell me all this and then just leave me in mid-air …' I've a right to know, she wanted to say, it's my husband who's involved in all this, not yours; the words were sitting on her tongue, when Josie snapped back.

'I'm going to,' Josie shouted. 'I'm going to tell you – but you won't want to hear it, I know you won't.' Josie took a gulp of her tea. 'Look – well, according to Billy, it seems that the War Office are really interested in this sort of thing because – well, because it means that they

116

could do things like flooding airfields – make them inoperable for an enemy air force – or they could bog down enemy troops in the field – trap them in saturated ground, so that they can't move or make advances on our outposts or our men …'

Alice could taste the wave of nausea rising in her throat. She had seen pictures of the trenches in the Great War, men up to their knees in the sodden winter mud, desperation on their faces as they tried to drag their weary bodies. But she had come too far now to leave the matter there. 'And what else?' she asked quietly. 'I can see by your face that that's not all …'

'It's terrible, Alice – after everything that's happened, you would think that we'd have had enough of this …' Josie sighed, tears welling in her eyes. 'Billy says … that if you detonate an atomic weapon into a one of these seeded clouds, the radio-active area will be spread with the massive amounts of rain - much further than with a standard atomic explosion.' Josie had turned pale, looked as if she might vomit at the words which had just passed across her lips.

Alice's instinct was to grab her jacket and run – back to a world where this wasn't happening to her, where she could bake apple crumble and get annoyed with Teddy for dropping his shirt on the floor, and water the sweet peas in the early morning. But as these thoughts ran rings around her head, Alice realised that there was another feeling completely which was overwhelming her. She was ashamed – ashamed of the fact that Teddy was right there - in the middle of all of this - making sure the experiments worked, so that disaster could be dropped with ease wherever and whenever someone sitting in the safety of an office decided it should.

And more than that she was angry, just *so* bloody angry with Teddy. Why had he got himself into all this … and how had she allowed herself to get mixed up this mess as well?

CHAPTER TWENTY TWO

'Oh, by the way, there's been a change of plan,' Teddy announced, almost smugly, as they were drinking coffee that evening.

'What's that?' Alice asked distractedly. She had been reading through a knitting pattern, a cardigan with a Fair Isle yoke, trying to decipher the complex instructions. She wasn't an expert knitter, had never got the hang of flicking the needles to and fro without looking at the stitches, but she had been desperate for something to keep her mind and her hands occupied and had taken advice from the woman in the haberdashery shop.

She stopped unwinding the skeins of blue and green yarn, and looked across as Teddy sipped nonchalantly from his cup. The thought crossed Alice's mind that he might not be going on this field trip after all, and for some reason she didn't understand, a tremor of alarm flashed through her.

'But you are still going to Rushcombe?' she blurted out.

Teddy looked up, surprised at her reaction. 'Oh yes, I'm definitely still going.' Infuriatingly, he picked up another ginger biscuit and started munching before he continued. 'It's just that Atkinson wants me to take the car now, rather than going by train.' He put the rest of the biscuit in his mouth, and for a moment was unable to speak.

Alice held the knitting needles tightly, subconsciously stabbing the points into the antimacassar on the arm of the chair. She knew she should have been pleased that there might be a chance Teddy wasn't going away; but her mind had been filled for so long with thoughts of catching Teddy "red-handed" with this woman he seemed to be having a fling with, that the thought of the whole situation suddenly being turned on its head left her feeling quite agitated.

'Steady on,' Teddy shouted, crumbs spraying from his mouth. 'I might be getting a pay rise, but we can't afford new furniture every five minutes.'

Alice thought this was rich coming from someone who had almost emptied the house of fittings, but she looked down at what she was doing to the chair and dropped the needles into her lap. 'Sorry, I was just ….' She shook her head, in an attempt to bring herself back to the present. 'Sorry – what were you saying about a train?'

'I wasn't saying anything about a train – other than I'm not going on it now. Atkinson has asked me to take the car …' He enunciated the words slowly, as if she were being particularly dense, but then must have registered and instantly misread the expression on Alice's face. 'Oh, don't worry about the money – Atkinson said they'll pay for the petrol - and a little more besides – wear and tear, that sort of thing.' He smiled to himself, looking pleased at his adoption into the world of petty cash and expenses. 'Anyway, it'll mean that I'll be able to get out and about a bit – monitor what's going on further afield, not just in Rushcombe. Which is really what they need, by the sounds of it … Rushcombe's just a base really …'

As Teddy wittered on, thoughts of the rain and the cloud-seeding and all the rest of it rushed back into Alice's head. 'Will it be …' she tried to think of a word that wouldn't give away what she had found out. 'Will it be – okay – all this work you're going to be carrying out?' It sounded feeble, even to her own ears.

Teddy looked up, confusion covering his face. '"Okay"? What do you mean – will it be "okay"? I'm only going to be taking a few readings here and there, making notes about what I see, reporting back anything unusual … It's hardly "behind enemy lines" stuff is it?' He started laughing, pulling faces at the absurdity of Alice's words. 'You're a strange thing sometimes you know, Alice Hathaway. I do wonder what on earth's going on in that little head of yours.'

He was so nonchalant, so light-hearted about the whole thing that Alice started once more to question herself. Had she read more into all of this than was really there – or was Teddy simply a much better actor than she had given him credit for, and was he, even now, just trying to put her off the scent?

She glanced over at him. His thoughts had obviously drifted; he looked as if he were already at the coast, driving his companion to some pretty little deserted cove, watching the two of them as they walked the shoreline, skimming sea-smoothed pebbles across the water.

'You look pleased with yourself...' Alice couldn't help but comment; it was the happiest she had seen her husband for some while.

'Well I am, to be honest old thing. I'm really looking forward to this trip.' Teddy looked over at Alice. 'I think my luck is turning at last – this will be a big step up for me you know, if it all goes well, and the extra money is going to make a big difference to my life –our life.'

The slip from "my" to "our" wasn't lost on Alice. But what struck her even more forcefully as she watched Teddy swig back the remains of his coffee was the feeling that they seemed to be in two altered worlds. She should have been the one in the dark, with no facts, no information about what was going on, but it seemed at that moment that it was Teddy who was existing in some fairy story world, where although there were evil spirits at play everything was going to turn out for the best in the end.

Teddy put his cup back on the tray, crashing the handle against the coffee pot in his eagerness to move on. 'Well, can't sit here gossiping – *I've* still got work to do,' he said as though it were Alice who had waylaid him with this conversation. He sauntered out of the room, whistling as he went. Alice glanced around her. Her mind wasn't on Fairisle patterns; she had excess energy twitching in her limbs, and she rolled up the wool and the needles and stuffed them back into the basket beside her chair. She began prowling the house, desperate for something to distract her.

CHAPTER TWENTY THREE

Alice drifted upstairs to the bedroom and dropped onto the stool in front of her dressing table. She picked up the tortoiseshell hairbrush and began pulling it through her hair, staring at her reflection, pondering the position she found herself in. She guessed that, in his own way, Teddy was fond of her, but he was such an enigma. When he was with her he seemed to enjoy her company, laughed with her, shared comments about wretched neighbours or nosy friends; in her view he didn't treat her any worse than most other husbands Alice had come across – but he obviously didn't see a problem with having another life outside of the one he had with Alice. She mindlessly picked up her compact and began to dab the soft powder on her cheeks. There was nowhere for her to go this evening – no need to put on make-up – but it made her feel better, the gentle perfume of the cosmetics, the healthy flush they brought to her skin. Thoughts began to run through her head – jumbled scenes in which Teddy went off permanently with this woman, mingled with the whole work thing going wrong and Teddy being publicly vilified and Alice trying to excuse his actions to the neighbours, and then Isobel interfering from the background, insisting that she move from the house because Teddy was no longer able to live there with her ….

Her head began to spin, and Alice sat on the bed and let herself fall back on the pillows. She closed her eyes, trying to blank out the tangle of images, but as she did so Teddy's earlier words drifted into her mind. "Atkinson has asked me to take the car". A smile came to her lips as she imagined him, Toad-like, tootling his way around the countryside, but as she did so the real significance of Teddy's words suddenly hit home. If Teddy was now taking their car to Rushcombe, then how on earth was she going to follow him?

'Damn, damn, damn,' Alice spoke aloud, slamming the hairbrush down on the dressing table. She pulled open the drawer and scrabbled around until she found the spare car key she had hidden there. 'After all my plans – what the hell am I supposed to do now?'. She looked again at her own reflection. The sensible person she thought herself to be seemed to have walked out of the room, and in her place was a vacant-looking blonde, biting her bottom lip. 'Oh pull yourself together for goodness sake.' Alice spoke directly to the eyes of the pathetic woman looking back at her. 'All you have to do – as Wing Commander Meredith was so fond of saying – is to regroup. No big deal – just a temporary hiccup, which you're more than capable of dealing with.'

Alice poked the key to the back of the drawer again – an insurance policy against further possible changes of plan – and picked up her handbag. She pulled out the small blue notebook she kept for shopping reminders and snippets of recipes or interesting-sounding books, and started to make herself a list. If Teddy and Mr

Atkinson could reverse their plans, she would simply have to do the same.

"1. Obtain train timetable" she wrote.

"2. Establish train times and length of journey" she continued, underlining the last three words.

She knew that Teddy had a train timetable – she had seen it in his jacket pocket when all this nonsense about going away had first started, but she doubted it would still be there. The obvious place for it would be his desk drawer, but after all Teddy's fuss about her being in his study, she had no intention of going in there again for a while. Even if she'd wanted to she couldn't check now anyway – Teddy was still ensconced in the room and would probably be there for the rest of the evening. Instead she went to the hallstand and grabbed at the fabric of his jacket, checking the pockets for anything thicker than a wallet, but there was nothing more than a handkerchief and a small bag of peppermints.

Teddy had probably abandoned it at work, she thought, or thrown it gleefully in the bin the minute he had found out he was to drive to the West Country. He would much rather drive, of course he would. He would be wallowing in that sense of being a "somebody", which driving a car still gave, particularly with petrol rationing having ended so recently. Everyone was still so cautious about driving anywhere at all, so an outing to Devon, with someone else covering the costs, would be a pleasure indeed for anyone, but especially for Teddy. No doubt he would be swanking about it already – dropping it into very possible conversation at the smallest opportunity. "Of course my seniors have insisted that I drive … I need to be able to get about down there, you see, let them know exactly what's going on, on the ground..."

The implied importance of it all would definitely fuel Teddy's ego, Alice thought, but in the meantime she needed to firm up out her own travel plans. She had no real qualms about travelling to Rushcombe by train, but her problem, she realised, was getting all the timetable information she would need. The journey up to London would be fine – the local trains went regularly into St Pancras station, and although she had no idea of the times she would surely be able to find that out easily enough. But further than that? She remembered from her WAAF days that trains to the West Country went from Paddington – but she was struggling to think of a way of finding out any more information without causing a stir. Previous experience had taught her that Mr Robinson who issued the tickets at Cotford station was quite an old woman when it came to tittle tattle. He had some sort of inner radar for potential gossip, and if she went along with her list of questions she knew he would remember every detail, and would make damned sure that he bumped into Teddy as he got off the 5.56, and make copious jokes about his wife wanting to run away from home and needing to know the times of the trains. Then of course Teddy would know immediately that something was wrong, and start bombarding *her* with questions, and her plans would be scuppered before they'd even started.

No, that wouldn't work at all. Alice thought and re-thought it, but every different scenario ended with Teddy uncovering her plans to follow him to Rushcombe. She tipped her head from side to side, trying to loosen the knots which had gathered in her neck and shoulders. She was tired of dealing with one hurdle just to find another one pushed in her way immediately afterwards, and the whole thing was giving her a dull thudding headache. She idly doodled the word "Paddington" in her notebook, elaborating the tail of the "g" and the tops of the "d's" as she let her mind wander round the problem. She would simply have to get up to London as early as possible, she supposed, then find her way across to Paddington, and discover the train times once she got there. The problem was that without any planning, there was every likelihood she would miss a connecting train and be hanging around for ages for the next – and then she might not arrive in Rushcombe until very late, with nowhere booked to stay once she got there. Alice slammed the notebook down on the table, feeling that everything was conspiring against her. For a fleeting moment she saw a picture of herself bundled up in a promenade shelter waiting for the first café to open. She knew she was being ridiculous, that dozens of people dealt with far worse every day, but as she looked up she was shocked to see the fearful woman staring back from the mirror, and realised she was working herself into a complete lather over the whole thing.

'Oh come on Alice Hathaway,' she said crossly to herself. 'What would you do if you were still in the WAAF?' And as soon as the words had entered her head she realised that she had a possible solution to her problem.

CHAPTER TWENTY FOUR

Had she known what was going to transpire later in the day Alice would never have gone out, but that Tuesday morning she had had enough of the house. The constant round of dusting and washing and peeling potatoes had begun to close in on her more than usual, and even the respite she had found in scrabbling around in Teddy's study was now just agitating her frustration. The garden too had lost its appeal, and she had been disinclined to go out there for fear of being chastised by Mr Atkins for the weeds she had allowed to run riot over the past couple of weeks. She moped around, finally, reluctantly, checking the calendar hanging on the kitchen wall. Her choices lay between the church jumble sale and the Women's Institute coffee morning. Neither appealed in the slightest, but she couldn't bear the idea of another day within these four walls. It didn't take long to consider the two options - the thought of sorting unwashed clothing and musty books at the back of the church hall made her cringe - and she grudgingly opted for the coffee morning.

'Ah Mrs Hathaway,' a woman in an over-decorated blue hat had called stridently down the length of the room as soon as she had walked in. She had continued to grill Alice on her lack of attendance for several minutes, and, even once the woman had been summoned to deal with a shortage of teacups, other similarly dressed matrons had taken over, with wheres, whens and whys being thrust into her face at regular intervals. Alice had escaped before the speaker had quite begun on her exposition of "Twenty ways with cabbage", leaving a half-finished cup of Camp coffee on the table by the door, along with the details of the next meeting. She had stuffed her hat into her basket as she freewheeled away from the town bridge, feeling an unfamiliar exhilaration as the wind rushed through her unruly hair, enjoying the exertion of pushing hard on the pedals to take her along Thursday Street and through the side lanes to the house.

As she jumped off the bike, fighting against the gravel and the overgrown privet hedge at their front entrance, Alice noticed that the garage door was slightly ajar. She knew that it was normally closed and locked – Teddy was very particular about that – so she propped the bike against the magnolia tree and crept around the edge of the driveway, attempting to avoid the crunch of the loose shingle. Just as she reached for the garage door it flew open.

Alice screamed, more in surprise than fear, but the pipsqueak of sound seemed to reverberate in the quiet street.

A face appeared around the door; a face Alice vaguely recognised but could not put a place or a name to.

'What the hell are you doing?' she barked at the man. Fear had always brought Alice's assertive side to the fore and the man who had so cheerfully poked his head out now looked affronted, terrified even. He stepped back into the shadows of the dusty space, which only encouraged Alice. She flung open the wooden door, setting a wide spotlight over the stranger and their little car, sitting neatly in its space, awaiting its regular weekend drive.

'What the hell do you think you're doing in our garage?' Alice stood, hand on hip, brokering no nonsense. The man froze, open-mouthed, apparently unable to mutter a syllable.

'Well, come on – out with it. You're trespassing – at least have the decency to give me an explanation.' Alice could feel her pulse pounding in her temple, but she wasn't about to stand down now.

'I – eh – I work with Teddy.' A voice, quiet but rich, sprung from the gloom inside the garage.

'And?'

'...And – er – he asked me ... Well, he indicated that he needed ...' The man cast his eye around as if looking for assistance from the garden tools, the oil can, the pair of Teddy's overalls hanging like a dead man from the hook in the corner.

'He asked you to break into our house did he – and do what?'

'No – no. I wasn't breaking in. It's just that Teddy has to go to ...' The man paused, pondering presumably how much he should say. He took a long breath and, as though the oxygen had brought him back to his senses, began to talk more coherently.

'Look. Teddy has been given this project at work – I can't give you the details, but ...'

Alice raised her eyebrows; she was interested to see how much of the story she had already uncovered would be revealed by this man.

'He has to go – let's say "further afield", and he was talking of using his car, but the boss isn't too keen – doesn't want the project being abandoned because of breakdowns, that sort of thing.' The man paused, but Alice had no intention of helping him out by replying. 'So – I just happened to be in the area, and I thought … I thought I'd check the car out, and then I could either back Teddy up or ….'

'Or tell tales to Sir?' Alice snapped. 'And why the hell would Teddy need you to back him – or otherwise? I've never heard such a cock and bull story in all my days,' she said, making to shut the garage door with the man still inside. 'I'm calling the police right now.' She scraped the door across the gravel and began to close the hasp in the lock.

'No – honestly – please Mrs Hathaway...' He sounded frantic.

Alice paused for a moment. Maybe it was the mention of her name, or the fact that her heartbeat and her anger were beginning to subside a little, but she hesitated about what she should do next. Slowly she undid the latch and pulled the door back again.

'Look, I know you won't believe me, but I can't tell you what I'm doing here – I really can't.' The man paused, trying a pitiful smile on Alice, but it met with just a stare. 'But if you call the police I'll lose my job.'

Alice remained silent.

'I haven't taken anything – you can search me if you like.' He held out his arms, but Alice didn't move. 'And

I haven't damaged anything either – I'd only just got here when you arrived - honestly.'

Alice's usual softness was beginning to return. He looked like a beaten puppy, soulful eyes looking pleadingly into hers.

'I'm going to ring Teddy - check out your story.' Alice turned towards the house. 'What's your name?'

'It's – it's …'

Alice's look defied him to issue another lie.

'It's Christopher, Mrs Hathaway, Christopher Frost. Teddy asked me to check out the car so that I could …'

'Well if that's the case why didn't he tell me you were coming?'

'Oh, you know Teddy,' the man laughed, relaxing a little. 'Memory like a sieve.   Never remembers from one minute to the next what you've told him.'

The accuracy of his picture of Teddy caused Alice's previously smooth flow of words to come to a halt, as if they had been dammed. He was absolutely right – she could tell Teddy at ten o'clock what they were doing that evening, and by lunchtime he would have no idea that they were doing anything at all and would have started making his own plans.

Alice could feel the man watching her, waiting for her to make the next move. He made her feel she ought to be offering him coffee, and the best biscuits. But she was still aflame inside, indignant at his cheek – his "brass neck" as Josie would have called it; his confident ability to be trespassing and yet still to make her feel as if it were she who was in the wrong.

'Well – I'd still like you to leave,' she eventually barked at him.

'But if I could just …' Christopher tipped his head towards the car.

'No.'

Christopher stood calmly, and to make it worse he was smiling beautifully, his puppy dog eyes beseeching her.

'No – definitely not.' Alice felt like stamping her foot. 'If there's a problem with the car you'll have to come back when Teddy's here – sort it out with him.'

The young man shrugged his shoulders and casually brushed some invisible cobweb from the sleeve of his well-tailored jacket. 'Whatever you say Mrs Hathaway. I wouldn't want to distress you.'

Alice wanted to slap his handsome face, boot his backside across the driveway and back through the privet hedge. But she noticed a curtain flicker across the road.

'Good day Mr Frost,' she said curtly, holding out an arm to indicate the exit route.

He saluted her, crunching his way across the gravel, whistling "Unforgettable" as he went.

Alice stood at the entrance, watching his back as he sauntered down the road. The conversation she would have with Teddy this evening was already taking place inside her head, all the questions, all the points about her safety and what the hell was he thinking of, inviting strangers into their house?

She stared angrily down the street, but, as if he knew she was watching, the young man looked back, and held up a hand in acknowledgement. She knew she had been duped, but she just couldn't work out how – or why.

CHAPTER TWENTY FIVE

Jack

Sod's law I suppose, because another thirty seconds and I would have been out of there and down the road before she was anywhere near. There was no way I would have even been there in the first place, whatever Teddy had been suggesting, if he'd hadn't told me so emphatically that she wasn't going to be at home. I checked more than once, and he fell over himself to assure me that he'd checked the calendar, that she'd be out all afternoon, so I nearly died, I can tell you, when everything was done and I slipped round the side of the house only to hear someone at the front gate.

If she hadn't made such a song and dance of trying to get that damned bike over the gravel I wouldn't have had any warning at all, and we'd have been dancing round each other at the front door.

For a minute, when I looked around me, I thought there was nowhere to go – that I'd be caught there like the proverbial rabbit, but then I saw the key – in the side door of the garage - and I thought I'd be fine in there until she'd gone into the house, got her pinny on and started dusting or baking or whatever. But those bloody front doors were so badly fitting – typical Hathaway –

that they sprung open, just at the moment she came up the drive. I could have killed him, leaving me exposed like that, while he swanned about in the background.

And why the hell did I tell her my real name? Well, at least I didn't say "Jack", I s'pose. I think it's only my mother who ever calls me Christopher, but at least that name put a bit of distance between me and the story. Anyone with any sense would take only five minutes though, to put together "Frost" and "Jack", but Teddy's little lady luckily didn't seem to make that connection – or at least not while I was there, anyway.

And that story that I came up with – what a load of old bull that was. I'm usually brilliant at thinking on my feet – always thought I would have made a good barrister actually - but maybe it was the stress of it all - and I can't deny it, a bit of excitement – because my mind just went totally blank. Checking out the car – who the hell was ever going to believe that? Although I have to say that she almost looked convinced, by the time I'd given her the puppy-dog eyes, and the pleading "I'll lose my job" routine. These eyes have got my out of no end of scrapes in the past, but I have to say, this was one of the less enjoyable ones.

I think I might have got away with it, no thanks to Teddy – although I'm pretty certain that he'll be for the high jump when he sits down to dinner tonight. Glad I'm not in his shoes, that's all I can say … but then, I wouldn't ever put myself into his particular shoes, would I?

CHAPTER TWENTY SIX

Dinner had somehow benefitted from Alice's anger. Instead of her usual half-hearted efforts, the kitchen had rung all afternoon to the clanging of pots, the clink of spoons against bowls. Sausages were violently stabbed and grilled, batter beaten into a turmoil with a hand whisk; the resulting Toad in the Hole was brought solemnly to the table, burgeoning and browned, with a jug of aromatic onion gravy.

'You've excelled yourself today, dear.' Teddy put down his newspaper, looking simultaneously delighted and dumbstruck at this change in his culinary fortunes.

'Hmm,' Alice grunted, hacking into the golden crust. 'More than can be said for some.' Her mouth was tight with the irritation she was trying to hold back, and her words came out as a mumble.

'What's that old thing?' Teddy looked quizzically at the plate which Alice had slammed down, teetering on the tablecloth. 'You'll have to speak up – can't hear a word over the rattling of the crockery.' He laughed, and that was enough to release the dam of Alice's rage.

'What the hell do you mean by sending your work crony round here to start rooting around our house?'

'My dear, I've no idea …'

'You know exactly what I mean,' Alice waved the pie slice which she still had in her hand from serving. 'You told that young man – what's his name – Snow or Frost or whatever it is – you told him to come over here and check out the car – *our* car. I found him lurking in our garage ...' Alice stopped to catch her breath. Teddy had slumped back in his chair, his skin as pale as the mash steaming on his plate, but that didn't stop her. 'He frightened the life out of me Teddy. He could have been anyone ...'

Teddy's had propped his head in his hands, rubbing his ashen forehead. But it was only a moment before he recovered himself, sitting up straighter, coughing loudly.

'My dear sweet thing – I can't make head nor tail of what you're talking about.' He waved at the food on the table. 'Sit down and let's eat this lovely meal and then you can tell me all about it.'

While Teddy munched and chewed, Alice could barely swallow a mouthful. She was fuming that Teddy had given himself thinking time – not to mention extra minutes for her temper to subside - so that when they spoke again he would have his calm rational answers lined up and ready.

She banged her knife and fork down on her plate, whilst he continued eating, adding a little more salt, pouring a second helping of gravy. Alice had forgotten to switch on the wireless and the silence of the room was oppressive.

'Now, I think I can see what has happened here.' Teddy didn't speak until he had started to refold his napkin into precise quarters. His face had recovered a little of its colour, but to Alice it still looked unnaturally pale.

'But …' Alice opened her mouth; Teddy held up a hand.

'It would appear that Frost – it *was* Frost that you met earlier – has got hold of the wrong end of the stick. He's just a clerk in the office – bit of a busy-body actually. He must have heard Atkinson quizzing me about our old jalopy. Cheeky little blighter must have decided to check it out and report back – bit of a toady if you ask me.' Teddy ran his finger round his collar, and loosened his tie a fraction. 'But nothing to worry about old thing – just someone getting ideas above their station.' Teddy pushed back his chair.

'Just a minute, Teddy,' Alice was red-faced. 'A complete stranger appears in our garage and I'm supposed not to worry? He could have been anyone – a burglar or ... or he could have attacked me.' Alice's voice had risen in decibels and octaves. 'At the very least you could have warned me …'

'But I told you, my dear' Teddy butted in. 'I knew nothing about the car being checked. I didn't arrange it – he just took it upon himself. There's nothing I could have done …' He paused for a moment, still looking uncomfortably warm. 'Anyway – no harm done, was there? So you needn't worry about it any more.' This time he pushed his chair fully back from the table. 'Now – any chance of a coffee, old girl? I need to go out shortly.'

Alice grasped one hand in the other, holding her fingers tightly to prevent herself throwing a plate at the closing door.

CHAPTER TWENTY SEVEN

Alice paced with the telephone receiver in her hand just as far as the plaited cord would allow her. Now that she'd had more time to think about it, the idea of ringing Lucy was becoming an increasingly mixed prospect.

Lucy had been in the WAAF with Alice and Josie – but so different from either of them in every possible way - statuesque and stylish, moneyed and totally immodest; one of those types who glides over every problem in life, and whose parents had bought her a place in London as soon as she was twenty one. Alice had often wondered how their three such varying threads had knitted together, but combine they had, and when their days with one another were coming to an end, Lucy had nagged Alice to go and visit.

'Oh come on Alice, it'll be such fun. We can be girls about town - paint London red.'

But the weeks had gone by, and then the months and Alice had never taken Lucy up on her invitation. 'But maybe,' she thought, 'this is just the opportunity to kill two birds with one stone ... or of course for Lucy to tell me to just get lost.'

She'd had it all worked out in her head - if she stayed with Lucy, just overnight, that would allow her to get an early train down to the West Country. She could arrive in good time to get her bearings and have plenty of the day left to find somewhere suitable to stay that wasn't going to blow her meagre budget. A good night's sleep and then she could start, fresh-eyed, on her quest to catch Teddy - red-handed, with any luck – dallying with his wretched fancy woman.

Alice doodled on her notepad as she thought the idea through. 'But even if Lucy doesn't think I've got the biggest cheek in the world – ignoring her for months, and then only ringing when I want a favour – I've still got the problem that I'm going to have to tell her where I'm going.' And she had done so well up until now *not* to tell anyone where she was following Teddy to – not even Josie. When she had first switched the location of Teddy's jaunt she had absolutely no idea why she hadn't told the truth. Maybe it had been the shame she felt at the impending failure of her marriage – or perhaps this was something she just knew she had to do alone; but whatever the workings of her subconscious mind, Alice realised that simply on a practical level she couldn't tell the same story to Lucy that she had told Josie. If she *had* been going to Derbyshire, Alice was pretty sure she would have been able to travel north and change trains without going into London; the same probably went for travelling eastwards. So she needed another decoy destination … and that only really left south.

She doodled a very rough and inaccurate map of the south of England on the telephone pad, trying to recall all the towns that lined the coast.

'Brighton – that would be good,' Alice eventually announced with enthusiasm, as if she would actually be strolling along the Palace Pier, or admiring the wonders of the regency Pavilion. 'But why?' she debated. 'What reason can I give Lucy for a trip to Brighton?' Alice paused, thinking through the possibilities. She had a sinking feeling that, whatever she said, Lucy would want to travel with her.

A funeral. That would do it. Highly unlikely that anyone would want to attend the funeral of someone they didn't even know. All Alice had to do was to create the right character to fit the bill.

She pulled out her address book and found the appropriate page once more – although by now she knew the number off by heart. The door to the dining room was ajar and she could see through to the garden; she stared out at two magpies fighting over something bloody and veined on the lawn knowing that she was prevaricating but not knowing why….it was obviously the best way of getting herself to Rushcombe, but something was holding her back.

'Oh, this is ridiculous,' Alice sniffed after a few minutes, pulling out a handkerchief and loudly blowing her nose. She dialled the number quickly and waited.

'Lucy?' Alice didn't recognise the voice which answered the telephone.

'Yes – this is Lucy Heatherington. Who's calling?'

'It's me. Alice – Alice Moore,' she said, reverting to the maiden name Lucy would remember her by. There was a pause, as if facts were being checked, photographs in the mind's eye being shuffled.

'Alice! It's wonderful to hear from you. How are you?'

141

For a few moments their conversation bubbled with names and dates and reminiscences, while Alice waited patiently for the right moment.

'Now Lucy – I have to travel down to Brighton next week, and I was wondering … would I be able to call in to see you on the way?' She crossed her fingers, hoping that Lucy would go down the route of generosity and not resentment.

'Oh that would be wonderful - but you must stay. There's plenty of room. And perhaps I could come with you – to Brighton …'

Alice throat constricted; no words would come into her mouth. It was just the response she had hoped to avoid, and for a moment all thoughts migrated from her head.

'That's really very kind of you Lucy.' Alice breathed out slowly, making an effort to relax her shoulders. 'I'd love to stay the night – have a good old catch up with you. But unfortunately … well, the reason I'm going to Brighton is to attend my great aunt's funeral …'

The easiness, the way the lie just slithered from her tongue, shocked her. The same easy lies seemed to be multiplying within her over the past few weeks, but she had no chance to ponder that as Lucy went on.

'Oh – that's a shame. I mean – I'm sorry to hear about your bereavement, but it would have been great to spend the day together … Never mind. Another time, perhaps …'

The disappointment was obvious in Lucy's voice and Alice felt a pang of guilt for spinning her a story, but there was no other way. She had already said far more to Josie than she should have done, and she really

142

couldn't deal with someone else asking questions, picking over the remnants of her life.

Lucy chattered on brightly, making arrangements, giving directions while Alice noted everything down on her notepad. Her instinct, once the call was finished, was to hide the notebook away from Teddy's prying eyes, until it occurred to her that she had already told him about her plans to visit Lucy. 'You're getting paranoid Mrs Hathaway,' she smiled to herself, pleased to see that the woman in the hall mirror was looking more positive, more like Alice's old self.

CHAPTER TWENTY EIGHT

'I was thinking …' Alice tried to sound casual, realising, as she listened to her own voice, that the roles were reversed and it was now she not Teddy who was playing a part, meting out words as she tested the reaction.

'Careful old thing – you know it's not good for you!' Teddy snorted at his own joke, sniggering as he waited for her to continue.

'Well, while you're away it'll be quiet here …' She didn't say 'It's always quiet; every single day is as silent as an empty playground, and most evenings too. Even when you're here it feels like no-one's home …' She didn't say any of that; she went on calmly, making the rehearsed words sound as natural as she could. 'So I thought I might make the most of the time and go and visit a friend.' She waited for the question – the one she had rehearsed an answer to.

'Sounds like a good idea. Can't have you sitting around here for days getting bored, can we?' Teddy carried on flicking through the newspaper, noisily turning the pages, making each one crack as he moved it on.

The lack of questions threw Alice; for want of anything else to say she slid into the response she had rehearsed anyway.

'You remember Lucy don't you?'

She paused, waiting to see if Teddy's head would snap up at the mention of the name. She had always thought that Teddy had had a bit of a thing for Lucy; for a while - before he got together with Alice – he had followed her around like a hungry puppy. Alice had never understood why – Lucy had not a curl or a curve in sight – but something about her had drawn Teddy irresistibly it seemed. She'd been even more baffled as to why there had been the sudden change – why from one Friday to the next, Lucy had been abandoned and *she* was suddenly the focus of Teddy's attention. It was as if someone had whispered in Teddy's ear that there was something inappropriate about Lucy, and he had dropped her like a stinging nettle.

'Well,' Alice continued, 'Lucy's living the high life up in London, and I thought it would be fun to catch up with her for a day or two …'

The mention of Lucy seemed to have no effect on Teddy. It was as if he had never known the woman.

'Splendid idea,' he said vaguely, appearing to be absorbed in some new article, only half-listening to her.

'So I thought I'd go the same day as you? Probably catch the eight thirty train up to London so that I'd have the whole afternoon …'

'Oh.' Teddy suddenly transferred his full attention from the newspaper to her. 'Oh – I wouldn't bother trying to get the eight thirty. Always a real squeeze – too many stuffy old men puffing on their pipes and droning on about the situation in Kenya or Korea.' He paused, deep in thought for a moment. 'No – you'd be much better off catching one of the later trains – the 9.45 or the 10.15 would get you there in plenty of time.'

"Got you!" Alice wanted to shout, as if she had trapped a particularly annoying wasp in a jar. She had guessed that if she suggested getting a train anywhere near the time that Teddy might be travelling, he'd want to shift her out of the way – not wanting her to be intruding upon his usual routine or mixing with his train cronies. Who needed a train timetable? Teddy had given her all the information she needed. Now she just needed to get things sorted out with Lucy and she could be on her way.

CHAPTER TWENTY NINE

There was a queue a mile long at the Market Street Main Post Office. Alice had thought it better to come into town rather than use the tiny local branch where everyone knew everyone's business, but as she watched the butcher's boy heave three bags of coins up onto the counter, and an elderly woman with a stick struggling even to get the teller's window, she wondered if that had been a good idea.

Having gone through her savings book at the kitchen table and carefully made her own calculations, Alice had already decided not to take everything out of the account. She didn't know, but she suspected that closing an account would be a lengthy exercise, with forms and signatures and a great deal of double-stamping on every sheet of paper – and a barrage of questions too, she had no doubt. Instead she had decided that she would leave at least ten pounds in the account, but that she would take the passbook with her when she went to Devon, just in case of emergencies.

The man at the desk had pock-marked skin and round finger-smeared glasses. He peered at her through the grime.

'I'd like to withdraw fifteen pounds please,' Alice said too quickly.

'How much was that – madam?' He seemed to be examining every inch of her face, her neck, her bare arms.

Alice moved her hands below the counter. 'Fifteen pounds please,' she repeated more firmly.

The clerk looked at her again, fingering the book.

'I can't do that Madam.' He stared through the grimy spectacles.

'But why ever not?'

'Had you ever taken the time to look at the details presented in the back of your "Post Office Savings Bank Book"' – he held the book so that she could see the final page. 'You would have seen that the maximum amount which can be withdrawn "on demand" is three pounds.' He sneered, a grimace for a smile.

Alice stood, open-mouthed, as he continued, reading from the book.

'Any larger amount by notice to the Chief Office,' he said too loudly, looking over her head to see if he had an audience. 'Sums up to ten pounds being normally payable the day after receipt of the application …'

Alice could hear people behind her in the queue, muttering, shuffling in impatience. 'I'll take three pounds now then,' she demanded, 'And I'd like to give notice to take a further ten pounds tomorrow.'

The nicotine-stained fingers reached for a drawer, and after some delay withdrew a piece of paper. 'You will need to complete this form,' he said, reluctantly passing it under the grille to her.

Alice reached for her bag to look for a pen.

'No –not here. It's far too busy. I can't allow a queue to form.' He had an oily smirk on his face, his eyes screwed into some pretence of a smile. 'You'll have to take it to the desk,' he indicated with a nod of his head 'Bring it back when it's completed.' He closed the drawer and shuffled papers together, dismissing her.

Alice looked at the queues, which were now knotting themselves together back to the door. 'I'll take my three pounds now please,' she said, pushing the savings book back across the counter. 'I'll come back with the form later.'

The clerk picked up his pen and began writing figures in the book, painstakingly checking his adding up before drawing a line under the new balance. He pulled out another drawer from beneath the desk. Alice watched his fingers linger over the notes and coins; he picked at them like a hungry bird, eventually gripping the fist full of money, and started to count it out for her.

Alice snatched it from the counter and put the whole lot into her purse, not bothering to separate out the notes into the wallet section. 'Thank you so much,' she smiled a gritted smile and turned before the wretched man could speak again.

She pushed her way across to the table the man had indicated and put down the form and her bag. There was a pen attached to a chain, but it was dried up and crusty; as Alice searched in her handbag for another she heard someone calling her name.

'Alice – over here, Alice.'

She scanned the crowd and saw someone waving. She waved back before fully realising who it was.

'Oh – Josie!' she said, smiling as recognition came at last.

Josie indicated that she would meet her outside. Alice couldn't explain about the form, across the congested room, so nodded her agreement and fought her way to the exit. But just as she pulled at the heavy door, Isobel appeared at her side.

Alice gasped, almost squealing.

'Did I startle you dear?' Her mother-in-law grinned salaciously, relishing the effect she had created. 'You look as if you've seen a ghost.'

'No – no - I'm fine. Just surprised to see you that's all.' Alice was doing her best to forget the last conversation she had had with Isobel. It seemed that her mother-in-law had put it from her mind too, although Alice knew this would only be a temporary state of affairs.

Nevertheless, Alice was aware that Isobel was intently studying her face.

'It's okay, I haven't robbed the Post Office or anything.' Alice knew she was talking rubbish, but she couldn't stop herself. She found herself still talking while Isobel was speaking to her. 'Plenty of money left for you!'

'I only need four threepenny stamps actually,' Isobel said dryly.

'Well I'll leave you to it then,' Alice gabbled. 'Must dash – lots to do.' And she bustled out through the door before Isobel could ask any questions.

She walked a few steps away from the Post Office, and stood, enjoying the dribble of sunshine which had penetrated the clouds. A boy and a girl were playing tag, and wound their way around her. She had to step into the road to avoid colliding with them. 'Careful you two – this isn't a playground,' she snapped and was immediately annoyed with herself for being such a killjoy.

But that's what happened, she thought, as soon as Isobel got inside her head. She quite expected her mother-in-law to re-appear, making some excuse to come back with her to the house, or to invite her for coffee so that she could probe and prod, eager to find out what Alice had been up to.

'Well, she can damn-well ask 'til the cows come home,' Alice spoke aloud, ignoring the strange look she received from the man sweeping lazily along the gutter.

'Here at last,' a voice said breezily behind her.

To Alice's relief it wasn't Isobel but Josie who tapped her on the shoulder, bright and bubbly as ever.

'Hello stranger,' she said. 'Time for a coffee?'

Alice couldn't think of anything she'd like better at that moment than a chat with dear Josie, and they walked arm in arm towards the square.

•

'So, it's all on, is it?' Josie said, concern creasing her face.

'Yes – oh, don't look at me like that Josie. I've got to do this, whatever the outcome. I can't spend the rest of my days wondering what Teddy's up to or if he's with somebody else.'

'It's just that - you look a bit stressed …'

'Oh, that's not Teddy. It's just that I've been trying to take some money out from my savings account, and that dreadful little man in there – she indicated back in the direction of the Post Office '– took the greatest pleasure in telling me I couldn't – well not without filling in forms in triplicate and giving a hundred year's notice and bowing down three times …'

The two women looked at each other and laughed.

'But seriously Alice, do you think everything will be okay?'

Alice looked at her friend, as if following an errant husband was ever going to turn out "okay".

'I don't just mean about Teddy,' Josie added hastily. 'I mean,' she looked around her, but no-one was the slightest bit interested in their conversation. 'I mean – all the other stuff. You know.' She looked meaningfully at Alice, eyebrows raised.

'I know what you mean,' Alice looked kindly at her friend. 'I asked Teddy exactly the same thing the other day …'

Josie looked up, shocked that Alice might have been discussing Teddy's work secrets openly with him.

'Oh, not in any detail – just generally saying "will it all be okay"; I think he thought I was mad,' Alice smiled, thinking how much everything had changed in the space of just a few short weeks.

''Well, make sure you let me know when you're leaving.' Josie said, pointing her cake fork at her friend. 'I'll come and wave you off.'

'I don't think you will,' thought Alice as she nodded at her friend, making out that her mouth was full of cake.

Josie needed to get back to work, and so Alice completed the form while she sat at the café table, finishing off the remains of the tea from the pot as she carefully filled in the details.

The queue was shorter when she returned to the Post Office, and to her relief there was no sign of the grimy man. She was assured by the snowy-haired woman at the counter that the money would be available for her the next day, and as she strode out along the lane on her way home Alice felt a sense of relief, but at the same time butterflies of excitement and anticipation were fluttering around her stomach and her head. Train, money, Lucy – everything was beginning to fall into place.

CHAPTER THIRTY

Breakfast was a strange affair.

For the first time Alice could remember since they had lived at the house, Teddy was out of bed before the alarm, and washed and piled into his flannels and his favourite blue tie before she had time even to struggle into her dressing gown and wander, bleary-eyed, downstairs. Despite her coaxing, he had only a small bowl of cereal, and even that was only half-finished when he rose from the table and started to collect his bags together.

'Must dash, can't be late.' He spoke breathlessly as he jammed his arms into his sports jacket. He was half way out of the front door before he stepped back and planted a hurried kiss on Alice's cheek. 'See you in a few days,' he yelled from the drive, as he threw his bags into the boot of the car. A spray of gravel spun from the wheels, and he was gone.

She was used to being on her own every morning - every day in fact - but the house seemed so much quieter today than it usually did as she drifted from cupboard to larder, gazing at odds and ends of food which might go stale before her return; she knew that she should really use them all up but in the end she opted just for a boiled egg and a thick slice of toast and dripping.

As Alice savoured the saltiness of the dripping spread - beef, her favourite - she smiled to herself, partly at the thought of seeing Lucy after such an age, partly at the pleasure of spending the best part of a day on trains, with no obligation to do anything at all – no polishing, no potatoes to peel, no-one to answer to, just the scenery to take in and other passengers to watch and daydream about.

She cleared away her plate and her cup and looked around the kitchen – everything neat and tidy, just as she would want it when she returned. She pictured herself walking through the front door in few days' time, and wondered whether it would be with relief or regret. 'Well, too late now,' she murmured. 'What will be will be.'

Her handbag, coat, hat and a battered suitcase stood ready in the box bedroom but it took her two journeys to bundle her belongings downstairs, and even then she had run back up a third time to check that she had left nothing behind. Teddy hadn't seemed to notice the inordinate amount of luggage she had for supposedly a short trip to London, and for once she was glad of his self-absorption. Finally she was ready for one last look in the hall mirror and, with a tweak of her best summer hat, she was set.

After all her planning, Mr Robinson at the ticket office seemed barely to notice her. He was distracted by the man behind her, who was signalling frantically that his train was about to arrive, that he needed a ticket before it departed again. The story she had rehearsed for the station master's curious ears didn't even get an

155

airing, and she trooped down the platform to the iron bridge feeling rather cheated. The steep flight of stairs towered dauntingly above her, but she gripped the handle of her case resolutely, ready to battle her way up and then back down to Platform 4. It was cumbersome, and she had manoeuvred it up only the first three steps, glad that she had left herself plenty of time, when a young man – no more than a lad really – stopped at her side.

'Take that for you Miss?' he asked, holding a hand out for the case. She passed it over meekly and trailed behind as he strode over the clanking bridge. Then she sped up, suddenly jerking into action as it occurred to her that he might board the wrong train with the case still in his hand; but he stopped at the foot of the steps, grinning at her.

'There you are Miss – all done.' He sauntered off down the platform before she had time to thank him properly. Unsure whether she should follow or let things be, Alice shuffled into the Ladies Waiting Room. It was empty and cold compared with the day outside, and Alice shivered as she perched on the edge of the hard seat. She wished she had bought a book with her, or even last week's copy of the Woman's Weekly. For now she could only stare from the platform to the minute hand of the clock and back again, ready to jump up and take her position as soon as it was time for the train to arrive.

For one awful moment, as she settled herself into her seat, Alice saw the back of a woman's hat in the corridor and convinced herself that it was Isobel. She squeezed herself into the corner, turning awkwardly to the window until the train chugged and rumbled into life. She knew

156

she was being ridiculous – that the chances of Isobel happening to be on the same train on the same day were probably a thousand to one; and that the chance of her travelling third class was even more remote. Only once the train was moving steadily forward though did Alice turn to look at her fellow travellers. In their WAAF days, she and Josie had come up with a game to pass the slow and crowded wartime journeys; "Carriage Criminals" Josie had named it, as they had used their fellow passengers for the final denouement of a murder, in the best Poirot tradition. She looked around at her would-be offenders –The young man with his hat pulled down and a newspaper held up, so that she could see only his highly polished shoes and the top of his head; the pale vicar, primly holding his knees together so that his legs wouldn't brush against the young woman by the window; the same young woman hiding her calloused hands. The newspaper man was the red herring, Alice decided; the hard working young woman was the one with revenge to be taken.

It passed the first part of the journey, and from there Alice was happy to have the views from the window as further entertainment. Although it had been a while since Alice had made the trip up to London she still loved the way that town faded into country and then back to town before it became city. Backs of high Victorian terraces, smoke-blackened, with bicycles, baths, kennels squeezed into their tight little yards; an apple tree fighting for air, an unexpected parade of dahlias, their colour shining out amongst the grimy bricks and chimneys.

Eventually the train began to slow. They still had some way to go before they reached St Pancras, but the man opposite was putting away his newspaper, and the vicar was retrieving his worn coat from the luggage rack. She had tried not to think of the enormity of what she was about to do, but as she gathered her bags around her, she took a deep breath to steady herself. When she had written down Lucy's instructions, she had also checked Teddy's map of the Underground system, scribbling down the details of every station between St Pancras and Putney Bridge at the back of her notebook. But that didn't stop her asking a porter, and taking just a brief glance at the route map on the wall before she made her way down into the Underground station.

The platform was surprisingly busy for late morning and Alice hung back, not wanting to be jostled nearer to the electrified line. A warm gritty breeze blew through the tunnel as the rumble of the approaching train increased. Alice forced herself to step forward, battering the young couple in front with her case as she made sure she got into the carriage. They didn't seem to mind – they even made room for her as she pushed the case into the corner and, holding the pole, stood guard over it. At the next station a young man offered her his seat, but she didn't want to leave her case. She thanked him, but he just shrugged his shoulders and looked away. At Fulham Broadway a man in a maroon turban, neatly pleated and tucked round his head stepped onto the train. Exotic amongst the beiges and greys, Alice struggled to take her eyes from him. He gave a hint of a bow as she glanced at him again and she realised she had been staring. She tried to shuffle round but it was difficult to move, and the humidity and staleness of the carriage began to overwhelm her. She desperately wanted to take off her coat; she wriggled and tried to shake her sleeves from her arms but there was little enough room to stand, let alone manoeuvre clothes, so she had to make do, blowing her breath upwards to try to cool her face. As soon as she saw the signs for Putney Bridge, she grabbed her case, clattering several shins as she did so, desperate to be out of that sea of heat and bodies.

CHAPTER THIRTY ONE

The platform emptied quickly as Alice looked up and down, unsure, despite Lucy's directions, which way she should walk. Eventually she noticed the tall dark-skinned man sweeping up litter. He reminded her of Joe – an RAF man who had come over from St Vincent and the Grenadines to work on the planes during the war. His accent had been soft, but this man's was harsher, stretching out some syllables, melodically knotting other words together. She asked him to repeat the directions, to Linver Road, but still she was struggling to pull apart the sounds, to arrange them into anything she could make sense of. She couldn't ask a third time, so she nodded sagely and watched as his hands flashed from pink to brown and back as he gestured and pointed out her directions. She thought she might have the gist, thanked him, knew he was watching, broom in hand, as she walked off more confidently than she felt. The first part seemed to make sense, to tie in with what Lucy had told her; Alice turned first down one street and then another; but suddenly the road names on the sides of the buildings were not those she had listed in her notebook and she felt swamped as the smaller and smaller red-bricked terraces seemed to crowd in on her.

There was no-one around except a child sitting on a doorstep. She couldn't have been more than three or four years old, singing to herself, rocking a naked doll in her arms. Alice looked round anxiously for someone else, anyone she could ask for directions; there were front doors ajar at intervals down the street, but not a single adult in sight. She took a few steps towards the child, hoping that the mother might be nearby, but at the sound of her footsteps the child gathered the doll in the hem of her dress, clambered awkwardly up the steps and ran indoors.

Alice noticed a small alleyway on her left; it had no name but as she peered along its length she could see houses of a more promising nature, with small gardens rather than front doors straight onto the street. She turned along the narrow passage and headed past the back entrances to the houses on either side.

A clang behind made her jump. She turned, but there was no sign of anyone, just an overturned dustbin, spilling its contents across the path. She pushed herself on, not inclined to look again over her shoulder, but at the same time feeling she must. A glimpse of a man, the tail of his jacket disappearing through an open gate. She speeded up, dragging the case as though it were an errant child, through the narrow passage. She turned right into the road she had seen from the other end of the alleyway; as she continued, alternating between a walk and a run, she was convinced of footsteps behind her.

Her thoughts jumped to the man she had found in the garage. Christopher. Was he following her? But why would he have followed her here … and how would he have known when she had left home – and where she was going? Despite the nonsensicalness, Alice couldn't shake the idea from her head.

She turned suddenly. The man was there; tall, greying hair, older than she had expected; he appeared to be studying the roof of a house intently. It was only a brief glimpse, but even that was enough to tell her it wasn't Christopher, that much was certain, but whoever he was, he was much closer to her than he had been in the alleyway. She couldn't walk any faster; she crossed to the opposite side of the street but he was almost behind her now.

Her heart was beating too fast. She gazed anxiously up and down the street as she rushed on, willing someone else to appear. Her best shoes were rubbing her heels; she knew she should have kept her everyday shoes from going to the cobblers until she got back; and the case felt twice as heavy as it had earlier. Alice searched again - for a friendly face, or a telephone box where she could escape and call Lucy.

She glanced over her shoulder again; this time there was no sign of the man. Maybe he lived in the street, she thought. Or maybe he was just visiting, trying to find the house he wanted? She felt ridiculously childish as her eyes swelled with tears. But as she sniffed and wiped a hand across her face, a flash of light made her look up. A boy was sauntering down the road, newspaper tucked under his arm; he turned almost immediately into a battered green door. Alice stepped forward, past the house, realising that the light had been the late afternoon sun, catching the window of a shop door as it opened and closed. Further down the road she could see the small corner shop, almost camouflaged amongst the rows of identical houses. She strode towards it, almost forgetting her fears and the pinching in her feet, focussed only on finding some help.

'Afternoon, miss.' The boy behind the counter greeted her as the bell on the door announced her arrival. He could easily have been the brother of the lad she had seen with the newspaper. 'What can I getcha Miss?'

'Oh – er – nothing …' Thinking only of her own questions, Alice was thrown by being asked something herself. 'I was just hoping you could help me …' Her voice faded away. The boy was evidently disappointed at a potential customer evaporating before his eyes, but he rallied quickly.

'Not from round 'ere Miss?' His eyes moved from her hat down to her shoes, taking in every detail. 'Didn't think I'd see you before.' The shop smelled of soap powder and vegetables and freshly baked bread. The shelves were crammed with packets and boxes, custard powder, Oxo cubes, tins of loose biscuits, and suddenly Alice felt hungry – and so thirsty that she could hardly move her tongue inside her mouth. A wave of light-headedness surged over her and she waivered.

'Ma!' The boy shouted out. 'Ma – give us an 'and.'

Alice was distantly aware of a voice, and then of an arm, pushing her gently into a chair.

'That's it – head down, dearie.'

The same female voice emerged from a darkness which had descended over her.

'There you go – bit of colour coming back now,' the woman observed. Alice tried to pull herself upright, but a firm hand kept her in place.

"You stay there for a minute, lovey. Don't try and move too quick. I'll go and fetch you a nice cuppa.'

The pressure lifted from her head and Alice was able to sit up. The wooden chair which had been produced for her was next to the shop counter, and jumbled in her eye-line were tins of peas, boxes of cotton reels, shoe laces, buttons, tea, boot polishes. The colours reeled in front of her and she tilted her head away, but as she did so it occurred to her that she couldn't see her case – or her handbag.

'Oh … where's my bag … and my case?' Alice called out to the empty shop. No-one responded. She held the counter and pushed herself to her feet.

'You feeling a bit better there, dearie?' The woman reappeared, carrying a large teacup in one hand and a small plate in the other.

'But my bag …?' Alice insisted; but it was as if no words had left her mouth. 'Is my case …?' she tried again, raising her voice.

'Now don't you worry lovey – everything's just fine. You just get that tea down you - and a couple of Rich Teas. Nothing fancy I'm afraid, but they'll fill a little gap.'

Alice gulped the drink down. It was syrupy sweet, but she was desperate to quench her thirst. She felt uncomfortable, munching the biscuits while the woman watched her, but she realised she hadn't eaten since her egg and dripping toast, and that felt like days ago. She drained the last of the tea and sat back, letting her body revive.

'Better dear?'

164

Alice looked over at the woman. She had an ample bosom beneath her flowered overall, and an unruly mass of dark curls. She was smiling at Alice, pleased with the successful outcome of her ministrations.

'You look all-in - you travelled far?'

'Not really,' Alice hesitated. 'Only from … just from Bedfordshire.'

'Ooh, I had a cousin from up that way – Fred – real country bumpkin he was. Funny boy …'

Alice could see that the woman was settling in for a long story. She knew that Lucy would be waiting for her, wondering what on earth had happened.

'You've been so kind, but I really must get going.' Alice stood, holding on to the back of the chair to steady herself. 'I'm going to visit a friend – she'll be wondering where…' Alice could feel the giddiness washing over her again. The darkness filled her head once more, and she was overwhelmed by the desire to lie down.

CHAPTER THIRTY TWO

It was the sound which penetrated through to her first. She didn't want to open her eyes but voices began to drift into her head, like smoke from a woodland bonfire.

'... Visiting a friend she said ...'

' ... Maybe an address ... can't be far ... Look in her bag ...'

Alice wanted to reach out, to snatch the bag away, but no part of her body seemed to be obeying the thoughts in her head. She was reluctant to open her eyes, but she wanted to get up, take her belongings and walk away; just as desperately she needed to stay, to curl up and sleep for ever.

Someone was stroking her face. She was dreaming, she knew that ... but somehow the fingers were real. And perfume. A scent was in the air which hadn't been there before.

'Alice? Alice – are you with us?'

She wanted to look at the owner of the voice, but her eyelids were heavy. With enormous effort she pushed them open, taking in a blur of colours, an unfocussed picture, before they closed on her again.

'It's okay Alice – you're fine. Are you going to wake up for us now?'

The stroking became a gentle patting on her cheek, and then an acrid smell punched her nostrils. She spluttered and opened her eyes, coughing.

'Lucy,' she murmured. 'How did you get here?' Her own voice sounded as if she were speaking through an army blanket. 'What's that awful smell?'

Lucy laughed as she put down a bottle of smelling salts and took Alice's hand.

'You got yourself completely lost, you mad old thing.'

'Where am I?' Alice asked, vaguely remembering a cup of tea and ginger hair and a box of buttons.

'You're in London – this is Mrs Massey's shop.' Lucy stared down at her. 'You frightened the life out of her when you passed out. Luckily she found my address in your bag and sent young Freddie here to get me.'

The faces continued to gaze at her, waiting for her response. She tried to piece things together – she remembered getting on the underground train but after that …? Somewhere, something was panicking her, tickling at the edges of her mind; something that she needed to do, to check …

She started to sit up, but Lucy grabbed her arm. 'Whoa - take it slowly,' she said, but Alice needed to stand, to …to what? Her bag - that was it, she'd been trying to locate her bag before she'd blacked out.

'Where's my case? … and my bag?' Her savings book and her small cache of money were all she could think of. If they were gone, she wouldn't be going anywhere.

'It's okay Alice – everything's through in the other room.'

167

Alice was desperate to go and check. No doubt Mrs Massey and her family were perfectly good people; and she knew it would be terribly bad form to check her purse while she was in their company, but still she needed to know.

A hand pushed a glass of water towards her, and Alice gulped down the cool liquid.

'I'm feeling okay now.' Her voice was abrupt, she knew it, but the more positive she sounded, the quicker Alice thought she might be allowed to go. 'Shall we get out of these lovely people's way?' she said, trying to soften the harshness of her previous words.

'Good job we're only round the corner,' Lucy laughed, 'Don't think you're ready for another trek round the block just yet.' But there was embarrassment in her voice, as if she knew exactly what Alice had been thinking.

Alice wasn't sure she could manage even six steps, but she was desperate to get out of the shop. 'You've been so kind,' she said, turning to the buxom woman. 'I don't know what I'd have done without you.'

'You take care of y'self,' she gave Alice a hug. 'Woman like you needs looking after,' she said, grinning broadly, and winking.

The woman's gestures and words were a complete riddle to Alice, but she thanked her again – and all the other faces who were still watching her intently.

Two boys appeared with her luggage, and although Alice could easily have snatched them away she reached in her pocket, assuming that one of the lads was Freddie. 'Here you are – here's threepence each for being my heroes,' she said.

The boys grinned and ran to the back of the shop, already arguing about how they would spend their money.

As soon as they were out in the street Lucy turned to Alice. 'What on earth have you been up to?' she whispered loudly.

Alice looked away. Had Lucy found something in her case? Did she know something about Teddy? She took the opportunity to unclasp her bag and rifle through; the post office book and her purse, still fat with her money, were tucked at the bottom, beneath her cotton gloves and her compact.

Lucy was talking, apparently oblivious to Alice's silence. 'I mean – collapsing in someone's shop, and frightening the life out of small boys – not to mention me …'

As they walked slowly on, Alice mentally unpacked her case, checking through what Lucy might have seen; eventually convincing herself that there *was* nothing for Lucy to find, but nevertheless …

'Right, let's get you back to Hurlingham House,' Lucy interrupted her thoughts, taking Alice's arm. 'Some food and a strong drink is what you need.'

'I don't think I could …'

'Strong whisky or strong tea – it's all the same to me,' laughed Lucy, pulling Alice gently along the road.

•

Alice felt so much better once she had some food inside her. While Lucy was preparing thick slices of Welsh Rarebit ('Don't even ask where the extra cheese "ration" came from, my dear'), Alice sipped a small glass of sherry, savouring the sweetness and the warmth

169

in her stomach, but after that she stuck to tea, which Lucy had made very strong and very sweet. By the time they sat in front of the empty fireplace with generous wedges of Dundee Cake ('courtesy of another good friend!' laughed Lucy) she felt quite normal again. They had been laughing over old times, remembering shared friends, but when a lull came in the conversation Lucy looked at Alice earnestly.

'Now I know it's none of my business, but is everything okay Alice dear?'

'Yes, of course – I just hadn't eaten …'

'No, I don't mean the fainting, I mean …' Lucy hesitated. 'It's just that – when you rang - you told me you were going to a funeral …'

Alice nodded, wide eyed.

'Yes - but when I got to Mrs Massey's, your bags were still open where they'd been looking for my address.' Lucy took a large swig from her glass. 'It's just that – I saw there were no … nothing black, nothing even vaguely funereal – a yellow polka-dot dress, sandals …'

Alice was silent, not a single idea of how to talk herself out of the hole she appeared unconsciously to have dug.

'I'm really grateful to you for letting me stay,' she said eventually. 'And I know I should tell you …'

'Look – you don't have to tell me anything. I mean you can if you want to – if you need someone to talk to, but I'm assuming things are obviously not …' Lucy hesitated again. 'Not *straightforward*, for you at the moment …?'

'No, you're right, they're definitely not,' Alice blurted out. 'But I ...'

'Honestly Alice - you really don't have to tell me a thing. In fact,' she said, taking another large swig of her whisky, 'Maybe it's better if you don't...' Lucy looked over at Alice. 'In fact,' she giggled, 'Don't tell me anything – not even which station you're going to tomorrow. That way, I won't be forever speculating on where you've gone and what you're up to. And then,' she said, draining her glass, 'Even when they come searching for you – trying to force your secrets from me – I won't have to lie!'

The two women fell into gales of laughter at the thought of Alice being pursued as some enigmatic character leading a dubious life. But as Alice prepared herself for bed, she thought about just how many secrets she was actually carrying around with her.

CHAPTER THIRTY THREE

Lucy's spare room was very much a "box" bedroom, filled to the ceiling with trunks and orange boxes. 'All Ma and Pa's stuff,' Lucy said matter-of-factly as she moved a photograph album from the bed. 'Haven't quite got round to sorting it out since …' Since the bombings in '44, was what she meant. Everyone had assumed that the Blitz in '41 had been the pinnacle of the German attacks on the capital, that those continuous savage raids had made the Fuhrer's point and that after that there would be no need for further bombing on London; but January '44 had seen the beginning of more massive raids, and Lucy's parents had been some of the first victims.

Alice remembered the news coming through; there'd been a sing-song one evening at a WAAF social; half of them were singing "It's a Long Way to Tipperary" and the other half "Pack Up Your Troubles" when someone came and whispered in Lucy's ear. She followed them, wordlessly, out of the room, and when she returned she seemed visibly shorter, caved in. Everyone had guessed at her news and the music had stopped, but Lucy had wanted to carry on, wartime spirit, just as her parents would have expected. Nevertheless, Alice had seen how

Lucy had crumpled inwardly and for a while her spirit had gone.

As she waited for sleep to come, that picture - of her confident friend dying a little, like a heatwave flower - dragged Alice's thoughts back to the cloud-seeding and the possible outcomes; the thought of loss and injury to innocent people and someone else's daughter having to bear that sort of news. She tossed and turned in the narrow bed, throwing the eiderdown off and then pulling it back up to her chin, as images of torrential rain mixed in her head with tomorrow's trains, and helpless victims appeared in hidden corners where she was already watching and waiting for Teddy.

In the end she forced herself out of bed and fumbled her way in the darkness to the kitchen. A glass of water was her usual bedtime routine, and Alice thought that if she had that, and maybe a read of one of Lucy's magazines in the living room for ten minutes, then her body would know it was time for sleep and would pack all these ridiculous images away for a few hours. But neither water nor reading helped. She was wide awake as the mantel clock struck one and then quarter past and then half past. She went back to her room and pulled the eiderdown from the bed. She dragged it back to the sofa and tucked it round her legs, laying back amongst the cushions, trying to think of "nice things", as her mother had insisted she do when she was eight and having nightmares. But birthday cake and party dresses no longer worked, and Alice pulled herself upright again as the clock struck two. She felt around for her glass of water on the side table, but as she did so, the eiderdown shifted and caught the glass, smashing it to the floor.

A light went on. Lucy rushed in, hair swept back in a bandeau and cream still shiny on her skin. 'What on earth … oh Alice, you gave me such a fright. I thought someone had broken in.'

Alice had never seen Lucy flustered before. 'I'm so sorry - I couldn't sleep. I thought a glass of water would do the trick …'

'Oh well,' Lucy sighed, bending to pick up the shattered pieces. 'At least you're not a burglar.' She pulled some newspaper from the magazine rack and began to wrap the pieces of glass. 'Don't walk about in your bare feet – I probably haven't got all the pieces yet.' She sounded cross, but as she looked up at Alice, her tone softened.

'Oh, Alice – what on earth is the matter?'

Tears were pouring down Alice's cheeks.

'It's only an old glass – nothing valuable. It really doesn't matter,' Lucy said, taking Alice in her arms. 'Don't fret old thing – worse things happen at sea as they say.' But Alice was truly sobbing now, great gulping moans.

Lucy rocked her. Eventually Alice found her words and began to tell Lucy almost the whole story.

CHAPTER THIRTY FOUR

A knock at the door woke her, and for a moment Alice couldn't think where she was. She was sure she'd had not even ten minutes' sleep, but the strange room was already light. It wasn't until she heard Lucy's voice that everything started to slip into place.

'Tea, my dear,' Lucy announced, energetically snapping back the curtains and planting the large cup and saucer on the tea chest which was serving as a bedside table. She looked down at Alice, concern sliding across her brow. 'How are you feeling?'

'I'm … well … I'm sort of okay,' she said, propping herself up on the pillow, reaching for the tea, reluctant to look Lucy in the eye.

'Are you glad to have got it off your chest? – well some of it at least,' Lucy asked, perching on the small bed.

'Oh Lucy – do you think I'm doing the right thing? I mean, just heading off to goodness knows where, in search of something I don't even really want to know about …'

'Alice my dear – you're not going to rest until you know exactly what's going on, so you may as well take the bull by the horns, as they say.' She inclined her head so that she could see Alice's face. 'And I'm here – at the end of a telephone line, any time you want me. I could even call in sick and come and meet you if you want me to – if it all gets too much …'

At this moment there was nothing Alice would have liked better – to travel with her old friend and have someone back her up, someone to share her thoughts and questions with. But she knew she had to face up to this – and to Teddy – on her own. And besides, she had only given Lucy part of the story about Teddy's work, and if that all started to reveal itself …well, maybe the fewer people who knew about it the better.

'Thank you so much Lucy – I really appreciate everything you've done.' Alice took her friend's hand. 'And I will let you know what's happening – even if it's just one of those naughty seaside postcards,' she said, a smile covering her concerns.

'Well, as much as I'd love a trip to the seaside, I've got to get off to work,' Lucy stood, back to her brisk and efficient self. 'But take your time. Pull the door to when you're ready – it'll lock itself.'

Alice sipped gratefully at the tea. She couldn't believe she was still thirsty, still not feeling quite right.

Lucy stood at the door, something evidently on her mind, words waiting to fly from her lips. '…And you make sure you have a good breakfast before you go,' she said eventually, softening the abruptness of her last-minute words with a smile. 'You need to look after yourself.'

Alice looked at her blankly, over the top of the teacup.

Lucy sighed, exasperated. 'Oh Alice – come on. I didn't want to say this last night – you were so upset … but don't you think there's just a tiny chance that you might be expecting?'

'No.' Alice immediately reddened. 'Definitely not,' she snapped.

Lucy looked at her, eyebrows raised. 'You are a married woman Alice. It wouldn't be beyond the realms of possibility you know.' She walked back to Alice and kissed her on the forehead.

'Yes it is,' thought Alice, smiling weakly. But as Lucy waved goodbye, with promises of visiting once Alice had returned home, Alice recalled that one night with Teddy. And shuddered to think what its outcome might be.

CHAPTER THIRTY FIVE

Alice was swept along with the crowds at Paddington Station, eventually finding her way to the ticket office where she obtained both ticket and train time from the man at the booth. She checked her watch; plenty of time before her train was due to leave, so she wandered over to the newsagent's kiosk, glancing at Woman and Home and Good Housekeeping, unsure whether a purchase even on this small level was wise. Two sets of train tickets had cost more than she'd expected, and she had no idea how much she would need to spend on a place to stay. In the end she decided that one of the cheaper magazines wouldn't make a great deal of difference either way, and bought a copy of Woman's Own. She would ration herself to reading part of it now, she decided, and keep the remainder for the next few days. Who knows what frame of mind she might be in on the journey back? - reading might be the last thing on her mind if she had uncovered what Teddy was up to, she thought, as she found a bench and made herself comfortable while she waited for the train.

There weren't enough people in the carriage to play Josie's "criminals" game, and anyway Alice felt unbelievably tired. She watched for a while as two small girls, clad in dresses identical except for their colour, played Snap in their mother's lap, shyly looking over to her between shouts. She must have dozed. She felt the train slowing to a halt and glanced up through bleary eyes to see that they were at Reading. She looked at her watch. It was only 11.30, but already she was quite hungry. Lucy had left some biscuits out for her, neatly wrapped in greaseproof paper, and Alice gladly pulled them from her bag. Two Digestives and two Gingernuts. She was rattled by how quickly she had become unwell yesterday, and nibbled away at the sweet biscuits, trying not to think about Lucy's suggestion that she might be pregnant. It might explain the nudges and knowing looks from the woman in the shop though – Mrs Massey, wasn't it? Alice immediately put the whole idea out of her mind – she couldn't even begin to think about such a thing, she decided, and stared determinedly at the scenery passing her by.

The man opposite had been reading intently, hat pulled down as though shading his eyes from some invisible sun. When she looked across again he was exchanging the book for a newspaper which had been stuffed in his coat pocket. There was something vaguely familiar about him, but Alice couldn't recall where – or even if – she had seen him before, or whether he just had one of those very easy faces which looked like a hundred others. She waited patiently as he shook out the folded pages; she had always found other people's reading material more interesting than her own, but this time the headline jolted her like a slap to the face.

"**WHAT ARE THEY DOING TO OUR WEATHER?**" the bold typeface of a local paper shouted at her.

179

Immediately she was back at Teddy's desk, with his files. She leant forward, trying to get a glimpse of the rest of the article, but it was difficult without being downright rude. Undaunted, Alice wriggled around until she was in a position where she could see more of the wording.

"Are they using us a guinea pigs? Rumours are emerging that government departments may be carrying out experiments which could affect the amount of rainfall in this area…." The crease in the paper blocked the next section, and Alice picked up the story further down the page… "… and perhaps it's no surprise that we are experiencing the wettest summer for fourteen years …"

She sat back. It was all too close to the truth. How on earth had this hit the headlines? Had someone been spreading rumours? She had heard of people selling stories to the papers for ridiculous amounts of money … and her thoughts went inexplicably to Christopher. She had never got to the bottom of his visit to their house, and there was something about him, something under the surface, like a splinter that refused to come out.

Just thinking about the situation that Teddy could be caught up in – that the country could be embroiled in - brought a clamminess to Alice's neck and her face.

'Is that lady all right?' As Alice closed her eyes she heard one of the little girls whispering to her mother.

There was a moment of silence, as if the woman were examining her, making a diagnosis. 'She's probably just

180

a bit hot, that's all,' she said quietly. 'Now you get on with your game.'

The train trundled on and Alice concentrated on its beating rhythms, allowing the regular gentle sounds to calm her. The voices in the carriage seemed to be coming from the end of a tunnel, but after a while she was aware that one voice had become more pronounced than the others. A polite cough forced her to open her eyes.

'I was just wondering …?'

She was aware of the man opposite – the one with the newspaper - leaning towards her. He seemed to be offering her something, but she was struggling to hear what he was saying.

'I'm sorry – I didn't quite catch …'

'I just wondered if you'd like a cup of tea …'

'No – no, that's very kind, but I'm fine thank you.'

But as she forced her eyes to stay open, she was aware of the man watching her, seemingly uncertain how to press the matter further.

'Well – maybe a glass of water …' Alice said drowsily.

'I'm afraid I only have tea,' he smiled, proffering a large flask in front of her.

'Oh, I'm sorry – I wasn't thinking …' Alice looked at the man. He wasn't elderly, but still probably old enough to be Alice's father. 'Avuncular' was the word which popped into her head, probably from some book she had read, but it suited the man perfectly she thought. While she dithered he seemed to have taken the decision into his own hands, and was holding out a steaming beaker to her.

'My sister,' he shrugged, as if that explained everything.

Alice reluctantly took the cup, but the tea was tempting now that she had it in her hand.

'I've been to visit her in London,' the man continued, rummaging in his bag. 'She always tries to feed me up …' He left the words hanging in the air. Eventually he put down the flask so that he could properly search his bag, and produced a neatly wrapped package, like an inadequate magician. 'Meat paste and tomato,' he said, looking at the paper square, 'Would you like one?'

'Oh no, I couldn't possibly ...' Alice was actually quite hungry, but somehow it didn't seem right, taking food from a complete stranger.

'Home grown tomatoes,' he said, eyes twinkling, 'And I know how hungry these train journeys can make you …'

Alice reached across and took one of the sandwiches. She nibbled at first, but the savoury saltiness whetted her appetite, and she was soon taking another from the proffered sandwich box, while she listened to the man relate something of his history. He mentioned a wife, but omitted her from the rest of his story; he was a doctor, once retired, then pulled back into service while the war had been on. 'I still do a few days here and there at the practice in Bankshead. I get to deal with all sorts,' he said, brushing crumbs from his jacket, looking up at her from under his eyebrows.

The mention of the town reminded Alice of the newspaper.

'I have to get my bus from Bankshead - I'm going on to Rushcombe.' She was surprised that the name of the town had left her lips; she realised it was the first time she had spoken of her real destination with anyone. 'I know this is a dreadful cheek … but have you finished with your newspaper?' Alice rattled on before she could change her mind. 'I don't really know this area, and it might be useful to read a bit of local news …' Her words faded, sounding rather false, even to her own ears, but the man appeared not to notice.

'Beautiful place, Rushcombe,' he was saying, pulling the newspaper from his bag. 'Wonderful views over the hills, pretty little bay. You'll like it there.'

'Maybe not,' Alice thought, but she smiled, thanking him profusely for his kindness.

●

The station at Bankshead was not as busy as Alice had expected, but even so the small clusters of people seemed completely absorbed in their own tasks – unloading luggage or gathering it around them, looking anxiously for the person who was due to meet them or the person they had come to collect – and no-one took much notice of her. She looked around for the doctor, hoping that he would show her the way to the bus, but as the steam billowed across the platform, the smell of coal mixing with something Alice couldn't quite put her finger on, she lost all sight of him. The guardsman's whistle coincided with an announcement; she thought she heard "Rushcombe" and "five minutes" and grabbed her case, looking for the direction of the voice.

'Rushcombe bus – All aboard who's coming aboard,' a conductor was shouting.

Alice rushed, anxious not to miss the waiting bus. When she reached the front of the station there were at least six people still gathered around the vehicle, forcing themselves and their luggage through the narrow doorway. As she mounted the steps she took one last look for the doctor, wanting at the very least to wave her thanks to him, but there was no sign across the rapidly emptying station.

She found a seat, managing to squeeze in on the sea side, hoping that she would get a good look at the views. The bus moved slowly along the seafront, and Alice was excited to see that the tide was in, and throwing itself against the drift of shingle. There was something mesmerising about the sea, but after only a few minutes they bus came to a halt; the driver jumped out and dashed into a small harbour-front café. 'Off for his usual tea and cake, while we sit here like lemons,' someone behind her tutted, and the busload sat, mainly in silence, until the driver emerged once more, wiping his mouth with the back of his hand. They turned at the end of the road, and to Alice's surprise, started off back the way they had just come, but this time, they turned away from the sea and into the small lively town.

A few grand Victorian houses stood at the bend in the road, and then the town gave way to countryside. Trees laden with apples, sheep speckling the sloping fields, a tiny bridge, the glimpse of a settlement nestling in the valley, hills rising up on either side, a jigsaw of green pieces.

Within twenty minutes they were winding their way through a pretty village, past tea shops and pubs, the garage and the church. But the quaintness of the scene was interrupted by the shout of the conductor.

'Hang onto your hats,' he called down the bus, in his broad Devon accent.

There were knowing laughs from one or two – locals presumably – and the bus began to labour its way up an impossibly steep hill. Trees arched out over the road, turning everything to gloom, making the whole thing seem like a dark parody of a fairground ride. It gave Alice the same creeping feeling in the pit of her stomach. Surely if they went any slower the bus would stall?

She snapped around, trying to see out of the rear window. Surely at any moment they must start rolling backwards? In her head she could feel the pull of the reverse descent already, hear the whining acceleration as they careered backwards and into the big white house sitting on the sweeping bend. And then all her effort, in getting herself here, would have been for nothing.

But the vehicle chugged on, like an old man, huffing and puffing its way up, dragging itself forward, the driver expertly negotiating the sharp bend and sharper incline which were thrown impossibly together.

The bus and all its passengers seemed to give a collective sigh as at last the road began to level. Alice had seen herself within an arm's reach of Teddy, about to tap him on the shoulder, then tripped at the last hurdle. But there, they had done it and were continuing on their way, and the chatter and the momentum of the bus resumed once more.

CHAPTER THIRTY SIX

Alice tumbled off the bus, suitcase in hand, blinking in the afternoon sunlight. She stood, scanning the scene which met her, taking in the little town. It was awash with light reflecting off the lively water and the whitewashed walls of the old-fashioned houses and shops which meandered around the foot of the hill.

She seemed to be an island, surrounded by people who knew exactly what they were doing, what they wanted; even those sitting on a painted bench, soaking up the sunshine seemed to have some purpose to their day. She had been swamped by planning and arrangements for so many days, and then by the journey itself ... and now that it was all done and she had arrived, she felt deflated, her mind suddenly as empty as a January diary.

As she tried to gather her thoughts, Alice watched a woman in a cream jacket and stylish sunglasses climb elegantly down from the bus and stroll over to her.

'Pretty isn't it?' the woman said, surveying the scene in front of them.

'Yes – it's lovely. I'm glad I came.' And Alice realised, as she slipped on her own sunglasses and forced a smile, that for the moment at least she was pleased to be here, whatever the next few days might bring.

Someone called from the other side of the road and the smart woman waved wildly.

'Oh, there he is – my *man*,' she said, suddenly unsophisticated and coy.

'He's booked us a room at the Waverley,' she whispered, waving again. 'Where are you staying?' she asked as she gathered her bags; but she was across the road and running into the man's arms before Alice could answer. Alice looked round once more; although she had known that this moment would come, she felt slightly sick now that it was actually here.

Over to her left were a couple of hotels that she guessed would be out of her league. And besides, one of them had to be Teddy's, she thought as she peered across, attempting to read the names. She wanted to track him surreptitiously - not bump into him over the scrambled eggs, or on the stairs with her suitcase still in her hand. Unless she could follow him from afar she would never get the true picture of what he was really up to – so he mustn't know she was here, not until she was absolutely ready for that moment.

And so Alice turned away from the hotels and wandered into a little café by the river. The lawn sloped down to the water, and small tables covered in gingham cloths were dotted around the grass. A plump young woman in a flowered apron was clearing teapots and cups from the deserted tables, licking leftover jam from her fingers.

'Oh, sorry – um, excuse me,' Alice wandered closer. 'I was just wondering if you could recommend somewhere to stay?'

The girl looked at her quaintly, raising her eyebrows to indicate the crowd of hostelries surrounding them.

'Oh – yes, I know - I've seen the hotels over the road,' Alice explained, 'But they're probably a bit …'. She hesitated to say "expensive"; she didn't want the girl to think she was completely unworldly. 'They're a bit *grand* for me,' she said, smiling far more than the situation warranted.

'Ah, you want something a bit more homely than they old places my dear.' The girl spoke like a woman three times the age she appeared to be. 'Mrs Westcott – that's what you need. That's her place over there.' The girl pointed to a double fronted cottage further up the hill. 'She does a good B&B. Nice and clean – very reasonable too.'

Alice's uncertainty must have shown on her face.

'Tell her Patsy sent you.' And with that she waddled away, her ample hips counterbalancing the overloaded tray as she made her way back inside the café.

Alice reluctantly picked up her suitcase, forcing her tired legs to tackle the steep pathway. She felt an overwhelming longing to be home, and not for the first time questioned her sanity in making the journey.

She stopped at the small stone wall in front of the house; there was no "vacancies" sign or any other indication that this was a guesthouse. Alice hesitated. She looked around but there was no-one to ask.

The red front door at the end of the tiled path was ajar and a ginger cat lounged lazily on the doorstep. It stretched itself at her arrival, but made no attempt to move. Alice leaned over it and knocked lightly on the door. The rattle of crockery sounded somewhere inside but there was no answer. She knocked again. This time a voice called from a distant room.

'Come in, come in, my dear,' a Devon accent beckoned, 'I'll be right there.'

As Alice pushed open the door, a woman almost as wide as she was tall, filled the entrance. Hair presumably intended to be caught back in a bun, most of it had broken free and was springing in pale auburn curls around her face.

'Lovely to see you my dear.' The woman spoke as though she had been waiting all week for Alice to arrive. 'Is it a room you're wanting?'

'Erm – yes. That is – how much …'

'Oh, it's 7/6 a night - with breakfast of course, and as much tea as you can drink,' she laughed. 'Shall I show you the room and then I'll put the kettle on.'

Alice remembered a rare holiday, with her mother insisting on rolling back the eiderdowns to check the cleanliness of the sheets before she would agree to stay. But there seemed little doubt in Mrs Westcott's mind that she would be staying, and when Alice saw the room there was no doubt in her own mind either. It was a pretty room overlooking the river, with a pale blue patchwork covering the ample bed and a small vase of asters sitting on the oak dressing table.

'It's lovely,' Alice said. 'I'll take it please.' But Mrs Westcott had already laid her case on the settle.

'Bathroom's just along the corridor – second door on the right. Come down when you're ready and have a nice cup of tea and a bit of my apple cake.'

Alice flopped on the bed. She had never felt more like sleeping in her life, but she knew that Mrs Westcott would be waiting for her – and besides, she realised, as she looked out of the small cross-paned window, she was as thirsty as she was tired.

She pulled her fingers through her hair in a half-hearted attempt to tidy herself up, and then ventured downstairs. She hesitated in the hallway, unsure which of the doors to open, but the smooth buttery voice called out to her again.

'Come through my lovely – just in here.'

Every inch of the small room was overwhelmed with Toby jugs and gaudy plates and glass bonbon dishes. The lace-covered table was laid for tea with an uncut cake taking pride of place.

'How did you hear about me dear?' the older woman asked, bustling in once more with a huge teapot.

'The girl at the café,' Alice pointed back down the river.

'Ahh, that'll be Patsy, Mrs Pinkham's oldest. She's a good girl – always sending people my way.' She filled two delicate pink cups and plonked a striped knitted cosy over the pot.

'There was no sign in your window…?' Alice started to ask.

'Oh you're lucky, my dear. Mr Frazer – one of my regulars – he was coming down from London, but wrote to say as he'd heard the weather was turning bad down this way. I ask you,' she waved the cake knife around as she spoke, before cutting two large slabs. 'Just a few showers here and there … I'd hardly call that bad weather, would you?'

Alice shook her head as she bit into the cake. It was moist, fruity, more flavoursome than anything she'd eaten in a long while.

The woman's chatter about the assortment of weather they'd been experiencing - sunshine then showers, drought then deluge – pushed Alice's mind back to the papers on Teddy's desk. Had it started already? Had Teddy's office dealt with a shortage of rain in the area by putting the cloud-seeding into action?

'Although they do say as the moorland is sodden as a sponge, up there on the top,' Mrs Westcott was continuing, barely stopping for breath. 'More water than the land knows what to do with just lately, but that's Mother Nature for you …'

The woman poured more tea, pausing with teapot in mid-air. 'Anyway, as they say – one door closes, another one opens. Mr Frazer's loss is your gain,' and she raised her teacup to Alice in celebration.

'So what brings you down to these parts my dear?' The woman continued between bites of cake. 'And what about Mr Hathaway – will he be joining you?' She slurped her tea and carried on, apparently oblivious or unworried by Alice's lack of response. 'How long do you think you might be staying? There's a lovely little walk up by the river if you fancy it – I'll show you just where to find the path; I'd come with you myself if I was ten years younger – and a few pounds lighter!' She laughed raucously, belly wobbling as she picked up the empty plates.

But despite the warmth of the afternoon trapped into the small overcrowded room, a shiver went down Alice's back. She wasn't sure she should be here at all.

CHAPTER THIRTY SEVEN

Unable to concentrate on her magazine, Alice had, for the past ten minutes, been staring out of the small square panes of the bedroom window. The weather continued in its indecision – one minute rain clattering against the windows, the next sun sneaking a look from behind the clouds. But restlessness was beginning to take a hold, and so she gathered up her blue mackintosh and her bag and plunged down the stairs.

'Oh - you chancing it then?' Mrs Westcott was carrying a large laundry basket through the hallway. 'This lot has been in and out to the line more times than a fiddler's elbow today,' she said, indicating the washing. 'Still, I s'pose a breath of fresh air wouldn't go amiss after all that travelling?'

Fresh air was exactly what Alice needed – and a decent meal she realised. Despite the apple cake she felt hungry again, and finding a café somewhere for an early evening meal would at least give her some purpose, something legitimate to do while she kept a watch for any sign of Teddy.

She decided on the first café she came to – freshly painted and homely - and chose a table by the window. There was a wonderful aroma of baking coming from the back of the shop and the thought of comforting pie made Alice relax as she perused the choices on the handwritten menu.

Having given her order she sat back, letting her eyes drift over the ebb and flow of the holidaymakers along the pavement outside while her mind wandered to the task ahead. She persuaded herself that this was the start of her search, that she was already looking while she was sitting there at the table, but she knew she wasn't really concentrating.

A man of Teddy's build loomed suddenly at the window. He leaned in further, holding his hand to his eyes, peering around. Breath was sucked like a tidal wave into Alice's body, only to come back out in short shallow gasps. It was as though he was coming through the glass, about to envelop her, pin her to the chair and demand to know what the hell she was doing there.

And then he was gone. Alice tried to control her breathing, deliberately pulling in long breaths and letting them out slowly. She could feel her pulse pounding in her temple.

Now a woman was at the window, pointing into the café and then calling back to someone across the path. Was this *her*? Was this the person who had caused so much heartache over the past few weeks? Alice stole a look. She was pretty – large almond-shaped brown eyes and sleek hair swept back from her face. She looked breathless, excited, full of fun.

'Maybe that's all he ever wanted,' Alice thought. 'A bit of fun.' And she tried to remember when she had last been "fun", when she and Teddy had last laughed or been silly together. Nothing came to mind.

Alice forced herself to look away. When she glanced back the woman was gone. Alice scanned the far side of the road – the spot where the woman had been calling to - convinced that Teddy would be standing there, but she saw only a family with two small boys, fencing with their beach spades.

The bell on the café door tinkled and Alice turned. It was early yet, and the café was still quite empty. But there she was, the fun-looking woman, by the door, beckoning someone to join her.

Panic engulfed Alice. There was nowhere to go. What should she do? Brazen it out, there in the middle of the café with the waitress and the old man by the counter both watching and listening to every word?

Alice turned her chair towards the window as far as she could. She knew it was a ridiculous thing to do – it wouldn't prevent them from seeing her; it was like a child covering their eyes, and thinking that they were invisible. It would simply give them the advantage - they could stare at her, snigger, and she would have to let it all go on, literally behind her back.

She sat, immobile, eyes unblinking on the scene outside the window. The waitress bustled up, a large steaming plate held with a cloth between her hands.

'There you are dearie – a nice big helping of our best pie, with potatoes and veg. You enjoy that.' The woman fussed around, bringing salt and pepper, while Alice willed her to go, to stop bringing attention in her direction. She picked up the knife and fork but she could hardly swallow, let alone eat.

'Ooh – that looks lovely – what's that d'you reckon?'

The dark-haired young woman was staring over at Alice's plate, talking to her partner. Her voice was surprisingly shrill, not at all in keeping with her Elizabeth Taylor looks.

'I think I'll have one of those too.'

It was the man who spoke this time – and it wasn't Teddy. *It wasn't Teddy!* Alice let out a breath she didn't realise she'd been holding. It wasn't him, and she was delighted. She'd come all this way, just to find him, and when she thought she'd done just that she realised she couldn't wait to run as far away as possible.

'Everything all right dearie?' The waitress looked concerned that Alice hadn't even started on their best pie. 'How about a nice bit of gravy? I'll just go and get you some.'

Before Alice could speak the woman had hurried off, returning almost immediately with a small blue and white jug.

'You tuck into that dear – do you the world of good.'

'Why did everyone think she needed feeding up?' Alice sullenly picked up her knife and fork. She felt fine. But as she began on the food she caught sight of her reflection in the glass of the picture on the wall. Her face looked pale, blank, as if someone had rubbed away her features. Lucy's words came back to her '… don't you think there's just a tiny chance you might be expecting …'

'That's just ridiculous.' The words had tumbled out of Alice's mouth before she could stop them. She looked around, but none of the tables nearby was occupied, and no-one seemed to be paying her the slightest attention. Miss Squeaky Voice and her companion were sitting in the window on the opposite side of the door, completely engrossed in themselves – holding hands and giggling into each other's eyes. As she looked on, the image of this couple of strangers, was replaced by a picture of Teddy and whoever his own Miss Squeaky Voice might be.

CHAPTER THIRTY EIGHT

To Alice's disappointment, the next morning was wet. She pulled the curtain back a little, still in her dressing gown, and peered through the streaks of rain. A few early risers were up and about - a boatman in his oilskins, a milkman with a crate, a man dragging a reluctant dog. It didn't look in the least like August, she thought as she got back into bed to savour another few minutes under the blankets. It was too early anyway to go down for her breakfast, and to be honest she didn't feel like eating. And then there was her plan for the day – or rather the lack of it - she thought, as she sat, arms embracing her knees, enveloped by the eiderdown. She knew that really she was afraid to start. It was like receiving exam results – while you left the envelope sealed there was still a chance that the outcome might be okay; but once you had opened it and looked, your fate was decided and no pushing it back in the envelope would change things.

Eventually Alice forced herself to get up. She bundled her dressing gown around her and made her way to the bathroom at the end of the landing. It was empty and she scuttled inside before anyone could appear and challenge her on who should use it first.

•

'You okay my dear? You look a bit peaky.' Mrs Westcott stood in front of her, teapot in hand. 'Never mind,' she continued before Alice could reply. 'A nice egg, that's what you need. I know you town folks are still finding it a bit difficult after the rationing …' She bustled about, making sure there was butter and marmalade on the table.

Alice was silent - torn between hunger and queasiness, determination and nerves.

'What's your plans for today then my lovely?' the woman asked as she put a large bowl of cereal in front of Alice. She stopped her bustling and went to the window. 'I would have suggested that nice walk up the river – always does you a bit of good when you're feeling under the weather – but it dun't look like it's the day for that. Old Mrs Hooper, she looks soaked through out there just getting her paper, that she do.' Mrs Westcott pulled the curtain straight. 'Mind you, bit of sea air, that always helps...' She continued clearing dishes from another table, already used. She didn't seem to notice that Alice had said nothing in reply.

Alice was still churning around in her head what her plan of action might be. 'Surely Teddy would want to be out and about, whatever the conditions?' she thought. After all, the rain and the changes to the weather were his main reasons for being here, weren't they?

She had only managed a few mouthfuls of Cornflakes before Mrs Westcott was back with a boiled egg and toast soldiers. 'Always made my George feel better,' she said, 'And there's some of my homemade whortleberry jam if you prefer.'

Alice was doubtful if she could manage anything more than a finger of toast, but she felt guilty for not eating the precious egg. She attacked it with her spoon, and surprisingly, the richness of the fresh golden yolk and the hot buttered soldiers did make her feel better; as she munched at the toast she began at last to make her plans.

•

She had her mackintosh, and Mrs Westcott had already offered her a rain hat and an umbrella. Wrapped up in a few layers of clothes, Alice felt ready to attack the world. Her guess was that Teddy was more likely to be around the river area, monitoring water levels, looking at any increase in flow which might demonstrate higher rainfall in the wider area. Nevertheless she started off back at the familiar spot where the bus had dropped her the previous day. From there she found her way through narrow alleys which soon meandered round to the main street again, to the little row of shops which tumbled down the cobbled road.

As she continued along, Alice tried not to be distracted by the holidaymaker fripperies for sale, concentrating instead on faces and possible meeting places. Between his observations and his note-taking, surely Teddy and ... Alice realised that she still had no idea of his flirtation's name and decided to nickname her "Jaffy" to incorporate the J and the F of her initials. Presumably the two of them would meet up at some stage, she thought, if only for tea or coffee. Somehow the rain seemed to dissolve the spice, the edginess of an affair she thought. Sodden coats and squelching shoes didn't make for passion, and the thought brought a small satisfied smile to Alice's face; the weather at least was on her side.

•

Several circuits of the small town brought no success – not even a vague sighting of anyone even vaguely resembling Teddy. The only slight positive was that the sun was working hard to win the battle with the clouds and the rain, and for the moment at least succeeding. Tired for the moment of the lanes and the shops, Alice was drawn back to the river.

The East Rush was stunning – gushing relentlessly towards the sea, grey wagtails jumping from stone to stone, flicking their yellow bodies above the waterline, hovering and jumping from place to place like bees. She remembered the walk which Mrs Westcott had mentioned and hesitated for a moment, drawn between the search which had brought her here and the desire to do something which was of her own choice, less stressful.

'He might be further up river,' Alice muttered to herself, trying to justify the decision which she wanted to make. 'I can come back to the town later – have another good look,' she said, as she turned away from the town and took the narrow riverside path.

She felt a sense of calm as she left behind the bustle of the town. The world was quieter here; it was as if the sound of people was gradually being turned down, and the sounds of nature turned up, like a retuned wireless set. Wind rattling through the trees, competing with the constant chattering of the busy water; a bird called and was answered by a companion. The surroundings gathered around Alice like a comfortable blanket, and the anxiety which had been constantly with her receded. The earlier sun was lost behind thickening clouds, and as Alice passed a cluster of cottages clinging to the steep bank above the river, a few drops of rain began to fall. It didn't come to much though, and Alice was determined to carry on. She relished the movement of her body, the slight breathlessness as she tackled the small inclines of the riverbank, realising that it had been a long time since she had walked – or done anything particularly physical for that matter – just for the sheer pleasure of it. Although her plans for the day were submerged for the moment, she took simple delight in her surroundings. She paused to watch the river cascading over the rocks; it seemed higher than she remembered it yesterday, but it was so full of life, of the positivity of knowing exactly where it was going. 'Unlike me,' she thought, continuing on along the path.

Whether it was the clouds or the rain, or the small bit of effort required, there were few people out walking. Occasionally Alice scanned the far bank, but even the smallest tag of coloured clothing would have flashed brightly against the intense woodland green, and there was little need for Alice to make much effort. Just once she thought she saw someone, a man most likely, someone in darker clothing anyway, emerging briefly into a clearing from the leafy cover of the shrubs which climbed down to the water. She stopped and let her eyes wander along the bank, but the trees in full leaf could conceal almost anything and there was no sign of any further movement. She continued to look for a few moments, almost out of a sense of duty – that she could justify the walk as a continuation of her search, but she was enjoying herself and didn't actually want to be reminded of her reasons for being here, for a while at least. No, whoever it was had gone she decided, and it had all happened so quickly that she began to wonder whether she had simply imagined it.

Eventually the woodland opened out, and the opposite bank widened to reveal a small hut with tables and chairs outside. Alice quickened her pace, eager now to take a rest and enjoy whatever refreshments the little café might have to offer. A pot of tea and a fruit scone was brought to her table, and Alice relaxed back into her chair, enjoying the tranquillity of the beautiful little spot.

•

By the time Alice was part-way back down the track the rain had begun to fall again, more intensely now, soaking her coat. She pulled Mrs Westcott's rain hat from her bag and tied it round her dripping curls, hoping she'd acted quickly enough that she wouldn't look completely dishevelled by the time she reached the town again.

The constant rain bounced off the river surface as if it were desperate to merge itself with the flowing water; Alice watched for a moment, mesmerised by the continuousness of it all.

Back in the town the streets were emptier than they had been earlier, and the café windows were steamed up, hiding the clutches of warm damp bodies inside. Alice peered in at a couple of shops but, seeing the tangle of people in each, she thought about taking the funicular railway up to Rockleigh, on the top of the cliffs. Reluctantly she decided that one trip away from the town was probably enough for one day. And it occurred to her, as she stood deliberating, that maybe she *should* be fighting her way into these crowded spaces, that these could well be the very places where Teddy might be with this woman of his, but she couldn't face all that uncomfortable wetness mixed with warmth, sucking oxygen from the air and filling her nostrils with the nauseating odour of damp wool and dogs. Just the thought of it made her claustrophobic and she began again the circuit of the town which she had mapped out earlier.

•

The back of a man's head caught her attention. He had no hat, but something about the sweep of his hair and the set of his shoulders shouted out "Teddy" to her.

Alice kept her gaze firmly fixed on the head as she followed along behind. He seemed to be walking with a purpose, not distracted by the homemade fudge and the watercolour paintings in the windows of the small shops. For a moment she lost him; she hurried on, convinced that he must have turned into an alleyway or a shop. She began to panic. What if this were her only sighting of Teddy and he was gone before she had barely found him? But no, there he was, further ahead now and Alice had almost to run to keep up with him. An old woman with a walking stick drifted out of a gift shop and Alice bumped into her.

'I'm sorry – I'm so sorry,' she called over her shoulder as she scooted past. The man stopped ahead, neck strained, head darting this way and that, like a bird. 'Looking for something – or someone,' thought Alice, desperate now to get a sight of this woman who was turning her world inside out.

He stopped again, fiddling in his pocket for something. Alice had to pretend to inspect the display outside the greengrocer's shop, glancing every few seconds over her shoulder to see if he was still there. The shopkeeper came out, re-arranging his stock. 'How about some apples my dear – local they are, sweet and juicy. You won't find better.'

'I – I'd – I'm sorry,' Alice stuttered, torn between politeness and her need to keep up with the man she was convinced was Teddy.

She turned again. He was gone. She dodged and dashed between the small crowds, all the time scanning for another sight of him.

Suddenly, a kaleidoscope of skirts and coats brushed against her; her arm and leg collided heavily with the pavement. She felt a pain in her knee, and wet grit biting into the soft flesh of her hand.

CHAPTER THIRTY NINE

An arc of heads peered down over her and Alice closed her eyes. She felt ridiculous lying on the pavement, everyone staring; a woman crouched beside her, taking her hand.

'You all right my lovely? You went down a real cropper there.'

Alice pulled herself to sitting. 'No – no, it's alright. I'm okay …' She winced at the pain in her hip as she swung her legs round, pulling at her skirt to cover her legs.

'These cobbles – they're the devil's own when they're wet,' the woman was saying. 'My Sally nearly did the same last week – and all this rain isn't helping neither.' The woman helped her sit up. Alice looked down and saw that her nylons were ripped, that there were drops of blood running down her shin. She wanted to run away and hide the mess she was in. Bizarrely, she wanted Teddy to be here – to pick her up and hold her, tell her she was imagining everything, and tease her for running after a strange man and falling at his feet.

Instead the woman had a hand under her elbow, helping her up. 'Come and have a cup of tea, my dear, and we'll get you cleaned up.' And she led Alice towards a tea room before she could find any words to argue.

They were able to dab away the blood and brush most of the grit from her clothes and her skin, but her pride - and her nylons – were not so easily restored. Alice sipped politely at the large cup of hot sweet tea which had been thrust at her, but now that she had pushed herself this far she was desperate to get back out there and pick up another sighting of Teddy.

'I think they've had it, my dear – even a good bit of darning won't mend those.' The woman was looking down at the ragged knees of Alice's stockings, shaking her head.

Alice looked too, and realised that she would have to return to her lodgings before she could go anywhere else. 'I'd better go and get changed,' she said, more enthusiastically that she felt. 'I look a bit of a sight don't I?' She tried to smile, but it was all she could do to hold back frustrated tears.

'Don't you worry my dear – shakes you up a bit, a fall like that. You'll be right as ninepence once you've had a sit down.'

Alice eventually managed to tear herself away from the kindly woman and the tea shop owner. She was cautious as she stepped back out onto the cobbled street, but was glad to see that the rain had strengthened. At least that meant that most people would have dashed inside shops and cafes to shelter, and those that were still out and about would be huddled under umbrellas or rain hats, so that their concerns and their eyes would be far from Alice's dishevelled appearance and she could creep back to the lodgings without further incident.

As she hurried along the near-deserted streets she couldn't help but go over in her head what had happened, and how she come to make such a fool of herself. Of course she had been too busy concentrating on Teddy, not looking where she was going – but even so …

Her shin had begun to throb and she huddled in a shop doorway, bending to dab at a new trickle of blood with her handkerchief; the whole area was sore, and the beginnings of a long bruise were starting to discolour her leg. It looked as if something hard had smacked against her skin, Alice thought as she hobbled on, trying to recall the pavement where she had fallen. Had there been a kerb? Was that what had created the heavy line across her leg? But the rain, now coming down in sheets, distracted her thoughts, and she was forced to make a half-hearted run for the house.

•

For once there was no sign of Mrs Westcott and Alice crept upstairs in her stockinged feet. She wondered if she could get away with a bath in the middle of the day – she longed to sooth her aching limbs – but she realised this would stir up an eddy of questions, and so, reluctantly, she made do with a stand-up wash after she had peeled away the torn and spattered clothes.

After she had put her skirt into the basin to soak, Alice considered what she should do next. The weather would keep people indoors wherever they could, and she couldn't keep going into tea rooms and cafes. She pulled her purse from her bag and checked how much money she had left. For a moment her heart lurched as she saw just a ten shilling note and some odd coppers, but then she remembered she had slipped more money into an envelope and hidden it at the bottom of her case. Even with that extra cash though, her days here would be numbered if she carried on the way she was. She pulled a cardigan round her shoulders, shivering; whether this was because of the rain or her fall she couldn't decide. She looked down from the window, racking her brain for a more specific plan, but she had to concede that she had no idea what Teddy's days might be like. Would he be working all the time, or would he be free to do as he pleased once he'd carried out his daily tasks? And the car, she suddenly remembered. That fact that Teddy had the car down here with him would of course give him far more options than she had. He might not even be in Rushcombe, she realised, while she was wandering up and down the crooked streets, hopelessly trying to find him. The thought made Alice want to pack her bags and give up, but the sound of her landlady, calling up the stairs, stopped her in her tracks.

'Mrs H – are you there my dear? There's a visitor here to see you …'

Alice stood, welded to the spot, unable to speak. Teddy had seen her, followed her, and now he was here to confront her …   It felt as if someone had tempted her with a titbit, then snapped the bars shut as soon as she had stuck her head into the trap.

There was a knock at her door, and Mrs Westcott's head appeared.   'Wasn't sure if you'd heard my dear…There's someone here to see you – shall I put the kettle on?'

•

After her landlady had retreated downstairs Alice sank back on her bed, staring at the back of the door.

209

She felt safe in her small blue room, comfortable with the country scenes on the walls and the asters and the eiderdown. Despite the reassurances she had given to Mrs Westcott that she would be down in a jiffy, she couldn't face an argument with Teddy, didn't want to be challenged, didn't want to justify herself and her actions; she wasn't sure that she could, really, not in any coherent way.

'Tea's ready – and there's a bit of caraway cake too,' Mrs Westcott called up the stairs again.

Alice knew she couldn't prolong the moment much more. She had no doubt that Mrs Westcott could talk to anyone – and at great length – but she couldn't leave him standing there indefinitely, and she might as well get it over with – his wanting to know, wanting to ask her what the hell she thought she was doing, following him down here. She grabbed her handbag from the bed and fumbled around for her compact and lipstick. There was no need to give him the satisfaction of seeing what a wreck he had made her, but as Alice looked in the mirror she realised that this small gesture was going to make little difference to her unkempt looks. But at least it made her *feel* better, the gentle scent of the powder, the creaminess of the lipstick. She took one final look at herself and pulled open the door.

Muffled voices wafted up from the sitting room, one of them definitely male - but was it Teddy? Alice blew out a long breath and walked gingerly downstairs, her hip beginning to ache now that she had sat for a while. She cracked open the dining room door, and there, sitting comfortably helping himself to cake was a face, at once a stranger and yet so familiar.

210

'Heard about your fall,' he spluttered through the cake crumbs. 'Just thought I'd see how you were doing.'

CHAPTER FORTY

The man she had previously seen in smart suit and well-brushed hat handing out sandwiches and tea in a train carriage was now sitting at Mrs Westcott's table dressed in a hand-knitted waistcoat, a lively blue tie, and a glow of self-assuredness on his face.

Alice had been so utterly convinced that it would be Teddy sitting here. In her mind's eye she had already witnessed him charming Mrs Westcott with his flattery, complimenting her outrageously on her cakes, while all the time his anger would be bubbling under the surface as he surveyed Alice's face, her clothes, her pretence, waiting for her to explain what on earth was going on.

The fact that a man who looked nothing like Teddy was sitting in his chair caused shudders of shock and relief to course simultaneously through Alice's body. She had been a puppet, with all the strings pulled to their ultimate tautness; now an unseen hand had let go the cords, and she barely had the strength to remain upright.

She had no idea how long she was standing there, but as her mind came back to her surroundings she realised that the doctor was staring at her, with something more than concern scrawled across his weather-tanned face.

'Are you all right?' His unexpectedly terse tone made her look up. 'That fall must have shaken you up a bit,' he said, more softly, rising now to pull out a chair for her.

'Um – yes – I rather think it must have,' Alice said vaguely, snatching his explanation like a prop, a side-step from having to explain the truth of the situation. 'But it's okay - I'll be fine. Nothing a good night's sleep won't sort out.' She flashed the broadest smile she could muster as she sat down. 'Oh – and thank you so much for coming to see how I was – it's really very kind of you …'

It was only as she was speaking that the oddness of the situation occurred to her. 'So how did you hear …?' she began.

'About your fall? Oh, it was one of those really strange co-incidences - I just happened to be passing by when it happened. I often come over to Rushcombe - bit of a day out, you know, change of scenery, take in the views across the moors, that sort of thing ...' His voice meandered on, but Alice was only half-listening. If he had seen her fall, and if he was a doctor, why hadn't he stopped to help?

As if he had read her mind, he responded to her unanswered question. 'Of course by the time I realised what had happened,' he said, picking up another piece of cake, 'there were plenty of people already helping. I didn't want to make a big fuss – you know – "stand back, I'm a doctor" he laughed. It sounded rather hollow to Alice's ears.

' – And I could see that nothing was broken, so I thought I'd let the dust settle and then come and see how you were doing.' He munched happily on his cake as Alice thought over what he'd said.

'And – well – that's very nice … but how … how did you know where to find me?'

'Oh, somebody in the town was saying afterwards that you were staying with Mrs Westcott here … It might have been that greengrocer chappie … or maybe it was the lady who helped you out at the café?' He took another sip of tea. 'You know what these small places are like – everybody knows everybody …' His words hung in the air as Mrs Westcott returned with a plate of jam tarts.

'Don't s'pose you'd be interested in a job as housekeeper, would you Mrs W? – I could do with a good woman like you in my house,' he laughed again, helping himself.

'Ooh, go on with you,' Mrs Westcott blushed as she soaked up the flattery, brushing invisible crumbs from the table.

The two of them chattered on, while Alice gazed blindly, ignoring their stories and replaying her own words and scenes in her head. She was sure she would have noticed if the doctor had been one of those faces peering at her as she had struggled to recover herself after the fall. But maybe there had been too much going on … maybe she had been more concerned with the mud on her skirt and the state of her nylons …? But why, she suddenly thought, would you choose a day like this, with the rain lashing and the clouds scraping the hills, to make a journey across the moors?

CHAPTER FORTY ONE

A small glint of sunshine, peeping through the gap between the curtains, woke her.

Full of tea and cake and unable to face supper, Alice had gone to bed early the previous evening, every bit of her aching from her fall. Mrs Westcott had given her two aspirin and they must have knocked her out, because she hadn't given another thought until now about what had happened.

Still in her nightdress she curled up in the chair by the window and examined her hand and her hip; there were only a few light bruises, not as bad as she had expected, but her leg was another matter. The mark which had appeared yesterday was now a dark red wheal - almost, she thought, as though someone had whacked her shin. An image of a detested game of school hockey came to her, when Jennifer Wrigglesworth had tried to take her feet from under her, determined not to allow Alice to progress down the field, and had left a similar mark on her leg. The picture for some reason brought the doctor to Alice's mind; something jiggled in the back of her head, something which didn't quite make sense, but she couldn't pull it to the forefront. Her train of thought was interrupted by a clock chiming eight somewhere in the house, and it jolted Alice into getting washed and dressed before she was late for breakfast.

●

Downstairs, Mrs Westcott was busy chatting to some new guests and Alice took the opportunity, while she buttered hot toast and spooned on a generous helping of homemade strawberry jam, to plan her day. She realised that seeing Teddy once was no guarantee that she would see him again, but she would be methodical, she thought – she would start at the seafront, and walk from one end to the other, from cliff to cliff.

She managed to escape from the dining room with no inquisition from the landlady, and, having collected her toothbrush and towel she sauntered down the corridor to the bathroom. As she cleaned her teeth, Alice convinced herself that today was going to be more positive; she even felt the notes of "Don't Sit Under the Apple Tree" begin to hum on her lips as she ran the tap and prepared herself for the day ahead.

●

From the bridge in the centre of the town Alice worked her way across the grassy meadow leading to the far beach. A man was trying unsuccessfully to launch a paper kite, ignored by a child who seemed to have long since lost interest and was chasing seagulls instead. Alice continued as she watched them, towards the end of the bay where there was a small crescent of pale sand. She stood at the edge, tempted to take off her shoes and cross to the gently lapping waves to paddle, but that would mean removing her stockings and she wasn't sure she wanted to mess about, releasing them from her suspenders. Instead she ambled along the flat sand which the high tide had washed and pressed into place, scanning her surroundings for that familiar outline. Eventually she drifted back along the seafront, all the time glancing around her, as she made her way to the little harbour. The sea wall was a handy resting place to watch the world go by, and Alice perched there for a while, watching from behind her sunglasses. Despite the ragged patch of sun which was filtering through the clouds, a chill wrapped itself round her once she stopped, and so she drifted back to the quaint row of shops where she had spotted Teddy yesterday.

A gift shop had its wares displayed outside, and the squeaking rack of postcards reminded Alice of the promise she had made to Lucy. She stopped and turned the stand, holding back a giggle at the bold cartoons and the suggestive words. Amongst the garish drawings there were over-coloured scenes of Rushcombe and the coastline. They might be more appropriate for the two girls, she supposed, but that would mean revealing her whereabouts; and, knowing Lucy, she might just take it into her head to turn up. The postmark might still give her away, of course, but there was no need to flaunt her whereabouts was there?

Eventually she selected two of the milder cartoons – one for Lucy and another for Josie. As she took the cards to the shop door, a waft of something unpleasant caught in her nostrils; the sulphurous stench of bad eggs. Several people stopped to look round, sniffing the air, trying to find the source. 'Drains,' someone announced authoritatively, and Alice assumed they might be right.

'Is there something wrong outside?' she asked the man behind the counter as she took a handful of coins from her purse. The smell seemed to have followed her into the shop.

'Blowed if I know.' The man was irritable, as if someone were deliberately undermining his previously irreproachable business. 'Started a while ago - nothing to do with us,' he added, waving a hand round as if to show a perfectly clean shop. Alice nodded sympathetically, not wanting to appear to push the blame his way. As she slipped the paid-for cards into her bag and wandered back to the sea front to continue her walk to the far cliffs, the foul smell still lingered in the air.

•

'Teddy.' She had almost cried out.

She'd been teetering on the edge of calling it a day; unsuccessful in her promenade walk she had sauntered back down towards the river, resigning herself to the fact that the whole trip had been a ridiculous mistake.

But then, there he was, turning up like a lost key or a forgotten sixpence. He was further along the street, but in her direct line of vision. And it was almost as if he were taunting her, appearing in clear sight like this, when she had been searching every hidden corner and crevice.

And, despite herself, despite everything that had happened, Alice had almost called out. She could so easily have rushed over – slipped her arm through his, taken him to look at the views of the distant cliffs, laughed about the tribulations of her journey, shown him the river path she had discovered. Just a few months ago, it could all have been so different, so enjoyable.

Instead she stopped herself, forcing her arm down to her side, feeling thin and insignificant, translucent almost; her words choked in her mouth as she watched someone else join her husband.

It was as though, having at last got to see the film she had anticipated, she found she was watching the wrong one. What was in front of her was not the picture she had expected to see – not the scene she had played in her head a hundred times. The face which she had anticipated, which she had conjured in her mind over and over until it was real enough for her to have reached out and slapped it, was not there. And the clothes were wrong, the stance was wrong – everything was wrong … except that she did recognise the face.

It was a face which seemed so incongruous and yet quite familiar, that it was almost laughably obvious that it should be here with Teddy, and she didn't know why she hadn't thought of it before.

She watched intently as the two of them strolled beside the river, stopping from time to time to discuss something, pointing down at the bank – perhaps at the grey wagtails flitting along the water, showing off their yellow bellies, just as she had watched them yesterday; laughing at a collie dog which had escaped its lead and was plunging eagerly into the lively waters.

And because it was so different from what she had expected, when they eventually turned from the river and made their way towards the beach, Alice had to chivvy herself to continue to follow them. Subconsciously she fingered her lips as she watched them share a comment, smile at each other's words; but for the most part they just walked, appearing to be absorbed in their amiable silence.

As she continued on, the light around her seemed to change, as though a switch had been thrown. Dark clouds had begun to roll together, menacingly colliding against each other, but amongst the gloom a tinge of pink had started to blossom, touching the edges of the grey, gradually taking over, turning the whole sky an ominous rose-yellow, sulphurous and unnatural.

Couples and small groups stopped to look up at the abnormal sight, pointing to strangers at the mushroom-like shape which seemed to be forming in the clouds. Alice, too, stared for a few moments, as mesmerised as everyone else.

'Want to take a gander?' A plump gentleman in moleskin trousers and braces, pushed the promenade binoculars round towards her. She didn't think it would give her any better view of the developing sky, but it seemed churlish to refuse his offer, and so she stepped forward and focussed her eye as the gentleman gabbled on. 'Strangest thing I've ever seen; been coming down here for years and never seen the likes of it before…'

She looked up at the painted clouds, but as she swung the binoculars back down she caught a glimpse of children on the beach. Without thinking, she moved the glasses to her right and there – there they were, the two of them. Forgetting about the man whose sixpence she was using up, she focussed on their faces and watched, totally absorbed.

Teddy's arms were flailing about; he had lost his footing, and toppled as he tried to find stability amongst the smooth stacked stones. Of course it would be natural to put your hand out to stop someone in this situation, and she watched as Teddy was grabbed and pulled upright; but Christopher's hand lingered on Teddy's rolled-back sleeve, on his suntanned arm, and there was a gaze, from one man's eyes to the other.

Strangely, for a second she didn't have a problem with it – one friend helping another, if you cared to look at it that way. The moment was like the touch of a butterfly's wing, there and then gone; but in Alice's mind it stayed, burnt into her memory. What hurt – what really seared her heart - was that Teddy had never looked at her in that way – with such softness, kindness, such caring and tenderness. Alice would have given everything she had to have been in the place of that man, just for that one miniscule moment in time.

And then the significance of what she had seen punched her. That look, that touch, between Christopher and Teddy, told Alice the story - pages and chapters and volumes of it - in just the flicker of a moment.

•

It was her legs which betrayed her first. She wavered like a sail taken by a sea breeze gusting unexpectedly.

'You okay Miss?' The portly gentleman swung the binoculars away from her and took her arm. Alice swayed again, and he guided her, half steering, half supporting, towards a bench on the jetty. 'Probably this weather, m'duck,' he said, taking his cap and waving it in front of her face. 'Can't make it's bloomin' mind up - sun one minute, rain the next - made it a bit sticky now, airless.' He spoke brightly, looking out to sea, not wanting to gawp at the pallid shade her face taken on, uncomfortable that it might be some "women's problem" that he would rather not know about. He stood

221

at her side like a sentry, although no-one was approaching, or even taking much notice.

'Yes, I'm sure you're right,' Alice spoke softly. 'I've walked a lot today - probably overdone it. I'll be alright in a minute.' She shivered as she looked again at the sky, even more inflamed now than before, an ominous parody of a sun setting, but at the wrong time of day. Her face and her hands were clammy, and searched in her bag for a handkerchief. She pulled out a neat laundered white square, and as she shook it free from its pressed state the letter "E" in one corner revealed itself.

The sight of Teddy's initial, which she had embroidered herself in those heady days before their marriage, finally galvanised her and she collected her belongings and ran.

CHAPTER FORTY TWO

She had no idea how she had got there; she felt as though she were in some sort of trance, but something must have compelled her to walk, stop, start, to follow the trail back, because eventually she found herself at the house with the cat and the red front door. It was as though she were replaying her arrival, except that the cat was no longer stretched out on the tiled path, but curled in the corner of the porch, its back to the rain which had now started in earnest.

Her hair was flattened to her head and dripping down behind her collar and onto her skin, but Alice was oblivious. A shiver brought her to, and she reached out a wet chill-reddened hand to the front door. All she wanted was to be by herself, to curl up on her bed, to replay and replay those awful scenes in her head until she was ready to obliterate them. She knew she should run for the stairs, bolt to her room before there was any fuss, but her legs seemed incapable of moving. She knew she needed to make some sense of what she had just seen; she knew she should pack her bags and leave. But nothing could happen; none of it was possible with a body and a mind which, at the moment, weren't her own.

Eventually she managed to drag one foot after the other, to pull on the ancient bannister rail and get herself to the top of the stairs. All she could think about was cocooning herself in the eiderdown, blocking the world out. But it was not to be. She had been in her room for only a few moments when there was a barely noticeable knock on the door. It was surely too quiet for Mrs Westcott and Alice ignored it, not wanting to speak to anyone. The discreet knock came again, and then a small voice.

'I don't want to pry dear …' an unusually reticent Mrs Westcott murmured. 'But I just saw you coming in – from the upstairs window – and you looked so pale and … not yourself at all.'

The room fell silent, but Alice knew the older woman was still outside the door. No words would come from her mouth; she didn't want them to, anyway.

'I thought you might want a nice cup of tea – warm you up a bit?'

Alice knew that if she opened her mouth as much as a wisp, a tangle of sobs and anger and wretchedness would fight its way out, and might never stop.

'I'll leave the tray outside the door for you, shall I dear? Just bring it down when you're finished.'

Alice heard the chink of china and then the woman's footsteps receding down the stairs. She was shivering; her head felt as though someone had tied a rope around it, pulling it tighter and tighter until it seemed it would shatter her skull in on itself. But she must eventually have drifted into some sort of sleep, and when she woke her throat and her mouth were parched. She stumbled to the door and saw the tray neatly laid with tea and homemade shortbread biscuits. Immediately she had to run to the bathroom. She knelt in front of the toilet bowl. She retched, and then, as the images of Teddy and the other man came back to her, she vomited violently, over and over. When there was no more left in her system she sat up and held tightly to the washbasin, splashing cold water onto her face.

The taste in her mouth was foul, and she wanted to spit and spit – not just to rid herself of the tang, but to expel the traces of Teddy from her body. Eventually she staggered back along the corridor and, desperate for something to eliminate the sourness from her mouth, pulled the tray along the floor and into her room. All energy was gone with the effort, and she left it where it stopped and threw herself back onto the bed. After a while she reached out and snapped a piece from the smallest biscuit and let it crumble in her mouth as tears slid down her cheeks.

She felt betrayed – no, more than just betrayed; she felt mocked, ridiculed. Teddy having another woman would have brought her world spinning off its axis, but at some point she might have begun to recover and put her life back on track. But this. How could she have got things so wrong? What had she done to make her husband turn to another *man* for his solace and his pleasures? So many things began to make sense – Isobel's willingness for her one and only son to marry a "nobody"; she had obviously been happy for an innocent lamb to come to the slaughter in order to give her son a shell of respectability, and the more unconnected that nobody was, and the more willing, the less questions there were to be asked. Had everyone known – everyone except her? Alice cast her mind around, dredging conversations from her memory. Surely Josie and Lucy would have said – would have hinted at least – if they'd thought anything was wrong? Everyone had seemed delighted when she and Teddy had announced their engagement – and of course, she had had no mother or aunt or sister to take her to one side, to say "are you sure?"

Alice played and replayed conversations with Teddy, pulling each picture to shreds, trying to find some clue she had missed, something she had said or done to turn his head the other way, until she had so many questions and images and words in her head that it was at bursting point. She closed her eyes, trying to push it all away.

•

Hours might have passed. The light through the window had dimmed. Alice pulled herself from her restless slumber, crept to the bathroom again and washed her face. When she returned she saw the cup of tea still on the tray, a dark skin formed on its surface. She sipped the cold liquid, her head full of wadding, of nothingness, as if a cocoon had wrapped itself around her and hidden her from what she had seen earlier. It wasn't that it was someone else's story, but her body had decided how she would deal with this – which for now meant blanking out everything so that at least she could function on some sort of level.

She found her compact and mindlessly dabbed powder on her sallow cheeks. She picked up the tray and walked shakily downstairs.

'Oh, there you are dearie.' Mrs Westcott was in her kitchen, mixing bowl fixed firmly in the crook of her arm, beating a yellow batter. 'You look a bit better – had a nap?'

'I slept for a while, thank you,' Alice mumbled. 'Sorry about the tea – I must have dropped off before I could finish it.' She looked blankly around her, wanting to sit but seeing no available space. 'Shall I wash these things up?' she said vaguely, not wanting to do anything, but not wanting to do nothing either.

'Oh no - you're on your holidays ...' Mrs Westcott put down the bowl and took the tray from Alice's hands. Alice moved a washing basket and sank into a chair, watching disconnectedly as the other woman busied herself running water into the sink, lifting in the crockery, wiping her hands; allowing the normality of it all to sooth her.

Mrs Westcott turned, hands on hips, as though deciding whether or not to speak. Eventually she took a newspaper from the table. 'I thought you might be interested in this,' she said hesitantly. 'I've got tickets – me and Mrs Hooper, we were going to the Pavilion to see the show, but she's not so keen now – not now that this awful weather seems to be set in for the night. Says she'd rather stay at home with her knitting.' The older woman's voice drifted to a halt as she looked over at Alice's face. 'I know you're not feeling yourself,' she said eventually, 'But p'haps a bit of music and a show might be just what you need?'

'No – I couldn't.' The words barely left Alice's lips; she turned and reached for the door, desperate to creep back to her eiderdown, but Mrs Westcott stepped forward.

'Look dearie, I don't know what's happened – and it's none of my business either.' The woman's words were kindly but there was no mistaking the firmness behind them. 'But I do know that you'll drive yourself to distraction just thinking and thinking about whatever it is.' She took Alice's hand. 'The best thing you can do, my dear, is think about something else for a few hours – and then tomorrow, who knows, maybe things won't look so bad?'

Alice was fighting back the tears. All she could do was to nod her head in acknowledgement of the other woman's words. She rushed from the room taking the newspaper with her

CHAPTER FORTY THREE

'How could she be so insensitive?' Alice raged as she threw herself down on the bed and hid her face in the bedclothes. How could that bloody woman have any idea what she was going through at this moment – and what the hell was best for her? 'I'm sick to death of everyone knowing better than I do what I should be doing,' she said, thumping the pillow, screaming into its feathered heaviness.

Why? Why was all this happening to her? The questions started buzzing round her head again, like an angry bee. All she had wanted was a happy marriage and a normal life, like everyone else. Instead she had married a man who was anything but normal, who probably right now was performing some unnatural act and … Just the thought of it made Alice cover her mouth, feeling like she was going to vomit again. She could see people pointing at her in the street, laughing at her naivety, whispering, hissing "She's the one, the one whose husband was, you know …" What were the words they would use? She didn't even want to think about it.

She stretched out and reached for her handbag. Scrabbling around, her fingers found a half-eaten packet of Polo mints, and gratefully she pushed one into her mouth, allowing the mint fumes to settle her queasiness as she breathed deeply.

Maybe it was the effect of the sugar, but eventually, as she sat up, Alice felt a little better, bolder. She would go downstairs and tell Mrs Westcott that she had made up her mind – she would definitely not be going to the theatre; she would spend the rest of the evening packing her bags and she would be leaving straight after breakfast. For the first time, Alice realised that this was what she really wanted; she had no idea what she was going to do once she had left, or where she would go - but maybe Lucy would let her stay for a day or two while she sorted something out?

Despite her firm stance, as she got to the bottom of the staircase her bravado abandoned her. She had so often heard the expression about having the rug pulled from under one, but now she knew exactly what it meant. She really didn't know which was up, and so, when Mrs Westcott opened the kitchen door and found her standing there, she could only nod as she heard the woman's words.

'Oh, good. You've changed your mind. I'm so pleased my dear. I really wasn't looking forward to going on my own, you know.'

The fight had gone from her as quickly as it had arrived. 'I'll go and get my coat,' Alice sighed. She hardly had the energy to climb the stairs again, out of breath and weary as she dragged herself slowly to the top landing. Once she was back in her room she slumped down on the bed; she found her comb and pulled it roughly through her hair, not caring whether her parting was straight or her curls were in place; she hadn't even the energy to put on a bit of lipstick.

•

She was sitting on the second step when Mrs Westcott came back out of the kitchen, face made up, best coat on, pinning her hat in place. 'We'll need this tonight,' she laughed. 'That wind's got up and the rain's coming down in stair rods - but it's only five minutes down to the Pavilion; we'll be there in two shakes of a lamb's tail.'

Alice double-knotted her headscarf and buttoned her mackintosh and they stepped outside into a very different world to the one Alice had left earlier. The deluge which hit her face brought her immediately out of her stupor, as if some drunkard had emptied a pint pot over her. One look at the conditions convinced her that she must be completely mad, going out on a night like this when she could have been curled up under the blankets.

'I'll come home early if...' Alice called out above the noise of the wind.

'That's my girl,' Mrs Westcott shouted. 'You'll be as right as ninepence by the time we get back.'

The rain was coming down so heavily that they couldn't even see the end of the street or the bridge over the river. They darted round one huge puddle only to find themselves inches deep in another. In the end they gave up trying to avoid the gathering water, concentrating all their efforts on just battling their way to the seafront and the doors of the Pavilion Theatre.

Despite the awfulness of the night, the little theatre was already busy, and the two women had to shuffle and

231

squeeze their way through the damp crowds before they could find their seats. But once their coats were on their chair-backs, and they had settled themselves, and Mrs W had produced a small bag of toffees, the brash stage lights and the garish colours and the noise began to wash around Alice. And even though her thoughts continued to dive and dart, tumbling through the spaces in her head, trying to find some sense in everything that had happened, eventually the proceedings on stage began to take prominence and such thoughts were pushed further to the back of her mind.

The troupe were surprisingly good - their costumes just on the right side of vulgar, the banter of Al Raie, the comedian, was quick and well-rehearsed, and they could all certainly sing.

It seemed to come so easily to them all - they would be meandering through a funny story when the words would suddenly take on melody and colour; the lyrics launched into the air like gas-filled balloons, floating effortlessly upwards. The notes faded and Al Raie stepped straight in with a joke, a rambling shaggy dog story with a punch line about Jack Frost, and somewhere in Alice's head something clicked, but was gone again, something which should have made sense, but she didn't know why. She allowed it all to wash over her, and half an hour must have passed before Alice realised she had hardly thought about Teddy or herself or what was going to happen next.

But then the show was interrupted by an announcement that the river was rising and giving some cause for concern. Alice was suddenly alert, elbowing Mrs Westcott, but only a few left the theatre and the older woman hardly took her eyes from the stage as she whispered 'It'll be fine.'

Alice tried hard to get back to her previous state of mind, to the point where she could be lifted away from the here and now by the performers and the music and the gaiety, but she couldn't make it come again. Like a longing for sleep, the moment had moved just beyond her grasp. The antics on stage seemed suddenly ridiculous; the female lead, who had been pitch-perfect showed a tremble in her voice; a note didn't quite reach its proper point, and she could see the stains on the well-worn costumes and the tears in the scenery. Her mind began to leap - dashing from one thought to another like a frantic game of Hide and Seek. She was hot, she fidgeted in her seat.

And then the lights went out.

CHAPTER FORTY FOUR

The stage and the auditorium were plunged into utter
darkness. Since the end of the war Alice hadn't known
nights this black – there was usually at least a lamp at a
window sending a puddle of light into the street, or the
flicker of a fire throwing shadows onto a wall. But this
– this felt as though the thickest cloak had been thrown
over her head, with not even a chink or a tear to relieve
the darkness. It was mid-song, the singer half-way
through "Unforgettable". And so, for a moment, Alice -
and Mrs Westcott and the rest of the audience judging
by their reaction - assumed it was part of the
performance. There was laughter all around them, but
Alice felt an anxiety deep in her gut.

She felt for her bag on the floor between her feet, as
if being able to hold on to something tangible would
reassure her that not all of her senses had failed. She
clutched the bag to her, which only seemed to accentuate
the pounding in her chest.

She sensed that this was more than a temporary
breakdown. Something was wrong, and for some bizarre
reason images of Teddy crowded her thoughts. She
turned her head as if he might be there, looming behind

her, but there was nothing more than the thick impenetrable blackness.

'Don't you worry my dear – it's not like the big city here you know.' Mrs Westcott grasped her arm. 'These sorts of things happen all the time down here in the country …'

But, despite the re-assuring words, Alice detected an anxiousness in Mrs Westcott's voice.

The singer had brought her previous song to an abrupt end, but now she launched into a sing-along medley, encouraging the audience to join her. For a moment there was silence, and then, voice by voice, a bass and then a tenor and then a group of light female notes joined her. The situation seemed bizarre to Alice, but no more odd, she supposed, than the masses singing in the Underground stations of London during the Blitz.

Eventually though, shouts began to burst forth, like sparks, around the theatre.

'Come on mate - put another shilling in the meter.'

'Yeah - If we have wanted to listen to the wireless we could have stayed at home. Get the lights back on.'

Alice was aware of fidgeting, rustling, people turning in their seats; everyone wanting to move but no-one willing to launch into the unknown.

A single streak of light appeared; a torch playing around the edges of the stage, moving hesitantly, to the centre. The singing faded, and a voice emerged from behind the light.

'Ladies and Gentlemen. Can I have your attention please.'

Jeers and catcalls rose and fell.

'Ladies and Gentlemen … I regret to inform you that – due to circumstances beyond our control … we have an – er – technical problem …'

'Oh – just get on with it mate …' an irate voice yelled from somewhere behind Alice's head; slow clapping and calls from up and across the theatre supported the sentiment.

'Ladies and Gentleman,' the harassed voice on the stage began again, straining over the growing babble from the audience, 'The, er – our electrical system has failed …'

'No kidding,' another voice called out.

' …Eh ..yes, and …' the voice gabbled on. 'It seems that the heavy rain has got into the system and shorted it out.' He stopped, presumably expecting another riposte, but the audience had quietened, begun to listen. 'And so I'm afraid tonight's performance will therefore - ' he paused, putting off the news until the last possible moment, 'be cancelled.'

The jeering and the shouting began again, and then there was a lull, the audience taking a moment to digest the words as if only slowly beginning to take on their significance. And then the mayhem started.

A clattering of seats springing back into place, coats being retrieved, bags being found, people shuffling blindly down the aisles.

Alice and Mrs Westcott both sat firm, unsure what to do.

'I want to go,' Alice eventually quavered. 'I don't want to be here anymore.'

'I know my dear, I know …' The older woman's words faded without an answer.

Alice wanted to join the stream of others leaving, but she had no inclination to move into the lake of blackness which surrounded them.

The voice behind the torch began again. 'Ladies and Gentlemen – please – I should let you know that the rain – the river, that is – there's no need for panic ...' His words were being swallowed by the rising volume of voices, shrill, shouting. 'The river has risen considerably now ... but there really is no need to panic.' His voice trailed away, beaten into submission by the overpowering surge of noise and movement in front of him. The torch was turned towards the auditorium and in the bursts of light Alice could see a wall of bodies surrounding them on all sides.

The announcer's voice was completely lost amongst the effect he was causing. The word "panic" seemed to have taken on its own life, spreading its wings across the auditorium, sweeping everyone up in its mischief. Shouts, voices, trampling footsteps, someone falling, cries, shrieks, thunderous as everyone tried to find their way to the exits.

More torches appeared.

'Don't panic – just make your way *slowly* towards the lights.' But the voice was again swallowed by the tide of bodies pushing and swaying and faltering along the rows and out into the gangways.

Alice and Mrs Westcott stood up, gripping each other's arms, finding their balance in the blackness. Although she could see the torches at the exit doors, Alice still couldn't galvanise herself to move. But a force was pushing towards them – people in the row as desperate to get out as Alice was to stay. They had no choice – they were taken along with the crowd, and as they met with the tide of bodies coming down the gangway they were jostled and elbowed and manhandled. Alice refused to let go of Mrs Westcott but this meant that their arms were twisted and wrenched as the movement of the crowd pulled them east and west. They could hold on no longer.

Her mind began to draw its own pictures out of the darkness, and Alice was convinced she could see Mrs Westcott's hat moving forward, being taken ahead of her; whether the image was real or imagined it was significant enough to make her panic. She had known Mrs Westcott only a few short days but she was probably the most dependable and unflappable person Alice had ever come across.

She fought her way like a dog through the tangle of bodies and coats, ignoring the swearing and backchat of those around her, in her determination to catch up with her companion. She pushed against a man in a tweed jacket and hooked her arm forward to force her way between a young couple who were desperately trying to cling together.

'Sorry – I'm so sorry – but I really need to get to my friend …' Alice pointed to Mrs Westcott's red hat.

The young woman shook her head, spitting words at Alice. 'We're all trying to get out you know, it's not just you …'

But her young man squeezed to one side and managed to hold back the crowd a little so that Alice could push her way through.

'Thank you, thank you so much …' Alice called over her shoulder as she reached forward and re-united herself with the older woman.   She didn't know why she had been so desperate to catch up – she knew her way back to the B&B after all, and the older woman knew the town much better than her, but the alarm which had surged through the crowd had taken over Alice as well, and suddenly she had felt like a helpless child, separated from its mother.

As the two women linked arms they smiled weakly at each other; Mrs Westcott patted Alice's hand as they shuffled along with the crowd, as it shoved and squeezed its way through the narrow space at the exit doors.

CHAPTER FORTY FIVE

Like a cork from a bottle they burst into the foyer. Most people were heading straight for the main doors, glad to be free of the trapped darkness, feeling as though they were able to see again, even if it was only through the opaque obscurity of the tempestuous night, glad to be able to breathe fresh air, even if it was damp and chilled.

Alice was perturbed though, to see some people pushing their way back into the building rather than out, pulling dripping hats from rain-streaked faces, shaking battered umbrellas, peeling off sodden jackets and rain macs, swapping all this for some sense of relief.

The foyer was filling from both sides, like a tub with two taps. People swarming from the auditorium while others pushed their way in from the street, all melding together in the middle, all wanted to be away from the place they had just left.

'Surely to goodness you don't want to go out there Miss,' an older man with a Welsh accent spoke as Alice pushed her way through the confused crowd. 'It's like the pipes of the heavens have been opened and no-one can find the valves to switch them off. Torrential, the rain is …'

Alice ignored his lyrical words, turning instead to her companion. 'I have to get out Mrs Westcott,' she pleaded over the hubbub. 'I have to get some air.'

The older woman nodded and shouldered her way forward, pulling Alice along in her wake.

'I wun't chance it out there if I was you Missus,' another man stood in front of them, half shouting in his cockney accent. He was drenched, his hair flattened against his head, coat soaked to blackness at the shoulders, rivulets of rain running down his sleeves and his nose. 'Bloomin' awful out there – ain't never seen anything like it in all me born days.'

'Oh, it's just a downpour,' Mrs Westcott turned to Alice. 'I'm sure it's nothing we haven't seen before in these parts,' she said, pouring scorn on the outsider's words. She heaved open the door and held it unsteadily for Alice to follow.

It was as though bucket after bucket of water had been thrown over her. There was no time for umbrellas or hats; her curls were unravelled immediately into rats' tails dangling over her eyes; dampness penetrated her coat and was soaking through to her skin. She looked over at Mrs Westcott; the woman's mouth was moving but no words were reaching Alice's ears. The noise around them was deafening, a deluge of rain, bouncing from every surface, thunder reverberating between the hills, round and round like ball bearings trapped in a drum. And there was something else, something which Alice couldn't identify. A roaring crashing turbulence like nothing she had ever heard before. Alice saw a change to the face of her companion - not worry now, but fear.

'What is it?' Alice yelled above the noise, forcing her voice to reach the other woman.

Mrs Westcott looked at her, confused.

'That noise – what is it?' Alice leant in so that her mouth was close to the woman's ear.

'I don't know – I've never heard the likes of it before …' the woman looked stunned, as if something or someone had battered against her head and forced all reason to abandon her.

They stood, caught between the proximity of the theatre building with its overbearing crowding, and the comfort of a distant home. Others were pushing past them now in both directions – some presumably looking for the familiarity and protection of their own houses, others wanting to cling to the first place of safety they had come across.

Despite tucking themselves into the shelter of the theatre doorway the two women were buffeted and battered by the weather. Alice could see the indecision on Mrs Westcott's face, but she too wanted the decision made for her. She was petrified at the thought of leaving the shelter of the building but she didn't want to stay in this almighty fury. She wanted desperately to be back in Mrs Westcott's cluttered living room with tea and toast, watching the weather from a place of warmth and safety – but the thought of the transition from this place to that was too much to contemplate.

A group of young women pushed their way out of the theatre doors, turning up the coat collars and laughing nervously, as they linked arms and made a run for it. They shrieked as the force of the weather hit them, but kept running across the road. Alice watched as their feet disappeared ankle-deep in mud and water as they reached the grassy bank. They hung on to each other as they tried to free themselves, but one lost her balance and disappeared into the darkness, away from Alice's sight.

'Come on my dear,' Mrs Westcott shouted at her, suddenly more decisive. 'We can't stay here all night. We've got to get back.'

Alice gripped the door, unable to let go. The sight of the girl disappearing into the night, and her friends' cries of horror forced home the severity of the conditions - she'd never seen rain like it. They'd had downpours and cloudbursts before which might flood the road for a few moments until the drains could cope again, but this – it seemed like the weather was trying to create a second river. Alice couldn't see the edge of the path now that the water had come level with the pavement, blending all into one as it gushed forward, some invisible force pulling everything towards the sea, regardless of what might be in its path.

A blinding flash of lightning ripped across the blackened sky. Like a searchlight it lit up the town for a second, and Alice saw the girls again, over by the river now, clinging desperately to each other as they called to their lost friend, trying to keep their balance against the force of the water which was smacking at their shins.

Mrs Westcott yanked at her – pulled hard, hurting Alice's arm. 'We have to go – if we don't go now, we never will.' And with that she dragged Alice into the street, following the path the girls had taken.

CHAPTER FORTY SIX

'You'd be better off at the theatre,' a young man yelled as he came towards them. 'It's a nightmare up there.'

They both looked where the man was indicating, further up the hill, but Mrs Westcott was insistent.

'We need to get home. We'll be fine once we're home.' She kept repeating the words like a prayer. Alice glanced over at her – her eyes seemed to be fixated on the roof of the house which she couldn't see but knew from years of familiarity was not far into the distance.

As they neared the river the noise, already loud, became overpowering, as if someone had scooped up the sound and was forcing it into their ears. Another flash of lightning lit the town and a tree, no longer waving proudly in the breeze but flat on its back, tumbled into the water, to be tossed, immediately, like a rag doll through the turbulent water. A boulder, the size of car it seemed to Alice, bobbed and tumbled, pushing its way against all in its path, as if in a desperate race for the sea. Anything and everything she could see was surreal, the world transformed into a nightmare of destruction.

The water was dragging her shoes from her feet as they tried to push through the fast-moving flow. They forced themselves through, wading, thrusting against the weight of the water which was tangling round their legs, as if a madman was trying to pull them any way he could towards the sea.

Alice felt that every ounce of her strength was being dragged from her, but still Mrs Westcott pushed on. As they reached the bridge the older woman dragged herself up the short flight of steps, struggling to find any breath she could to fill her chest. She hesitated and it was Alice's turn to push; she leaned against the solid roundness of the woman's back, forcing her towards the apex of the crossing.

As they reached the high point and looked down the river they both faltered, overwhelmed by the sight that greeted them. Impossibly large boulders were tumbling their way downstream with the lightness of paper, and in front of one, like an elephant pushing along its young, was a car. Its headlights were inexplicably shining, eerily lighting the water from beneath, a spirit below the waterline rushing to escape the mayhem.

The two women dragged and pulled and pushed each other, exhausted by the weight of their saturated clothes and the strength of the rain swiping and slapping them from every direction they turned.

Alice realised that, if they didn't move soon they would be trapped, taken into the claws of this unseen giant which was throwing around vehicles and trees and rocks as if they were children's toys. Holding on to each other they stepped down gingerly from the bridge, but the second that their feet left dry land the water hit them, as if someone unseen person had taken a shovel to their shins, determined to upend them.

Mrs Westcott lost her footing, stumbling headlong, and Alice lurched forward, grabbing at the older woman's coat, attempting to drag her from the water's edge. But she was too solid, too heavy, and the ground beneath Alice's feet was slipping away from her, like an escalator step. She couldn't get a foothold, couldn't maintain a hold on the weight of the two of them; but their clothes and their limbs were so intertwined and fastened by their wetness that Alice was unable to free herself either.

Suddenly her legs were pulled from under her. Her thighs and then her hips and then her whole body was thrashed by the water. The coldness, the fierceness of it, stole her breath away. As she gasped for air something heavy pushed against her – she had no time to see what it was before it dragged her away into its path; Mrs Westcott was no longer in her arms. Alice's hands reached out, grabbing for anything – but there was nothing except the strength of the water, dragging her away.

CHAPTER FORTY SEVEN

Teddy

'We're never going to make it.'

The two men strained to see, looking for a way back up the hill towards the hotel where they had been staying for the past three days. Teddy held his hand to his face, shielding his eyes from the driving rain. The river had taken a huge bite out of the bank and was pushing itself across the road, adding to the water already streaming towards them.

A child screamed somewhere along the road, and as they turned they saw a family approaching, completely focussed on ploughing forward. The parents were holding fast to their children, one scooped up in its mother's arms, the other pulled close by its father and eventually raised onto his shoulders. They scooted in front of Teddy and Jack, and headed straight for the steps of the Combe Dale Hotel.

The men watched for only a split second before following closely behind. All six clustered round the door just as a wave of water washed over the path where they had been standing; the older child squealed again, although whether in fear or delight, Teddy was unsure. Jack reached for the door and pushed his way in, holding it open for the rest of them to follow, before ramming it shut against the awfulness of the night.

A young woman was standing at the desk, lit only by candlelight. It gave her a startled appearance, and she looked as though she might object to their sudden presence, but before she could speak a bald-headed man appeared carrying a bundle of towels.

'We're not residents …' Teddy started to say, 'But we can't ….' He pointed up the road, incapable at that moment of speaking a full sentence; struggling to take in what was going on around them.

'Come in, come in….' the man waved his free hand. 'You're not the first.' He was evidently a local man, and his gentle Devon accent had a calming effect, for a moment at least, making Teddy feel as though what they were doing, what was happening, was all completely normal. 'It's filling the cellars,' the man was saying, matter-of-factly, 'But we put through a call to the Fire Brigade a while ago. They'll come and pump us out soon.'

Teddy couldn't see for the life of him any way that a fire tender would be getting through, but the confidence of the man overruled and he kept his negative thoughts to himself.

'You're soaking – here take off your coats and dry yourselves down,' the proprietor said, thrusting towels at each of them. 'And perhaps the children …'. He had presumably been about to make an offer that he had made a thousand times before, of some treat or other, but then appeared to remember the predicament they were all in. 'They might be able to find you a glass of lemonade, through there.' He pointed to the bar area, adjacent to the reception, and the parents gratefully moved their shivering children forward.

'Come on – room for two more,' the landlord said, holding the door open for Teddy and Jack as well.

They took off their drenched jackets and rubbed themselves down with the towels as they huddled near to the fire. Others who had been grouped there shuffled around to make more room, and for a moment everything seemed ordinary – a jumble of locals and holidaymakers, gathered in the bar on a Friday night. The candles on the tables flickered as the door opened to yet another bedraggled stranger, ushered in by the landlord and made to feel welcome. Teddy couldn't help but wonder if people in his own town would be so hospitable, but before his thoughts could continue Jack was prodding his arm, pointing to the floor.

'Look – look, old man,' he hissed. 'It's getting through.'

Teddy looked down at his feet and saw a thin wash of water covering the wooden parquet floor. He gazed around at the others, grouped and exchanging stories; they didn't seem to have noticed. He wondered should he say something, draw their attention, and was about to speak when a lad, no more than twelve or thirteen, came bursting through the door.

'It's coming through – the river's coming through the front door!'

For a moment no-one moved. Then, as if orchestrated, they rose and began to push their way forward. Teddy lost sight of Jack for a moment, but he was wedged in by the crowd with no choice of where he might go.

A torch beam played across them all, and the landlord shouted.

'It's fine, everyone – no need to panic. We'll just move ourselves upstairs. Take it carefully now.' He started to indicate with his hands, 'Back into the lobby then up the main staircase.'

They moved as one, following the directions, but as they edged into the entrance hall they saw water pouring through every crack and joint of the front doors. It was as though someone had opened a sluice, and they found themselves ankle deep, then knee deep, within seconds. The children had already been scooped onto shoulders and their carriers were pushed to the front and hoisted up the stairs. The small crowd followed behind, desperate to escape the violent cold water before it took hold of them completely.

Teddy's sleeve caught on the door handle, and for a moment he was held fast as countless bodies jostled round him, but someone behind tugged at his arm and somehow managed to release him. He waded towards the stairs, all the time looking round for Jack, but was taken with the momentum of the throng, striding and scrambling up the steps, desperate to be out of reach of the raging monster which they knew was just biding its time before it surged forward and flung open the doors. A child slipped and the mother screamed. Teddy was suddenly incapable, even though the child could have been within his grasp. He froze as he watched four pairs of hands reach down and pull the child up. A man took the boy in his arms and strode to the top of the stairway; the mother pushed blindly through, frantically trying to keep her child in view.

They funnelled their way into a large function room, some finding floor space, others perched on seats as they gathered their belongings and their companions around them. Teddy felt suddenly alone.

'Could I just borrow...?' He looked beseechingly at a young waitress, still in her black dress and white pinafore, who was half-heartedly waving a torch backwards and forwards.

He scanned the room with the light, looking for Teddy but, caught for a moment by the sight of the landlord, utterly exhausted, but still wearing his waistcoat and tie, handing out towels and blankets.

'Um – sir – I need the torch back now ...' the girl prodded his arm, and Teddy reluctantly returned it. He found himself a space on a window ledge as he tried to catch a glimpse of Jack through the flicker of candles and the waves of torchlight. He knew Jack would be fine – he had the nine lives of a cat - but Teddy couldn't help but think about the speed with which the water had taken over the ground floor.

Someone had had the forethought to grab Tilley lamps from the bar downstairs, and as they were ignited, people clustered round the tables to share the pools of light. It flickered across elaborately draped curtains and red velvet chairs scattered incongruously between the rag-taggle groups, like prim maiden aunts at a raucous family party. The crowd continued to build, filling the gaps between furniture, settling into every crevice.

'At last. I've been looking everywhere for you.'

Teddy looked up and there was Jack, hand on hip, reprimanding, as though Teddy had deliberately gone off

251

without him. He waved something in front of Teddy's face.

'Couldn't carry on without supplies.' Jack, obviously pleased with himself, held up a half bottle of whisky.

'I thought you'd be more worried about saving your skin,' Teddy snapped, churlishly wishing that Jack had had as much thought about rescuing him as he had obviously had for finding the alcohol.

They hunkered down in a corner, and sat in silence, each taking swigs from the bottle before Jack slipped it back into his pocket.

'Better keep some for later,' he said, and again Teddy felt rebuked, as if it was he who had purloined the bottle and was indulging in irresponsible amounts of drink. But there was no opportunity for any comeback. Jack had turned to the hopeful young woman who had wriggled in beside him, and was already chatting while Teddy, left to his own thoughts, began fretting about his papers and his reports, and how he was going to retrieve them from a hotel that might, by now, be under water.

He was brought back to the present by the incongruous cheer which arose from a small group at the far end of the room. Teddy strained his neck to see what was happening, borrowing a torch from a sturdy old dear who had also latched on to them, and was rewarded by the sight of a soaked and bedraggled young woman emerging from the crowd. It reminded him of a new calf being born, flopping, wet and bedraggled from its mother's body. He was slightly nauseated at the sight, but Jack quickly grabbed the torch and hauled himself up, eager to see what was going on.

A human chain had formed, and a second and then a third half-drowned body was manhandled back into the safety of the room; men at the front were swapping places as each in turn became exhausted by their efforts.

'Bit of a silver lining amongst all this chaos.' A heavy-jowled man in tweeds had dragged himself from the front of the group, and spoke breathlessly as he removed his sodden jacket. 'Water level's up to the window now; a few poor beggars are being washed this way and we've been able to hook 'em in.' As he flopped into an empty chair, another fellow, sleeves rolled up and exhaustion etching his face, staggered over to Teddy and Jack.

'We could do with a hand over here, gents – bit of fresh muscle wouldn't go amiss.'

He glanced back at the attempts of the small crowd to revive the latest dishevelled body, and Teddy glanced at Jack. Jack shrugged his shoulders and held out a hand to pull Teddy up.

'Only too pleased to help,' Jack said heartily, taking off his jacket and moving towards the window.

CHAPTER FORTY EIGHT

There was an almighty thunderous crash. The building shook and every person stopped in their tracks. The room fell silent, as if fifty people were holding their breath, as though concentrating on their stillness might prevent the next – possibly fatal - move. But it came again quickly, a shudder that felt as if a colossal pair of hands had taken the hotel and shaken it like a baby's rattle. More than one woman screamed; a child called out, asking the question they all wanted to ask.

'What's happening, Mummy? Why is the room moving?'

The silence fell again as fifty pairs of ears listened to the timber of the entire building groan. No-one moved, worried that their weight might be just enough to tip the floors and the walls into the floodwater.

For five full minutes they stood or sat as still as they could be. The creaking gradually faded and someone began counting, under their breath, like the moments between lightning and thunder; but there were no further crashes. Eventually one of the men crawled to the window and cautiously rose, peering over the windowsill.

'Dear Lord God Almighty' he called out, although it was not clear whether his words were in prayer or despair. 'We've been hit by a boulder – giant of a bloody thing; must be the size of a house.' He waved another of the men to take a look, and then they were all there at the window, craning and stretching to see what had happened.

A gabbling and chattering began, rising in volume, as the relief and shock translated itself into sound. Everyone was suggesting and wondering and "what-if-ing" until the babble became almost unbearable.

'Come on,' Teddy pulled at Jack's arm. They both walked tentatively to the window, and other men shuffled aside so that they too could look at the sight.

It took Teddy's breath away. Huge boulders had wedged themselves against the wall of the hotel, and a complete tree, uprooted from its original home, had jammed itself between the rocks, appearing bizarrely to be growing there amongst the mayhem.

'Here comes another one,' one of the men shouted out, pointing across the water. At first Teddy assumed that another boulder was headed their way, turned to move aside, but he realised that the man was pointing to what looked like a bundle of rags.

'Grab 'em,' someone shouted, and the surging of the group spurred Teddy and Jack to reach out as far as they could. They managed to haul a young boy through the window space, allowing him to slither through their arms to the floor. Others grabbed him, pulling him away and into the warmth of the room.

They turned, scanning the water with torches to search for others.

'Look – there,' someone shouted again, and they turned in the direction of his shaking finger. Another bundle was being tossed about in the cauldron of water, churning and eddying around the massive boulder. For a moment it swung away from them, and they gazed hopelessly as it seemed as though it would be taken straight out to sea. They swore, holding out helpless hands. But then the water flicked backwards on itself and the bundle came round again.

Teddy leaned out, as far as he could manage. The swirling torrent grabbed at him, and something, sharp and heavy, caught him full on the side of the head. For a moment it seemed as though the water had claimed him as well, as his torso drifted helplessly.

'Get him,' Jack screamed, and grabbed round Teddy's waist. Others took his legs and heaved, and he was back inside, face down on the floor.

He was aware of a woman bending over him, of his eyes not focussing on her blurred outlines. He could hear a voice, questions which he wasn't able to answer, and then a searing pain as someone touched his head. It might have been seconds or minutes - he had no idea – before he was able to raise himself to sitting.

Nothing was clear, but he forced himself to concentrate. There was a knot of men, still gathered round the window, and Jack – he knew that frame, that muscular back - Jack was there with them, in the thick of it.

And suddenly all Teddy wanted to do, in his frail and feeble state, was to stand close to him. Ignoring the protestations of the woman who had been tending him, he drew on every ounce of strength, pulled himself to his feet and staggered back to the window.

He was aware of the other men, grappling to hold Jack's legs as he stretched out of the open window. Teddy peered out into the night, with the torchlight playing across the tumbling water, unsure whether what he was seeing was real or imagined. Real he decided, as he watched in horror at the bundle being tumbled to and fro.

'We can get her,' he called, aware suddenly that Jack seemed to be hesitating, as if he had given up hope. But suddenly Jack was elbowing Teddy out of the way, ordering men to hold their torches higher so that he could see.

'It's alright – I've got her,' he shouted, thrusting himself forward. 'I just need to get a bit of purchase.' He brought a foot up against the window frame, and then seemed to stop, staring at the bundle which had now turned face upwards. Jack thrust himself forward again, grabbed the hands of the poor creature, and for a moment, before Teddy slid once more to the floor, he could see them locked together, as if about to dance.

CHAPTER FORTY NINE

Teddy groaned as he tried to prop himself up on his elbow. His head felt as if it had been repeatedly kicked in a street brawl, and his stomach churned. For a fleeting moment he thought he must have been drinking - a night out on the town with the boys - but as he took in the reality of his surroundings he knew that this was about as far from the truth as it could be.

He turned to see Jack still sleeping at his side, and his immediate instinct was to shuffle away, putting space between the two of them. But then he looked around and there were dozens of people sleeping alongside each other – quite naturally children curled in the arms of their mothers, but there were also women in the arms of women, and men propped against other men. He pulled himself to sitting, fluttering his eyelids in an attempt to shake away the double images which were dancing in front of him, trying to run his tongue around his parched mouth, rubbing his damp cold limbs. He had no idea of the time, except that the morning light was already pushing its way through mud-splattered windows. He tried to recall everything that had happened, and at first he thought he could remember, and then a moment later he thought he couldn't. His head was full of rocks and boulders and swirling water, and faces, but none of it made much sense.

A door opened somewhere, and voices began to build.

'Water level's gone down.' Someone on the other side of Teddy spoke; and then he heard it again, and then again as bodies began to stir, and conversations began to swell. He shook Jack's arm, anxious to talk, but Jack turned away, seemingly determined to hold on to sleep just a little longer.

All around Teddy people were standing, gathering their meagre belongings, looking towards the doors.

Jack eventually roused himself, and patted his pockets for cigarettes. He looked around, taking in what was happening.

'We need to get out of here, old man,' he said quietly, pushing away a water-stained blanket. As he gathered himself together, he continued muttering, but Teddy caught only parts of it – something about leaving the mayhem behind …. getting their stories straight, stories that might have to stand the test of time…

With a great effort Teddy pulled his aching body to standing, half-heartedly brushing himself down, running a hand through his hair. They shuffled along with everyone else but his head was thudding. They staggered out of the doors and down the stinking mud-covered stairs. The fresh air hit him like a slap, but that was as nothing, compared to the effect of the sight which greeted them.

It was as though they had been lifted in their sleep and taken to a war-torn state. They stared, open-mouthed, at the broken buildings, the boulders, the upturned vehicles and trees; the road had been taken away, and so had the bridge and everything which had been familiar, and it had all been replaced with heaps of brick and stone and wood, broken and splintered like kindling. It was almost impossible to walk; everything was covered in layers of mud, and there was not a flat surface to place down a foot. In every direction were hillocks and mountains of rubble and detritus.

Teddy found himself unable to move, jostled by those coming behind him, those who had not yet seen the nightmare which awaited them. But Jack had already stepped forward, had begun to clamber across the impossible landscape.

He had to sit down; his head was spinning and for a moment he had thought he could hear Atkinson's voice barking at him, asking for explanations; a wave of nausea washed over him.

Teddy forced himself to concentrate, trying to take in the scene around him, but other incongruous thoughts fired off in his head. Would they already know – at the Ministry – what had happened down here, would they still want his notes and graphs, would they expect him to explain all of this?

He needed to be able to point to his figures and say "look – this is where it all started", although even in his hazy state he realised his paperwork was probably out in the Bristol Channel by now. He wanted to be able to say "here's where it all went wrong," but he guessed that right now those were probably the last words anyone at the head of operations wanted to hear.

Teddy stood amongst the debris, totally helpless, searching around for some sign of Jack. He spotted him eventually, heaving himself up on a pile of bricks which only yesterday had been someone's home, surveying the scene. He seemed eager – like a child looking for the best spot on the beach, or the best vantage point at the match. Teddy found himself reluctant to join him, not wanting a better view of the carnage which had already rendered him incapable of action or speech. He realised he was shaking.

'What are you doing?' he called feebly to Jack, narrowing his eyes against the sunlight.

'Looking for the car,' he shouted back down. 'With any luck it'll still be drivable, and we'll be able to get out of here PDQ.'

Resigning himself to the fact that Jack had no intention of returning to him, Teddy tentatively began to move across the rubble, slipping as a child's tricycle dislodged itself beneath his feet. As he neared, Jack stretched down and pulled him up onto the ruins; he made a half-hearted attempt to look as well for the small black saloon, but his eyes weren't focussing; nor were his thoughts.

Jack looked at him, a wave of concern crossing his face as Teddy held his head in his hands. 'Tell you what, old boy – you hang around here, I'll go and try to track down the car.'

Teddy began to protest, but then realised he was happy to let the words dissolve in his mouth. He had no desire to fight his way across this nightmare, and he wasn't sure he wanted to see the car. He really just wanted to hide himself, to bury his head.

Jack strode away, leaving Teddy marooned on the pile of boulders. He started to pick his way forward, sliding and tripping, feet becoming wedged between the belongings which had fallen from the open sided houses, where beds were still made, clothes still suspended on their hangers from the picture rails. He couldn't help but stop and stare – the exposed wallpaper, and the chest of drawers hanging on the precipice of the open floors – yet it felt voyeuristic somehow, peering into the bedrooms of strangers. Eventually he found an upturned tin bath and perched himself there, unwilling to move any further.

Teddy knew that his car could be anywhere – in the same way that the bicycle perched on top of a fallen tree was "anywhere". But the thought of the car – and of Jack looking for it – made him think of Alice, and the dressing-down she had given him when she'd discovered Jack in their garage. He sniggered to himself, but then stopped abruptly, shocked that he could be laughing in the face of what was around him, floundering at the thought that if Alice had followed – if his suspicions had been right – then she would have been caught up in all of this as much as he was.

He watched disconnectedly as men in overalls sifted through the wreckage, starting to move some of it, trying at least to clear some sort of pathway. Teddy wondered vaguely about asking one of the men if they had seen a woman with blonde curly hair, but his thoughts were disturbed by Jack waving and yelling at him.

'No sign of the car, old man – but I have just spotted what might be the cavalry.' He pointed to a small group gathered at the top of what had yesterday been the road. 'I've just seen a truck taking people out,' he called over optimistically.

And so they joined the handful of waiting men and women - dazed, mud-streaked and crumpled, some still with blankets round their shoulders, others in clothes which looked as though they had been through the trenches of the Somme. Teddy looked down at himself, and then at Jack, realising for the first time what a state the two of them were in as well.

'Jack,' he said, as he made a futile attempt to brush mud from his jacket. 'About Alice ... do you think we should look for her – at least make sure she's okay?'

The battered farm truck had returned and was reversing towards them. Jack had started striding out towards it as soon as it appeared at the top of the hill, but now he stopped in his tracks, and turned to Teddy, his face pale and drawn. 'Look old man – you're in no fit state to go gallivanting anywhere. You couldn't even find your own front door at the moment.' He helped to release the tailgate, then clambered up onto the truck and held out a hand. 'Let's just get out of here – then we can think straight,' he said, but the hesitation in his voice was not lost on Teddy.

He looked back across the carnage. He had no desire to stay, but just walking away from all this – from Alice, if he really had seen her – it didn't seem right. But no sooner had he climbed up onto the back of the truck than the driver revved the engine and began to pull away. They wound their way up the steepest and narrowest of tracks, the truck straining with the weight of its load, but gradually, steadily, it ate up the yards beneath it and managed to carry them in a shudderingly slow procession up to Rockleigh.

Only two days before Teddy had taken the funicular up to this neighbouring village. It stood high and proud at the top of the hill, and had presumably avoided any of the flood damage – for as they clambered out of the truck it was as though they had travelled back to yesterday or the day before. There was no sign of water or mud or debris here – everything was as it had been on Thursday or Wednesday – before the rivers broke their banks and turned the world upside down. Every person who had been in the truck stood silently as they stepped down, taking in the scene of normality, unable to comprehend that within a few minutes they had travelled from carnage to calmness.

'Town Hall's just over there,' the driver was saying, as he prepared to make the journey back down the hill to collect his next load. 'They'll be able to sort you out.' And with that his exhaust billowed and he was gone.

Jack strode out, making his way in the direction the driver had pointed, beckoning to Teddy. 'Come on mate – breakfast is calling.'

Teddy looked up to see that there was a WVS van parked at the side of the town hall, where uniformed women with huge teapots were pouring out mugs of tea. They each took one gratefully, together with a doorstep of bread and jam, warming their hands against the cups as they drank. The sun had started to poke its way through the clouds, and although it was only the smallest amount of heat penetrating through to them, it was enough to generate some energy in Teddy. He wandered back over to the van and spoke to the older woman before rejoining Jack.

'What was all that about?'

'I was just asking where the nearest telephone kiosk might be …' Teddy noticed the look of surprise, maybe even dismay on Jack's face. 'I just thought that we … well, I … should make some effort to contact Atkinson.'

'What the bloody hell for?' Jack snapped. 'It's not as if they won't have heard what's happened … I should think the whole damned world knows what's happened by now.'

'Yes, but he might want to …'

'You gents might want to make your way inside before the next truck load arrives, otherwise you'll miss your turn' the older woman called out as she turned to refill her pot, interrupting Teddy's reasoning, and giving Jack a good reason to move on.

CHAPTER FIFTY

The Town Hall was as busy as a Bank Holiday market.

'It's like demob all over again,' Teddy muttered to no-one in particular, as he surveyed the sight. Women were unpacking bags and boxes, stacking shoes, piling clothes, efficiently sorting men's shirts from women's dresses.

Teddy's head had begun to throb once more, and he pressed his hand to his temple, massaging the pain. He felt a wetness on his fingers and realised it was bleeding, but as he pulled his handkerchief from his pocket he knew that he couldn't put the filthy mud-splattered rag against his wound. He looked around, but it seemed his predicament had already been spotted, because a woman in Red Cross uniform was bustling her way to his side, and took him by the elbow. She ushered him to a makeshift bed, collected a bowl and cloth, and began bathing his head, chattering about nothing in particular.

'Once I've finished with you, you must go and find yourself some new clothes,' she said as she applied some lint to his skin.

Teddy looked at her, aware that he was not speaking, unable to get his thoughts into any comprehensible order.

'Are you okay?' she said, lifting his eyelids and staring into his eyes before folding a blanket into a pillow and pushing him to lie back. 'Maybe this bump to your head was a bit harder than you thought?'

Gently but firmly she held Teddy's shoulder to the bed, insisting he stay where he was, and he had no choice but to view the room from his supine position. Eventually he spotted Jack, rummaging through a pile of garments, pulling out a shirt and then discarding it, searching for another.

'Where have all these clothes come from?' he asked as the nurse took his pulse, studying the fob watch on her chest.

'Oh – local people have been coming in since first thing, bringing stuff, but vans are starting to come in now from all over. Soon as the news went out on the wireless first thing this morning it seems the whole country wants to help. Red Cross went into action straightaway – and even Byremead hospital has sent over dozens of pairs of pyjamas from their stores!' She laughed as she went about her business, not phased at all by the generosity and kindness of others.

But it got to Teddy – this compassion for neighbours and strangers alike. He was sure that although Rockleigh hadn't been flooded, there would be those here who had lost people – missing or dead – and yet they were still digging in, offering what they had, whatever they could do to try to restore some degree of normality. He rubbed a hand roughly across his eyes as the nurse took away the bloodstained cloth and bowl.

'How're you doing old man?'

Jack had arrived at his side, presumably having waited for the nurse to disappear. He had changed into clean set of clothes, holding another bundle out to Teddy.

'Cast offs for the most part,' he was saying, pulling a face at the donated clothes, 'But I managed to sort out some of the best.'

Teddy looked at Jack. He appeared to have found himself a shirt and trousers which looked practically brand new. He took the clothes from him and struggled to sit up. But as he did so, a woman brushed past him, carrying a dress, chattering to a friend. The folded material over her arm triggered something in Teddy's head.

'That woman, Jack – the one … you know … that we couldn't help – in the water …?'

'Don't worry about that just now old man.' Jack helped him stand. 'Go and get yourself changed. I've been told that there's buses being laid on to get us all out of here, so the sooner you're ready the sooner we can be on our way.'

As Teddy pulled off his muddy trousers his head swam. He held on to a chair and let things settle, and as he did so he realised that all thoughts of finding the car seemed to have been forgotten by Jack; for a moment he was resentful, angry even. It was his car after all, and why should he just abandon it …? But he couldn't get his head round the logistics of it all, there was just too much to think about. Maybe they could come back in a few days and sort out the car, he thought vaguely as he pulled off his filthy shirt and slipped into the new one.

There were dozens of people milling about, waiting for one of the buses which were shuttling people away from Rockleigh and Rushcombe, and the hubbub of it all was too much. Despite Jack's protestations that they should stay where they were, keep their place in the queue, Teddy wandered over to a stone wall and let his aching body sink onto it. While he sat amongst the throng, fleeting pictures came and went in Teddy's mind - like skimming though a picture book, but allowing the pages to flick past so quickly that only a glimpse, a remnant of colour, or a shape, caught one's eye. But two things came back round again and again; one was Atkinson. The other was Alice. He screwed up his eyes, trying to shut out the images, but nothing would stop them appearing and re-appearing, sometimes blurring on top of each other.

If Alice really had been in Rushcombe, then she would have been at the mercy of the floodwater as much as they had. And where might she have been staying? - in the centre of the town, on the outskirts, in the path of the river, or tucked away in complete safety? He thought of the little terraces of houses he had seen which had been completely untouched by the ferocity of the water; and of others which he knew only too well were now just a pile of bricks and dust.

'What about Alice?' he blurted out.

Jack hesitated, just for a moment. 'We've already had this conversation old man...' He looked at Teddy, saw his expression. 'Look – we'd just be making things worse, if we went back down there – just getting in the way. And besides, the Army's arrived now – the woman on the WVS van said – they'll get it all sorted.'

There was something about Jack's expression which didn't sit well with Teddy, but Jack had already turned to a man with a clipboard, asking him questions about the buses and where they would be taken.

'Do you think ...?' Teddy grabbed Jack's arm. He had been about to challenge him, but just as he did a bus swept round the bend in the road and stopped to mop up as many as it could. They squeezed their way on, Jack finding Teddy a seat, then pushing his way down the aisle. Everyone was straining to be positive, but soon the banter died to a gentle silence as they pulled up the steep hill and were able to look over their shoulders at the sight of broken Rushcombe.

•

As they chugged across the moors Teddy stared at the sheep munching endlessly at the roadside, at a pony whisking its tail as it watched the bus pass by. There was a strange sense of calm, of nothing changed, and the raging river and the shattered town might well have happened in another century.

The bus wended its way back down the hills and through the villages, eventually dropping them at the station in Bankshead.

'Where do we go from here?' Teddy was rubbing his temples, looking helplessly at the crowds milling about.

Jack strode off in the direction of a harassed porter, who gestured this way and that.

'Down here, first left,' Jack repeated back his conversation. 'He said it might not be the best, but all the world and his wife are looking for digs right now.'

They found "Sunny Lawns", a down-at-heel house with a vacancies sign just about holding on to its fixings.

It certainly wasn't perfect, but it was a bed for the night, and a base from which to make arrangements.

As soon as the landlady had shown them their rooms, Teddy pulled his jacket back on. 'I'm going to try Atkinson,' he insisted, searching through his pockets for change.

'Well, I think you're completely bonkers, old man. He won't be expecting to hear from us – from you – for days yet.' He stopped, looking Teddy in the eye. 'But if it'll make you feel better – be my guest ...' And he slapped a handful of coppers onto the chest of drawers.

CHAPTER FIFTY ONE

The telephone booth at the station was in constant use, and there was a queue waiting – everyone wanting to let their families and loved ones know what was happening. He asked a porter, who directed him to another booth, further along the promenade.

It seemed to take an age to get through. No-one at the office seemed to be where they should be, no-one seemed to know what was going on. Eventually someone asked Teddy for the number of the kiosk phone, saying that they would get Atkinson to call him back as soon as possible.

He tried to look busy, pulling out a directory while he waited, blindly running a finger down the lists of names as he tried to ignore the vague smell of urine and the woman banging on the window. As soon as the phone rang he snatched it up.

'It's me – Hathaway,' he began, realising that he had no idea what he was going to say.

'Yes Hathaway – *I've* just called *you*. You and Frost need to …'

'We're in Bankshead, Sir,' Teddy blurted. 'We're unsure … I mean we don't …'

'Stop blethering Hathaway. Meet me at the Beach Hotel.' Atkinson's manner was terse. 'Five thirty.'

Teddy was taken aback. 'Um – well – will that be tomorrow … or when? Sir,' he added belatedly, in his confusion.

'For goodness sake, Hathaway. No, this afternoon. We need to get all this under wraps as soon as possible.'

The telephone went dead. Teddy absentmindedly pressed button B but no coins were returned to him. He drifted back to the shabby boarding house, his head full of pieces which he seemed incapable of fitting together.

'Atkinson wants to see us this afternoon,' he blurted out, almost before Jack had opened the door of his room. He plonked himself down on the end of the sagging bed and Jack came to sit beside him. He took Teddy's hand in his, stroking it gently, then pulling a finger towards his lips.

'Didn't you hear what I said?' Teddy snapped, pulling his fingers away. 'How the hell can Atkinson get here …' He paused, thinking. 'You don't think he's been down here all along?'

'Wouldn't put anything past him.' Jack said vaguely, searching his pockets for cigarettes. 'Probably had second thoughts about giving us the job – well, you the job.' He looked sheepish. 'Keeping an eye on things himself, knowing him.' Jack inched closer, massaging the flesh on Teddy's thigh, but Teddy pushed him away.

'But what if we've done…'

'Look old man,' Jack sat up, lighting two cigarettes, handing one to Teddy. 'Nothing you or we have said or done could have made the slightest bit of difference to what happened over there.' He pointed vaguely in the

273

direction of Rushcombe. 'It was the powers-that-be that came up with the damned cloud seeding idea - and Operation Cumulus; we just followed orders … then watched the awful bloody fallout.'

Jack went on, not giving Teddy a chance to argue. 'Atkinson just needs to debrief, get a view from the ground, that's all.'

Teddy looked at him, frowning at the fact that Jack seemed to know too much about Atkinson and his plans.

Jack glared back, took an imperceptible breath and continued. 'I've seen it before - standard practice for operations like these,' he said airily, lying back, blowing out a long elegant stream of smoke. 'Get this done, maybe we can wangle a few extra days down here - you know, R and R – before we're back to the grindstone.' He paused. 'In the meantime, I'm bloody starving – let's go and find a bite to eat,' he said, jumping up again and pulling on his jacket.

•

Every café and public house in town was packed to the rafters. They tried at least four before they found one with any space at all, and even then they were pushed into a corner on the smallest table at the Copper Kettle. Teddy could see that Jack was about to start some sort of altercation with the harassed waitress; he pulled at his sleeve.

'It's fine miss – we're just grateful to get a bite to eat.' He looked meaningfully at Jack, who had the grace to look shamefaced. They ordered, and sat back, both suddenly exhausted. They sat in silence for a while, each thinking their own thoughts, but the sight of the large plates of egg and chips and a pot of tea revived their spirits.

'I've never been so glad to be out of somewhere,' Jack said, squeezing four chips into his mouth at once. 'That must be the hardest night of my life.'

Teddy was about to point out to him the hardships that he and so many others had endured during active war service, but he knew this would mean nothing to Jack. Instead he said grudgingly, 'Well, I s'pose it wasn't easy – dragging them out … and that one – you know – the one you couldn't save …'

Jack's face immediately coloured up and a look of terror was momentarily obvious in his eyes before he managed to get himself under control. Nevertheless, he was squirming in his seat, glancing constantly towards the door like a cornered rat.

Teddy put down his knife and fork, stared at his companion. 'What?' he demanded.

'No – nothing – just that it was a bit - you know – harrowing …'

'But that's not all is it?' Teddy, now oblivious to the cooling plate of food in front of him, was staring at Jack.

'No – I just meant - you know …' Jack too had stopped eating. He looked away, scanning the crowded room.

'No, I don't bloody know. Look at me,' Teddy hissed as he grabbed Jack's wrist. What I do know is that no-one looks embarrassed or guilty for having tried to save someone's life.' He tightened his grip, forcing Jack to turn back to the table. 'Something happened there …something you're not telling me.'

275

Jack was silent. He looked at Teddy with eyes that flickered from guilt to sorrow to fear and then turned away again.

'What in God's name was it?' Teddy saw the couple at the next table staring; realised that the manageress at the counter was glaring, that his voice was too loud. 'Tell me,' he struggled to reduce his voice to a whisper. 'Tell me, or I'll create such a scene in here …'

'I had to do it.' Jack murmured, head bowed.

'Had to do what?' It was all Teddy could do to contain himself.

'It was too good an opportunity, Teddy – a chance like that would never have come round again.'

A knot clenched tight in Teddy's stomach, a fear that they were on the tipping point of something from which there would be no going back. He stared at Jack, waiting for him to go on.

'I couldn't believe it when the water spun her round.' Jack was almost inaudible. 'But once I knew, once I was sure it was her – then there was only one thing for me to do.'

'Once you knew …once you knew it was *Alice* …. Is that what you're saying?' Teddy could barely let himself say the words; he wanted so much to be wrong.

'She *knew* everything Teddy,' Jack murmured. 'You told me yourself that she'd been rooting about in your study. And once that whisper came back to us that she had been asking around about silver iodide … well, we knew the cat was out of the bag on that score as well. And then, when you saw her down here, when she started to follow you that day … it was obvious that she was on to *us* as well …'

276

Teddy was stunned. He couldn't believe what he was hearing, didn't want to hear any more, and yet he couldn't let Jack stop there. He dug his nails into the pale skin on Jack's wrist.

'Don't you think we were condemned, right from that moment? You seem to be forgetting old man ...' Jack's voice was barely audible. 'What we're doing – it's against the bloody law for God's sake ...You've only got to look at what they did to Turing... chemical castration, and that was him getting off lightly ...I don't know about you, but I couldn't face any of that ...'

A woman in a blue mackintosh brushed past, then hesitated. 'I don't suppose I could join you...?' she began to ask.

Teddy closed his eyes, unable to speak. Jack managed a "Sorry, love – not a good moment ...". She sighed irritably and turned, looking around for another space in the crowded restaurant.

Teddy thumped a fist against the table. 'I can't believe what I'm hearing here.' It was all he could do to stop himself shouting. 'That woman – my *wife* actually - was fighting for her life in that bloody awful water and some stroke of fate brought her to the hotel window.' Teddy buried his face in his hands, rubbing vigorously as if trying to scrub the images from his mind. 'You could have saved her and you chose – you actually made the decision not to ...'

'I couldn't Teddy...for God's sake man, haven't you listened to a single damned word I've said?'

'Of course you bloody could, you bastard; of course you could.' Teddy exploded, grabbing Jack's lapels, shaking the other man like a dog with a rabbit, not caring who might be watching or listening.

They barely escaped being thrown out. It was only Jack pleading their overwrought state after their experiences in Rushcombe that saved them, but they paid quickly and got out anyway. Teddy fled, like a released wildcat, towards the promenade and disappeared into the shadows of an unlit shelter. Jack pursued breathlessly, arriving just as Teddy smashed his fist into the walls for the first time, a primeval wail of despair escaping from him. He tried to take Teddy in his arms, but Teddy pushed him away, wanting no false comfort and Jack was left to sit helplessly, staring out to sea.

It was he who eventually broke the silence, but Teddy's head remained down, his eyes closed, no sign that he was listening. 'She only had to say one thing – you must see that … just one word out of place, one slip of the tongue – and we'd be completely finished.'

Teddy's head snapped up at this; his lips were clamped together, as though he couldn't trust himself to let any words come out. But Jack was in full stride.

'…And do you think *she* would have been happy – to carry on playing the part of your wife, but knowing full well that she was continually living a lie?'

Teddy still made no response, just staring, glassy-eyed, into the night.

'Well – do you?' barked Jack, frustrated that his words were having so little impact.

But Teddy was elsewhere. He was back in his garden, watching Alice, resplendent in old clothes and wellington boots, carrying a tray out for him, coffee slopping into the saucers, but a happy grin lighting up her face. He angrily brushed a tear from his cheek.

'I know it's upsetting, old man,' Jack rubbed the sleeve of Teddy's jacket. 'But what you've got to remember ...

'Upsetting! You have no bloody idea,' Teddy shook his head, and then a fresh bout of anger seemed to surge up in him. 'And I know what I've got to bloody remember – that's easy,' he shouted, spittle flying from his mouth. 'I've just got to remember that *you* didn't want to suffer the same fate as Turing, because of course this is all about *you* ...'

For a moment Teddy's thoughts went to the newspaper on his desk, the trials that poor man had had to go through for his illegal homosexual acts; the shame, the ignominy, the disgrace. He knew he wouldn't be able to face a similar treatment either, that it wasn't just Jack being cowardly ...but Alice - she didn't deserve any of this ...

'And it's not just us, Teddy.'

Teddy's looked up as Jack's voice brought him back to the present. What the hell was the man talking about? Surely nothing could be worse than the position he was already in; he felt as if he'd done ten rounds with Freddie Mills, with every punch directed straight to his head.

Jack continued, swivelling round to look Teddy in the face. 'There's the job as well ...'

Teddy felt his head sway, as though someone had landed yet another blow, this time to his jaw. 'What the hell do you mean – "the job"..?'

'All that,' Jack hissed angrily, waving his arm towards the coastline. 'That was a bloody disaster to end

279

all disasters – and you seem to have forgotten that, despite the reality, we might not be seen as innocent bystanders …'

Teddy opened his mouth to speak – to argue again with Jack, but Jack grabbed his shoulder, pointing towards Rushcombe. 'The rains, old man – this flooding – we did that, with our experimenting and our cloud seeding. This is all down to us.' His voice was raw, and it finally cracked.

'Well you've changed your bloody tune … it wasn't *us* who dropped the silver iodide, remember? We were nowhere near any of that stuff. We didn't …. We were just monitoring it all, you said … and the river bursting its banks – none of that was down to us … you said.'

'But it doesn't matter who actually pushed the button,' Jack said frustratedly, 'Alice saw all that stuff in your study – went through all the details presumably. She knew what was going on – she could easily have gone to the newspapers, blown the whistle …'

'But she wouldn't – not Alice …'

'Oh come on old man - hell hath no fury like a woman scorned – that's what they say, isn't it? Who knows what she might have done after she found out what you'd been up to, what was going on behind her back.'

Teddy sat in silence, another tear running down his cheek. He took another swipe at the wall of the shelter, smashing it again and again, until blood dripped from his knuckles.

Eventually Jack put out a hand to stop the onslaught. 'I know it's a shock – and an utter bloody awful mess…' he paused. 'But she could have slaughtered us, Ted - not to mention dropping The Ministry and the Government in the proverbial as well. This way …' Jack sighed heavily, looking out to sea. 'This way, you've done your bit for your country – by trying to keep the whole thing under wraps; and at least she'll be saved the humiliation of … of us. And give it a few days and you'll be the loving widower, pining the loss of his sweetheart, and everyone will love you for it; no-one will expect you to look at another woman – you're set up for life …'

Teddy slumped back against the wall, dazed at Jack's outpouring, at his matter-of-factness, and finally unable to control the tears his sobbing. 'But we were just doing what the likes of Atkinson told us…' He pulled a sleeve across his face, wiping the mucus and the tears. 'And I *did* love her Jack … in my own stupid, perverse, incompetent way I loved every inch of her. And now she's gone.'

CHAPTER FIFTY TWO

Teddy had no real memory of finding their way back to their lodgings - only of sitting on the bed while Jack removed his jacket from him and produced a bottle of whisky from somewhere, pouring him a large slug into a tooth-mug. He suspected Jack's motives were more to do with shutting him up than in consoling him, but he was desperate for the oblivion it might bring, if only for a couple of hours, an escape from the constant pictures in his head of Alice being wrestled by the water and taken off into the angry sea. He had taken the whole lot down in one go and then curled up on the eiderdown, fully clothed, and watched in his dreams as he saw himself in a boat, rowing hard and rhythmically against the tide, following her crown of blonde curls, but never getting any closer.

'Teddy ... Teddy, wake up. We need to get going.'

He was aware of someone in his dream shaking his arm, vigorously pushing his shoulder. He tried to push them away, tell them that he was about to save Alice ... but when he looked back she was gone.

As he raised himself from the bed, what seemed like the worst hangover of his life engulfed him even though he only recalled taking one glass from the bottle Jack had held out to him. He shook his head, trying to remember where it was they needed to be. He was aware of Jack's voice, somewhere in the background, giving some sort of commentary, and snatched at the word "Atkinson". The name forced him to open his eyes, trying to focus, but the room around him was more of a hazy dream world than the world he was trying to pull himself from.

Eventually, with some heaving and pushing from Jack he managed a dizzy path to the musty bathroom on the landing. He stared at himself, aware that his reflection was swaying in and out of focus in the mirror; he gathered a handful of cold water and threw it at his face, then again and again, until he felt some sort of consciousness returning to him. He ran water through his hair, feeling the cold drips on his scalp as he looked at himself in the foxed mirror. He looked half dead, he thought, as he peered at his ghostly green skin, splashing more water on his face, desperately trying to wash away thoughts of Alice, just for the moment, so that he could prepare himself for the meeting with Atkinson.

•

They pushed their way through the doors of the Beach Hotel at two minutes to half past, to find the older man already pacing the foyer. Apart from cricket whites they had never known him in anything other than a dark grey suit, but here he was in shirt sleeves, a knitted waistcoat and jaunty blue tie, as if he had been interrupted in his stroll along the promenade. But the man's mood was anything but casual, Teddy thought, as he watched him check his watch and the hotel's clock as he marched towards them. With few words he beckoned them down a short corridor and led them into a small room. The walls were scuffed and there was a motley assortment of furniture which looked as though it had been abandoned in other parts of the hotel, and had found its way there because no-one knew quite what to do with it. A young waitress followed them in, as if she too had been lurking in the hallway awaiting their arrival, but Atkinson barely waited for her to place the tea tray on the table before shooing her from the room.

'Okay – no sense beating about the bush,' he said, pushing his fingers hard into his brow. His face was dangerously red, like a bottle of homemade wine about to explode. He looked back and forth between the two men, as if deciding where to pounce. 'Hathaway – I want every detail - from the day you arrived. A blow by blow account of the whole thing – every kit and caboodle.'

Teddy's head was still pounding. He was struggling to remember anything of what he had planned to say. He fiddled with his shirt cuffs, trying to dredge something – anything - from his mind; he sipped at the tea to wet his dry mouth, and eventually – amongst much sighing from the more senior man - managed to meander his way through to the end of his story, leaving out only the parts which involved Alice.

'And you're sure that's all - you've omitted nothing?' Atkinson probed, for some reason looking at Jack rather than Teddy, but Teddy was excused from answering by a knock at the door. The hotel proprietor stuck his head round, like a hungry bird of prey.

'Yes?' Atkinson snapped.

'We'll be serving dinner shortly,' the man used an exaggeratedly superior voice. 'I wondered whether you gentleman might be joining us, Sir?'

Jack looked up optimistically, but his hopes were dashed.

'A plate of sandwiches and another pot of tea will suffice – in here please,' Atkinson said, indicating the pictureless room in which they sat.

While they waited the older man began to go through the whole story again, this time with Jack, making endless scribblings as his pen scratched its way across the pages of his foolscap notebook.

The refreshments, when they arrived, seemed to ease the tension, just a little.

'Did you notice anything odd or unusual about the sky on the Friday?' Atkinson's tone was almost conversational as he picked up a fishpaste sandwich.

Teddy and Jack looked at each other, as if this might be a trick question.

'It's just that – members of the public have been reporting a strange cloud formation – almost mushroom-like, they say – appearing in the sky on Friday afternoon?'

Both men were silent, weighing the repercussions of truth against lie.

'Well – was there or wasn't there?' Atkinson barked. 'The two of you were on the ground – *supposedly* making observations – did you see something or didn't you, or have the British public at large been telling fairy stories?'

'Yes, yes – there was something a bit odd – about the sky – now you come to mention it,' Teddy squirmed at his omission of this presumably significant meteorological detail. 'Was that something …?' He had been about to ask about its connection to their project, but Atkinson was already on to his next point.

'And then there was the smell …' he said, looking again between the two men.

'Smell?' Jack looked offended, as if he personally was being held responsible.

'Yes. Those far-too-observant members of the public again.' Atkinson's tone was sarcastic. 'Reported noticing a distinct sulphur-like smell – you know, like bad eggs.' He stared hard at Teddy, then sighed in exasperation as he almost threw his cup back into its saucer.

The cup continued to rattle as Jack launched in.

'Well, now you come to mention it, there was a bit of a whiff on Friday afternoon, but I just put it down to drains or rotting seaweed or some such …' He looked innocently up at Atkinson as he took the last sandwich.

Teddy could see that Jack's flippant approach appeared to be doing nothing to calm his boss's agitation. 'Is it significant, sir?' he asked, trying to show what he hoped would sound like professional interest.

'Significant? Never mind bloody "significant",' Atkinson bawled. He looked around, presumably aware that his voice could probably be heard outside the door. He continued in a stage whisper, rising out of his seat as he stabbed his finger repeatedly at Teddy. 'The fact that it has featured in neither of your reports is what is "significant" to me.' Atkinson he slammed his notebook down on the table, his face almost purple. 'And even more to the point – more "significant" in your words

Hathaway - is the fact that neither of you has seen fit to mention *Mrs* Hathaway.'

CHAPTER FIFTY THREE

It took them some time to unravel that particular knot.

Teddy sat, open-mouthed, as he realised the significance of what his superior had just said. But it was left to Jack to put into words the stream of questions which were surging through his own head.

'So – sorry, Sir – but I'm just a little confused here...' Jack had leant over to help himself to a Rich Tea biscuit, but stopped mid-track. 'Are you saying ... you were aware of Alice – Mrs Hathaway - being here all along?'

Atkinson gave the briefest of nods.

'But that means ... so why didn't ...and anyway, what about? ...' Jack blustered dramatically, his thoughts appearing to run faster than his mouth could deal with them, and eventually he had to stop.

'But - how did you *know* she was here?' Teddy's voice was almost inaudible, even though a silence had fallen on the three men.

Atkinson sat, fingers laced together in an arch. He pondered, looking from one man to the other. 'You must have realised that the news of Alice's prying into the question of Silver Iodine came back to us as quickly as it did to you. People are still used to keeping that sort of information – any sort of information - to themselves, after six years of wartime activity – "Careless talk cost lives" and all that. Anyone appearing to operate outside of the "rules" tends therefore to stick out like the proverbial sore thumb.' He took a sip from his teacup, in no rush to continue, although Teddy and Jack were staring hard at him.

'Once the matter had come to our attention, we started to keep an eye on your wife.'

Teddy looked up, surprise and then shock spreading across his face.

'Actually she made it quite easy for us,' Atkinson went on. 'We knew of her connection with Miss Moorehouse – she was the one given the task of finding out about the chemicals after all – and by monitoring her, and your wife, we were easily able to put the pieces together.' He put his cup down and poured more tea. 'And of course, you gave us plenty of information yourself, Hathaway.'

Teddy looked indignant, as though he had been accused of some sort of disloyalty to Alice.

'Oh - it was nothing deliberate on your part – but you did keep *mentioning* things.'

Teddy started to but in, but Atkinson held up a hand. 'For example - you happened to say in the office that Alice was thinking of staying with a friend in London, while you were away – and although this didn't seem to bother *you*, it set alarm bells ringing for the rest of us.' He paused, watching Teddy's incredulous face. 'But it did make things a whole lot easier, in a way.' Once we knew your wife was on the move, we were easily able to follow her.' He put the cup down again, deliberately.

'And of course by that point, we had guessed that she planned to follow you to the West Country.'

Teddy's head was throbbing again. The double vision that had started yesterday had returned, and he was struggling to take in most of what he was hearing.

'But ... even *I* didn't know that that was what she had planned,' he said eventually. 'As far as I was concerned, she was going up to London to stay with ... with Lucy ... and then ...' Teddy paused, realising he hadn't given the slightest thought to what Alice would be doing after that. '... Well, I suppose I assumed that she would just go back home ...'

'And that everything would return to normal?' Atkinson asked, a strong note of sarcasm accompanying his words.

Teddy opened his mouth to respond, but recognised that he had no argument - nothing of any value to say, anyway.

'Quite,' said Atkinson. 'Moving on then –' He looked between the two men, as though they might simply be discussing the weather forecast or the best menu choice at Lyon's Corner House. 'Of course we can't condone Frost's actions at the hotel – far from it ... and, needless to say, the Department extends its condolences to you Hathaway – but under the circumstances, Mrs Hathaway's ... demise ... is of some considerable help to us, in trying to contain the situation.'

It was then that it hit Teddy. He realised he had been completely naïve, but now he knew he was on his own – that Jack was not only supported by the Establishment – indeed seemed to be part of the whole thing - and that whatever he thought, Alice's passing had simply become a convenient conclusion to an irritating problem.

He couldn't sit there any longer. He rushed from the room, knocking a cup as he passed, felt the tea spilling on his leg, heard the clatter of the china as it hit the floor; but he couldn't spend another minute with either of those two men.

•

It was only the setting of the sun which gave Teddy any idea of how long he might have been sitting on the bench on the seafront. He found himself staring at a squawking seagull, which was fighting for pieces of bread - discarded sandwiches that had been tossed onto the promenade path. He was aware of someone sitting down at the opposite end of the bench, someone who tipped his head back to take in a long breath of air, and realised from the familiar sound that it was Jack.

Jack didn't speak but shuffled down the wooden slats, handing over a lit cigarette.

'I know this sounds crass,' he said eventually, 'and that the whole thing absolutely stinks, but it really is for the best.'

CHAPTER FIFTY FOUR

'Post. Come on Edward – sit up. There are things to do.' Isobel thrust a pile of letters at Teddy. 'Moping around is not going to do the slightest bit of good. Things need to be sorted out.'

Teddy's eyes remain closed as he listened to his mother sweep from the room. She had been waiting for him at the house when he had returned from Devon, dressed in an appropriately mournful grey dress, and had burst through the front door at some ungodly hour every day since, organising, checking on the daily woman she had drafted in, tutting. When there was no-one else around but him there had been a considerable amount of tutting, although Teddy had noticed that this turned instantly to sympathy and cake as soon as he was "on show" to visitors.

He had been given compassionate leave from work since the nightmare of the West Country and had taken to dozing on the sofa, in the middle of the morning, and again in mid-afternoon; anything to fill the haunting gaps between waking and returning to bed. The scent from the pink and purple flowers which his mother had arranged and set on the table penetrated his nostrils – the heady perfume of sweet peas – and his head was immediately filled with images of Alice, tending her garden.

'Come along.' Isobel's voice jolted him. She didn't shout. Teddy had never heard his mother raise her voice; she didn't need to. She had a way of talking, steadily and decisively, which was far more ominous that any screaming banshee of a woman. 'There are bills here that need your attention – urgently by the look of most of them.'

The skin of Teddy's eyelids pulled as he attempted to open his eyes. They were heavy, caked together, and he rubbed at them as he glanced over at his mother. She was plumping cushions, brushing imaginary crumbs from the armchair.

'She has no idea,' he thought, 'About money or Alice or the damage that has been done. None of it had made even the smallest mark on her, he realised, as he watched her gather up newspapers from the floor, and return books to shelves, pulling and pushing at the volumes until they were in uniform lines. The fact that she had lost a daughter-in-law, had a son who was in all manner of difficulties – none of it seemed to have caused even a scratch on her resilient skin.

'I can't Ma – you see ...'. He knew he needed to tell her about his precarious financial situation, knew he needed his parents' help to drag himself out of the mire. His mouth was open and the words were on his lips, but Isobel was already taking the conversation down another lane.

'Nonsense. It'll do you good to focus your attention on something mundane. Come along – chequebook, pen ...' she chivvied, as though marshalling a disobedient dog. She dropped the letters into his lap and whisked away his half-finished coffee.

Reluctant to raise himself, Teddy eventually lifted the bundle of post to his eye-line, dropping each letter in turn to the floor, as he glanced at the profusion of red ink. Each one that is, until he reached a white rather than a brown envelope. He sat up slightly, pulling a freshly plumped cushion behind his head. The name and address – *his* name and address – had been neatly written in block capitals, black ink. There was nothing on the back and he ripped it open. Inside was a postcard – a picture of the Doone Valley on the Devon moors. On the reverse, in the same block capitals, was the address repeated, as though the sender had intended to send the postcard in the usual way, and had then changed their mind and enclosed it in an envelope. He read the message, then read it again -

SILENCE IS GOLDEN, BUT IT IS NOT FREE.	MR E HATHAWAY 26 PHILLIPS LANE COTFORD BEDFORDSHIRE

'What the hell is that supposed to mean?' Teddy sat up, speaking aloud, then immediately turned to check over his shoulder for the whereabouts of his mother, but Isobel had already left the room. He returned the card to its envelope and stuffed it in his trouser pocket; whatever it meant, he needed to consider it in peace without Isobel interfering.

He gathered up the pile of bills from where they had fallen and went to his study. It was the first time in weeks that he had been in there, and he tried not to think of all that had happened in the interim as he took in the stale tobacco smell mingling with the dust. He turned the captain's chair away from the window and began slitting open the brown envelopes. He even picked up his pen and began to write cheques which he knew full well would be returned. But the questions the postcard had raised were nibbling at his brain, awakening something which has been slumbering since he had returned from Rushcombe. He pulled the envelope from his pocket again and flipped it over, checking the postmark. "London SW1", dated yesterday. He didn't know anyone in London - not any more. 'Although that doesn't mean a thing,' he muttered. Anyone could have bought the card, had it for months or years in a drawer; could have given it to a stranger on a train to post ...

After a fruitless half hour he collected up the bills and stuffed them into his desk drawer. As soon as Isobel was out of the way he would ring his father – perhaps arrange to meet him in town, and do his best to set down a tale of woe which would have his father transferring money into his account. Douglas had always had a soft spot for Alice, and he was probably finding this whole situation as difficult as anyone. It wouldn't take a lot – a reminder of the possibility of Alice lost in the floodwater – to get him to roll over and cough up the much-needed cash.

●

Over the next few days Teddy waited anxiously for every postal delivery to drop on the mat. He even met the postman out on the drive on more than one occasion, eager for some further information that might throw more light on that first message. Most days just brought more brown envelopes, and then another white square arrived on Tuesday, and Teddy rushed immediately to his study, keen to open it in the privacy of his room. But it was only from Aunt Margery, hoping that all was well and inviting him to Hove for afternoon tea. Just like her sister, he thought, she too was living in never-never land, and had no idea that things would never be "well" again. By Thursday, when he had almost given up, when he had gone back to the original missive again and again, and checked a dozen times to make sure he hadn't imagined what he had read, or missed some vital clue, there amongst the postman's bundle was another plain white envelope, another "London SWl" postmark.

He rushed to his study, slammed the door, grabbed the paper knife and slit open the envelope.

This time, it was not a postcard, but an illustration – something which looked as though it might have been cut from a child's picture book; it was a colourful drawing of a bevvy of magpies, or whatever the

A HALF SHARE IN EXCHANGE FOR
SILENCE. A FAIR SWAP
WOULDN'T YOU SAY?

8/9/52, 18:00 HOURS.

collective noun might be - with a sheet of white paper glued to the back.

At first he thought that the date and time referred to the timing of the message, but then Teddy checked the calendar. The 8th wasn't until tomorrow. Did that mean that something was going to happen tomorrow then, and at 6 o'clock?

The something which had been tickling his brain since the first message, now became a full-blown itch. He flicked the letter over to look again at the illustration; seven birds. Was that supposed to mean something? He screwed up the picture, launched it at the waste paper basket, then, after a few seconds of staring at it, he hurriedly retrieved the paper, smoothing out the creases and folding it into the back of his diary.

CHAPTER FIFTY FIVE

He slipped into the hallway, checking for signs of Isobel; he could hear her upstairs, giving instructions to the Daily woman over the noise of the ancient vacuum cleaner.

He snatched at the telephone, the number he needed long ago familiarised so that there had never been a need to enter it into his address book.

'Jack – Jack we need to talk.' The words tumbled from his mouth too quickly, blurring into a whirlpool. 'I need to – we need to meet … urgently…'

'Okay, okay old man, take it easy. I thought we weren't …?'

'This won't wait Jack. Meet me at …' Teddy's mind, unaccustomed in the past few weeks to making any decisions or arrangements, was suddenly blank.

Jack filled the void. 'Bricklayers Arms, six o'clock – will that do you?' he said, ending the call before Teddy could say more.

●

'You do know they listen in, don't you?' Jack slammed his whisky glass down on the table.

'Who?'

'The girls at the exchange ... well, MI5 for all I know - but you can't go blabbing your mouth off. The point is, anyone could hear ...'

'But I didn't say anything incriminating – I hardly said anything at all for that matter.'

'But you would have done – if I hadn't cut you off ...' Jack signalled to the barman for another round, despite Teddy's full glass. When the drinks had been set down in front of them and the landlord had returned to his post behind the bar, Teddy whispered behind the fingers covering his mouth.

'She's alive Jack.' There was a shiver in his voice, perhaps glee, perhaps panic.

'Who's alive?'

'Alice,' Teddy hissed, his hand shaking as he moved to pick up his glass.

'Don't be ridiculous man.' But despite his scorn, Jack returned his own glass to the table untouched.

'No really – I've heard from her. Twice, in fact, two letters ...'

Jack searched Teddy's face, examined his whole demeanour. 'Look man – I know that this has all been a bit of an ordeal – and the mind can play funny tricks when it's under pressure, you know.'

But Teddy's face was set, would broker no argument. Jack turned, reached out, but then let his hand drop into his lap again.

'You saw the state of that floodwater.' Jack's voice was gentle now. 'There's no way on this earth that she could have survived without being ... dragged out to sea.'

'I'm perfectly aware of what I saw.' Teddy snapped. He wanted to add "And I'm perfectly aware of what you did, too …". But instead he simply said 'You can't argue, Jack - not with two letters.'

'Let me see them then,' Jack demanded, his demeanour changed.

'I don't have them with me.'

'What? You summon me out here and then you don't bring along the very thing you want me to talk about?'

Well – no – I don't really know why I … I suppose I just thought you'd take my word …'

'I'll come back to your place then – they are there I presume?' Jack, ignoring Teddy's feeble reasoning, was already draining his glass, a challenging expression on his face.

'Of course they're there …'

'Come on then - let's go. Let's get this sorted.'

'But my mother's still at the house … we can't …'

'Poppycock. If it's as you say – then this takes precedence over any snide remarks of your mother's.'

Teddy still had a drink and a half to finish. He made a half-hearted attempt with the emptier of the two glasses, while Jack took a swig from the other.

'Come on, leave those man – we need to go.'

•

Isobel opened the door before Teddy had a chance to put his key anywhere near the lock. 'There's a Detective Sergeant Christie here to see you.' She looked pink, harassed, scanning the street for signs of prying neighbours.

The two men looked at each other.

'I'll eh – I'll go and get a pint of milk from the corner shop,' Jack said. 'You'll need more milk I'm sure Mrs Hathaway – with all these visitors.' He'd gone before Isobel could point out that she had two pints already, on the cold slab in the pantry.

Teddy hesitantly pushed his way into the lounge. 'Is there any news?' he asked, genuine interest in his voice.

'No sir, regrettably not.' The detective sergeant seated himself again, turning his hat between his hands. 'I came to let you know that we've spoken to everyone on the list you gave us – and while several people knew that your wife was going away –' He made a show of consulting his notebook, ' "for a few days", it seems that there was some confusion.' He spoke the last word with some degree of scepticism.

Teddy looked askance at the prematurely balding man.

'Well – shall we say that none of the individuals concerned appears to know *exactly* where Mrs Hathaway was going.' The officer waited expectantly, presumably for Teddy to throw more light on things, but he was met with silence as Teddy slipped into his now familiar chair by the grate, deflated once more.

'I don't suppose ...' The sergeant paused long enough that Teddy eventually lifted his head. 'I don't suppose *you've* had more thoughts, sir, as to where she might have gone?'

'I think he's told you already officer, that apart from going to see this Lucy person in London, Alice mentioned no other journey.' No-one had noticed Isobel re-entering the room. 'Surely, constable, it really isn't necessary to keep bothering my son like this? Isn't it

301

obvious that he's still in shock, after all that's happened?'

'Sergeant, Ma'am ...' the officer tried to correct her.

Isobel looked over her spectacles at the policeman, trying to fathom what it was he was saying.

'It's Detective Sergeant – Ma'am. And we do feel it's important to keep in touch. Sometimes – after a shock, as you say – people take days – weeks sometimes – to remember something vital.'

Both officer and mother looked across at Teddy, who could only bury his face in his hands.

CHAPTER FIFTY SIX

'Where did you get to?' Teddy had been walking the streets of Cotford, looking for Jack. He had tried The Red Lion and The Swan, and even the run down Bootmakers Arms and had been about to give up, when he found him at last, sitting on a bench by the river, throwing stones at the water.

'Well, I needed to keep out the way, didn't I? Didn't know how long old PC Plod would be there, so I thought I'd better make myself scarce for a while. Didn't want him questioning *us* as well.' Jack managed to get a stone to skim three times, bouncing half way across the river in the wake of a group of rowers. 'Anyway, did he have anything useful to say?'

'There's still no trace of her …'

'Great. So we can forget all this nonsense about "she's still alive" then?'

'She is.' Teddy was insistent, tired of Jack's scepticism. He pulled the two white envelopes from his inside jacket pocket, and held them out.

Jack looked taken aback that the letters actually existed. He took them in silence, and pulled the contents from the top envelope.

'Well – this could be anyone,' he laughed, flicking a finger at the card. 'Just some tactless person having a laugh at your expense.'

'It's her – I know it is. Open the other one ...'

Jack read the second card; and then re-read.

'See – it's obvious,' Teddy was animated, now that he had presented his evidence.

'Well – I wouldn't exactly say obvious.' Jack turned the message over. 'What makes you so sure that this is ...?'

Teddy butted in before Jack could finish. 'At first I thought the same as you – somebody playing some tasteless joke. But something kept niggling at me, once I saw that second letter. And then I remembered; did I tell you – I'm sure I must have done - that story that Alice kept going on about? I'm sure I did ...'

'Well, if you gave me some idea what you're damned well talking about I might be able to give an opinion,' Jack snapped.

'The birds – the ones she saw in the park that time – you know – after I told her I was going away.'

Jack shook his head, sighing. 'Not a clue old man, not the foggiest idea what you're ...'

'Magpies.' Teddy shouted irritably. 'She saw a group of magpies in the park, she said it looked like a funeral service ...' Teddy looked over at Jack, waiting for some sign that he remembered the story. But Jack just shrugged.

'It made quite an impression on her at the time. She went on about it for days.' Teddy paused, closed his eyes, the thought of Alice threatening to overwhelm him. He took a deep breath, and started again. 'And now she's sending a picture of magpies – giving me a sign without having to actually say it's her. And the rhyme – don't you see – one for sorrow, two for joy…'

' … Five for silver, six for gold, and seven for a secret, never to be told …' Jack finished the verse off. He sat in silence for a moment, rubbing the back of his head. 'Well, I suppose I can see how you might come to the conclusion you have … and shock can do strange things, as I said before …'

'Don't give me any of your mock sympathy – I know you don't believe a word of it…'

'Actually Ted, I was going to say –,' Jack hesitated, obviously still thinking something through.

The two men sat in silence for a few moments, until Teddy could contain himself no longer.

'Well – out with it – what were you *actually* going to say?'

'I was going to say – if this really is Alice … and you know that we would have to find some way of proving it …?' Jack said, pointing to the envelopes. 'But if this is Alice – well then, I can see this might be a good solution all round.'

Teddy stared in disbelief. 'What – Alice coming back?'

'That's not what she's asking for, is it old boy?'

'But…'

'She's asking for money – something to set her up presumably, something so that she can start again - without you.'

'But I don't have any money …'

'Hmm.' Even Jack had to call a halt to his theory at this obvious statement of truth. He picked the letters up again and re-read them both.

'Insurance,' he suddenly exclaimed, stabbing at the letters. 'You must have life insurance?'

'Do I look like I have money to spend on something which might never happen…?'

'Well, we're all going to die old boy, so strictly speaking that's not true– but Alice – if this is her - does seem convinced in these letters that there's a fortune just waiting to be had …'

Teddy snatched the letters back; reread them, several times. He shuffled them between his fingers as his mind whirled.

'Mother,' he said eventually. 'Alice did keep wittering on about Mother asking her for stuff. And then,' Teddy suddenly became animated, waving his arms around as he remembered more. 'Then one day Mother demanded to have birth certificates - mine and Alice's – but she was being so damned mysterious about what she was up to that I lost my rag with her, and Alice made me invite them to dinner to make it up …'

'There you are then. Alice was ahead of the game. She knew what your Ma was up to – or she wheedled it out of her. Either way,' Jack said, taking back the letters, 'Now it looks as though she's planning to reap her reward.'

'Reward?'

'Oh Teddy, you can be so incredibly bloody dim at times. Do I really have to spell it out? She's offering to keep shtum about everything – about us, the cloudseeding, the – "incident" with the rescue, the whole damn shooting match, in return for the money. She's obviously planning to disappear and start a new life … presumably.' He considered the point. 'That's what I'd do anyway – if I was her.'

Both men sat staring at the darkening river, almost imperceptibly flowing. Perhaps in both their minds was that other river, raging, totally out of control, destroying all in its path, including - up until this moment - Alice.

'But there is just one fly in the ointment,' Teddy said eventually, still staring at the water.

Jack sighed, shaking his head, but Teddy continued. 'She's not actually … you know ...' Teddy struggled to get the word out of his mouth. 'And if she's not … dead, there's no death certificate, no proof. So then surely, no insurance money …?

CHAPTER FIFTY SEVEN

Jack had the look of someone who had already churned the same thoughts, except more quickly, more effectively, and not only produced his pound of butter, but had it wrapped and ready for sale as well.

'There are times, Edward Hathaway, when you are indisputably – ' He scoured the riverbank, searching for the right word; 'Look – we work with the Air Ministry, do we not?'

Teddy nodded. 'Yes, but …'

Jack ignored the interruption. 'And so, my dear man, what better organisation to make people disappear? There's plenty of stories doing the rounds …'

'Stories? What stories?'

Jack pressed on, ignoring Teddy's interruption. 'People vanishing or popping up in fortunate or unfortunate places. Rogers was telling me only the other day about some bigwig at the Admiralty …' He stopped, glancing over at Teddy, checking that he was listening. 'He's writing a book about some poor dead fellow who they trussed up to look as though he had just drowned, and they chained a briefcase to him, full of supposedly revealing documents…'

'I don't see what that's got to do with us – or with Alice,' Teddy snapped.

'They staged all that just to fool the Nazis – but my point is, anything's possible, old chap. The right people in the right places can make just about anything happen – if they choose to.'

'Well, that's as may be.' Teddy looked as though he didn't accept a word Jack had said. 'But why would they *choose* to do something like that for us? You're talking there about people who might make the world of difference to national security, not two-a-penny people like us. *Especially* people like *us* …they'd just as soon send us the same way as Turing, wouldn't they? And from what I hear on the QT, he did far more for this country than the two of us will ever do.'

'Forget the "us" for a minute, old man.' Jack took a packet of Senior Service from his pocket and tapped a cigarette on the box. 'They've got a whole lot bigger fish to fry than that. Surely you must have thought about what would happen if this whole damned thing came to light – the cloud seeding I mean.' He struck a match and let it catch the end of the cigarette, inhaling deeply. 'A national disaster is bad enough – but a disaster created by a Government Department, 34 lives lost, a whole town and community wrecked…'

Teddy tried to speak, but Jack held up a hand.

'It was a disaster on a massive scale – but one which could have been totally averted if we'd experimented somewhere else – some remote island in the middle of the ocean - or waited until the conditions were better, or not sent the bloody plane up at all…'

As the steam of Jack's argument dissipated, Teddy let out a sigh. He massaged his temples, fingering the scar there which was still refusing to heal. The list of victims which had been in all the papers flashed in front of him - Robert, aged five, Richard aged eleven, and all the others – men and women, old and young. And all for what? Operation Cumulus had been cancelled, almost immediately after the affair in Rushcombe, but that had done nothing to help the broken families, or to distil the terror that had shaken a whole country.

'So we just go ahead and get Alice "dealt with"? Is that what you're saying – take the money and tie up all the loose ends? It just doesn't seem right, Jack – us taking money when …' Teddy looked up, unable to shake the thought of those families from his mind.

'But it won't bring them back old man – not a single house or shop – or child. Whatever you do next – whether you claim the insurance money or live in saintly poverty – it won't change a single iota for any of them … except perhaps for Alice of course,' he said, grasping Teddy's shoulder.

As the two men sat in the evening gloom, the toll of the dead of Rushcombe came into Teddy's mind again. There at the bottom of the list of losses, he had read three words which might now just be the answer to so many things – "An unknown woman".

CHAPTER FIFTY EIGHT

Teddy had been pacing the hall long before the six o'clock deadline which had been given in the letter. He wasn't sure whether to expect a visitor or a call, but either way he wanted to be in the right place to intercept before his mother could get involved. In the end it was the telephone which had summoned him, but when he heard the unfamiliar voice he had almost told the caller to ring back, to clear the line so that Alice would be able to get through when she rang.

'It's Lucy …'

Of course it was. Had he really expected Alice to be there, bright and breezy, outlining her expectations as though they were discussing arrangements for the annual cricket tea?

'I said, it's Lucy – are you still there Teddy?'

'Yes – yes, I'm here. Just wasn't expecting it to be you, that's all.'

'Did you get the letters?' The cogs began to slot into place in Teddy's mind, but conversation continued - efficient, business-like; she wasn't going to allow awkward silences or hushed tones.

'I – well – yes…' Teddy had been about to prevaricate, to keep to non-committed phrases until he had heard what Lucy had to say… but somehow, now the moment had come, it seemed quite pointless.

'So you do understand – what is being asked of you?' There was no indication in Lucy's voice that she and Teddy had ever been acquainted, but he remembered; even in their carefree days, her decisiveness, her assertive manner when there were things to be done – and so he was sure that this was all of her doing.

Nevertheless, Teddy was struggling to deal with the matter-of-factness, the lack of any … well emotion, he supposed it must be. He wanted to ask questions, to know more about Alice.

'How is …? What's …?'

'It's probably better you don't have the details, Teddy.'

'But …'

'Teddy,' she started again, an exasperated tone in her voice. 'If someone comes asking questions, what are you going to say?' She paused, waiting for her words to sink in. 'At least if you have no facts to give you can't drop yourself in it – or anyone else for that matter.'

Teddy noticed that she hadn't mentioned Alice by name – in fact hadn't referred to the situation or arrangements in anything other than the vaguest of terms.

'Can we get this settled as quickly as possible?' She carried on as if the previous few words hadn't been spoken. 'Do you understand …?'

'Yes,' he butted in. 'Yes, I know what she's asking for …'

'And you'll go along with it – with the deal?'

He was silent for a moment, felt the lump in his throat which was preventing his words from coming out.

'I – hhmm,' he coughed, trying to clear his throat. 'She ... she can have what she's asking for ...' It's the least I can do, he wanted to say, but didn't.

'It's the least you can do.' There was anger now in Lucy's voice, just a hint, as though she were doing her best to keep her feelings at bay, but enough to confirm that she was appalled by the run of events, was fighting on behalf of dear Alice, who, Teddy realised, probably wouldn't have done any of this herself.

'Yes ... yes, of course,' Teddy stuttered. 'But I'll have to – I'll have to speak to ... to someone – to make it all happen ...' He'd been about to say "make it all right" but that would never be the case.

'How long will that take?'

Teddy was struggling to get his thoughts in order. 'I'll speak to someone tomorrow – get the wheels in motion. But I don't know how long that will ...'

'Well, I'd suggest as quickly as you can,' she interrupted. 'She has nothing, in case you'd forgotten. I'll call again in two days.'

He guessed she was about to put the receiver down. 'Lucy – just a moment – before you go ...' A thought had occurred to him and he had to speak before he talked himself out of it. 'How do ... how do I know that she's ...'

He heard her sigh, unclear whether it was in sadness or disgust. 'You'll have to take my word.' There was nothing for a moment, and then she sighed again. 'I'll send something,' she said. And with that the line went dead.

●

The two of them went to Atkinson. He and Jack had talked long into the night, aided by whisky, but Teddy had been unable to get his head round the right form of words.

In the end it was Jack who did most of the talking. He was pretty good at it, Teddy thought, as he listened to him outline the situation in flat factual terms; he could just as easily have been explaining a budget proposal or an AGM report – but it was exactly what was needed – no emotions, no ifs or buts.

Atkinson seemed remarkably unsurprised. Teddy hadn't looked up at all during Jack's speech, afraid that if he lifted his eyes from the hands resting uselessly in his lap that it might break some sort of charm; but when Jack had finished and there had been no explosion of words from the older man, Teddy tilted his head and stole a glance from the corner of his eye.

Atkinson was sitting in his customary position, hands steepled, nodding almost imperceptibly.

'Hmm' was his only sound for some minutes. Teddy wanted to jump in, to fill the silence, to re-explain what had already been explained, but Jack signalled to him to hold fire.

'Well – it's a fine state of affairs,' he paused, obviously considering his choice of words. 'But not totally unexpected,' he said eventually.

Teddy's head shot up. 'Do you mean you …'

But Jack put out a hand, silencing him once more.

'No,' Teddy shouted, pushing Jack away, 'This is not – I can't just pretend, like the rest of you, that any of this is normal …' He stood, picked up his hat, turned to the door.

'Sit down Hathaway.' There was a threatening note in the quietness of Atkinson's voice.

'Teddy.' Jack waved him back to his seat. 'We can't sort this out on our own,' he said, tilting his head meaningfully towards their superior.

Teddy slouched back into the empty chair.

'Leave this with me for a few days, Hathaway.' Atkinson continued as though there had been no interruption to their conversation. 'We'll have words in some of the right ears.' He picked up his fountain pen and moved some papers towards him. 'Nothing more to be said at the moment.' And with that he began writing.

CHAPTER FIFTY NINE

It wasn't until the Thursday that Teddy got the okay. He'd been called into Atkinson's office – without Jack this time; he had sidled into the polished quietness, wanting to ask the how's and where's of it all but there was no small talk, no invitation to sit down in the hard wooden chair in front of the desk.

'It's all settled,' Atkinson said, handing Teddy a manila envelope.

His hand shook as he reached out for it.

'It's all there – everything you need.' Atkinson picked up his pen.

'But - Sir – how do we deal with … I mean - there's no …certificate.' He was reluctant to say the word death. It still felt to him as if Alice had simply gone away, a little holiday perhaps, with her girlfriends – and that one day soon she would bustle through the door, talking about dinner and her vegetable patch.

'It's all sorted.' Atkinson put the pen down again. 'You may remember that some bodies at Rushcombe were never recovered – and that one in particular was found but could not be identified – she was listed just as "unknown woman"?' He looked at Teddy, not wanting or needing any answer, but simply indicating that the context of the facts need not be spelled out. 'Well, that all worked quite well for us, in the circumstances.' He took the pen and rolled it between his fingers. 'We can never announce it formally of course – too many repercussions – but we've managed to convince the powers that be that there was good reason to think that that unidentified person might have been … Mrs Hathaway.' He took a sip from what must have been cold tea on his desk. 'Took a bit of arm-twisting, I can tell you, but we managed to get a death certificate issued – and that's what really matters.' He looked up at Teddy as though he expected another outburst, but Teddy was still trying to absorb it all.

'So it shouldn't be a problem with the insurance company – but you'll have to sort that bit out yourself – it'd look damn strange if the Ministry got involved in that bit of business.'

Teddy stood, staring at his superior, the brown envelope still shaking in his hand.

'Well, come on man – no time like the present.' Atkinson's tone was gentler than his words. 'Get yourself along there now and let's get all this sorted.' He almost smiled. 'Report back as soon as things are completed.'

•

And that was it. Teddy went through the motions, filling in forms, accepting the lines of grim faces and the mounds of condolences. It had actually helped to think that Alice really was gone – and, as far as his life was concerned, she was. He would never – could never – see her again, and the sadness this brought to him stood him in good stead when he was faced with any sort of

317

officialdom. Thanks to his mother they had even managed a funeral – well a memorial service at least – and with the hymns and flowers most people seemed to accept it as one and the same. Friends of his mother cooed and fussed over him, and here and there they sent a spare daughter with a fruit cake or a dry Victoria sponge, all of whom he could legitimately turn away in the name of grief.

●

The insurance cheque had slid anonymously through the door with the rest of the post. When Teddy first saw the figures written there, he had to admit that there was a moment when he was tempted. He could, in those few minutes, have easily pocketed the whole payment, and walked out of the door to a new life of his own. But it didn't take long for his conscience – and, more convincingly, the thought of Lucy – to get the better of him, and he walked briskly into town and directly to the bank, knowing that most of his own half would barely cover his debts. His mother was in the process of signing his grandfather's house over to him – presumably happy now that Alice wouldn't be getting her hands on it. But Teddy didn't want to stay there – didn't want to stay anywhere in Cotford for that matter. He thought he would be better losing himself in some anonymous conurbation somewhere – and selling the place might get him solvent again, blur the financial tracks, so that his mother wouldn't query the disappearance of so much money. But for now he would stay on – until everything was settled at least.

It had felt strange, sitting in his study once more – at the desk that had contributed so much to the whole sorry story – but, as he watched the ink from the pen flowing into the words on the cheque, Teddy felt some strange comfort in being there, in being able to make some recompense to Alice for all that had gone before.

He tore the cheque from the book and blotted it carefully; for some reason he didn't understand he patted the cheque – wanting really to plant a small kiss on it – before he slipped it into the envelope.

It wasn't in Alice's name of course – it wasn't even in her new name; he had no idea what that would be, and he never would, he supposed – but between Atkinson and Lucy they had arranged where the money was to go, and how it was to make its final journey to Alice.

He placed the stamp carefully in the corner and picked up his jacket from the back of the chair. Without a word to his mother he left the house and sauntered down the road, glad to feel the autumnal breeze on his cheeks. A new season - a new beginning perhaps. He was reluctant, at the last moment, to allow the small envelope to drop into the post box, as if it were a final farewell, a last wave goodbye. But as his fingers finally let go, he heard a whistling from the other end of the street, and looked up to see Jack, leaning against the tree which was just beginning to change into its russet coat.

EPILOGUE

Della watches as the visitor places the expensive chocolates on the table and puts the purple and pink sweet peas into the old woman's hands. She fingers the petals, holding the scented blooms to her nose.

When she first worked here Della had assumed that the man was her son – a son who didn't visit often. But as she has come to know her, the woman has mentioned, in her melancholy moments, only one child – a child who had been lost before its birth.

He greets the white-haired woman gently with a soft kiss to her cheek; he holds her hands in his, his troubled expression relaying to Della that he has unhappy news. He pulls something from his pocket – a small piece of paper - and watches as the woman unfolds it. She searches the table, and the man finds the magnifying glass and hands it to her, looking away as she scans the cutting.

'So – he never re-married,' she hears the woman say as she turns to look at the younger man. 'Never had a child, or found a "special someone" as your Aunt Josie would have said?'

'Apparently not,' he says, taking her hand in his once more.

'It was your mother,' she hears the woman's words. 'I wouldn't have done any of it – wouldn't even have thought of it - without Lucy, you know.'

He looks as though he does know, as though he has heard the story many times, but still he nods and answers.

After he has gone the woman sits, her mind and her vision a long way from home.

Della has seen her this way before, and fetches the book from her room - the only thing which seems to bring her solace.

Journal
April 1956

I didn't think I would ever be able to return, and yet all the time, since I left Lucy's, something has been pulling me back to this part of the world. More than once I had climbed aboard the bus, and then, just as the engine shuddered into life, my stomach churned and I'd rushed past the other eager travellers and jumped off before the bus had chance to leave.

Just last week I finally managed it. I stayed on the bus for the whole journey, gripping the seat in front until my knuckles turned white, staring through the window at anything which would distract me – the sheep scattered across the fields; the ponies on the hill - trying not to think of what was to come.

Stepping down at the end of the journey felt as if time had moved backwards - to that day, four years ago, when I had stepped off the same bus. My eyes turned to see if the girl – the one who had directed me - was still clearing the tables on the lawn; and immediately I spun round in the direction of Mrs Westcott's house. By some strange quirk of fate it had remained standing when many higher up had been taken by those dreadful waters. But I couldn't go there – there was no way my legs would carry me in that direction - but even if I had wanted to see that house again, with all the memories which were wrapped up in it, I couldn't have made myself known to the poor woman, could I?

I didn't want to admit to myself either that she might not actually be there. I had thought about her many times, feeling so much guilt that I hadn't been able to hang on to her or stop her from being taken by the floodwater; I had scoured back copies of the newspapers, over and over, but there was no record of her being found. I can only hope that she, like me, experienced some sort of miracle, and survived. But of course I am no longer the Mrs Hathaway she would remember, and I would not have been able to explain to her who I am now, or why. So I kept on my dark glasses and my sun hat and mingled with the tourists, all the time fighting to lay the ghosts of everything which had happened there.

Journal
September 1956

Now that I have broken the nightmare, I have been able to come back here again. I know others might thing it strange – macabre, even – but there is something surprisingly therapeutic about this place – perhaps in

322

the way it has so quickly rebuilt itself - that makes me feel I too can eventually move on.

Sitting on this bench, away from the town but still by the river, I find it - healing, I suppose you might say - to go over everything which has happened, and I realise I need to tell the story one last time. I have told it only twice – first to Lucy and Josie, and then to Lucy again, at her insistence, when she was dealing with the whole thing – and now I realise that there is no-one else I can tell the facts to, it is left to this journal to be my confidante.

•

I was barely able to get through one day into the next, even once they'd patched me up; the bruises and the beating I'd had from the rocks and the unrelenting river were all that occupied my waking hours. My ankle and my ribs had been broken, and my arm – but luckily my left one, so I could still manage the simple tasks of tea or toast, but anything more was completely beyond me.

It wasn't just my useless limbs which held me back; my mind was everywhere. And of course the child never arrived. At first I thought I could deal with it – after all, I had denied the poor thing's existence since the very start, but as I slowly came to terms with my own impossible survival it made me think about life and mortality and about what might have been … a boy or a girl? Teddy's looks or mine? The thoughts multiplied in my head, and often took me by surprise, particularly the longing for a daughter which I hadn't known was there, and which crept up and almost smothered me, so that on a daily basis I had to force myself from considering names.

323

When they had first dragged me from the shallows I was really not in this world at all. I had no recollection then of what had happened and quite honestly I was glad to have that blankness within me so that I need give no thought or consideration to anyone or anything.

But gradually, as my body came to heal a little, so did my mind, and small snippets began to re-appear, like snapshots recovered from the back of a drawer. They questioned me – very gently of course – those who had found me and nursed me, keen to link me back to my past, to where I belonged. But the more the pictures returned to me, the less I wanted to go back. Increasingly, I couldn't even bear to think of Teddy's name, let alone his face.

I knew though that I couldn't stay with those kind generous people for ever, and eventually I pretended to recall Lucy. She had been on my mind for some days – and Josie too, of course. The three of us had been such a gang, in our WAAF days, each complementing the other, never apart except when work dictated.

So when I was up and pottering in the kitchen one Tuesday morning I made mention of Lucy's name and how she had "suddenly" come to my mind. Of course they wanted to know everything – and I could see that they were clinging to her like a life raft, a way out of their predicament, despite their kindness. I genuinely struggled at first to remember her address, but then, like a switch, it came to me, and I found I could recount the whole incident of getting lost and the corner shop and the two lads and the happiness of being in Lucy's company.

•

They found her surprisingly quickly. Apparently a bored girl at the telephone exchange tracked down Lucy's number with little difficulty. And then it was as though a trolley had been put under me – one of those wooden carts that boys loved to make from pram wheels and discarded wood – and I was launched back into real life with a speed that made my head spin.

It was only with Lucy's gentle prodding, over days in front of her comforting fire ... I never seemed to feel warm enough after everything that had happened ... that I came to acknowledge that the baby no longer existed. And once she had got me thinking about life as it once had been – what seemed a decade before – then she began to push me for details of how it had all come about.

She invited Josie for the weekend, and I was so delighted to see her smiling face that I didn't at first realise that they were effectively ganging up on me.

Of course the tale of my "almost-rescue" was the thing that decided the two of them. I had turned down a trip to the Lyons Corner House at Marble Arch – feeling that a bus trip, even with my fellow amigos, would shake my bones more than I could bear - but felt that I could make it as far as the teashop on Wandsworth Bridge Road, close to Lucy's flat.

The two of them were outraged when, over tea, I quietly told the tale which, in my own mind, had happened to some other woman, or maybe not even in the real world. And immediately Lucy's determination took over. Where I was happy – prepared, at least – to leave it all hidden in some dark corner of my mind, she was determined that some serious reparation must be made.

They nagged and cajoled me for details – for some way of getting from Teddy what they felt I was rightfully owed. I despaired, because I knew they wouldn't give up until the matter was settled. Maybe it was their constant pestering, but eventually Isobel and her demands for birth certificates and information came once more to the forefront of my mind. This had been exactly what they needed, and between them, Lucy and Josie quickly established the possibilities of insurance money.

I wanted to walk away from it all – in fact, it was the first time since my rescue that I had been so sure of anything – but the two of them were persuasive, and I was becoming increasingly conscious that I couldn't hide away in Lucy's box bedroom forever.

And that was it. Lucy sent off the postcard to Teddy – although it was Josie who had recalled my story of the magpies in the park, and, thinking that it would be sufficient to make Teddy realise that the request was genuinely from me, found a suitable picture, in a jumble sale book.

•

The two of them seemed to revel in the challenge, while I sat back and waited for some sort of backlash. If I knew Isobel she would be on to the whole thing like a shot and would have them all tied in knots before they knew what was happening.

But after the phone call, Lucy just turned to me and smiled. 'Wait and see,' she had said; 'You just wait and see.'

I have no idea how they managed it – how they persuaded an insurance company to pay out for someone who wasn't actually dead – and it was that thought which shocked me most. The fact hit me so hard I couldn't breathe ... that I would never – could never – be Alice Hathaway, ever again.

It set me back, even once I saw proof that the money had come through.

Josie sat with me quietly one Saturday – we had taken a bus to Hyde Park and slouched in deckchairs on the grass in the warm spring sunshine, and she began slipping names into my head ... Shirley or Patricia or Margaret. I didn't want any of them, didn't even want to consider it, but I knew I had to be someone else.

Della looks in on all "her ladies", just before she leaves for home. The woman is still there with her journal, but this time she is writing rather than reading.

Journal
June 2001

Write your memoirs they are always saying - before it's too late. And they bustle on, collecting tea cups and half-eaten biscuits, and I wonder.

I suppose I do have a story to tell ... the circumstances of my "renaissance" certainly might attract a passing curiosity ... but who will really know or care about the effort it took to seize hold of my life, to find myself a job at a minor prep school, where fortunately they thought more of life experience than paper qualifications, and where there was a certain prestige attached to the title of "war widow" which I had assumed?

And did I find solace with other men? I'm sure the pages might be turned to find an answer to that question. Yes, there were some – dalliances, you might call them – but I never allowed them to go further. I thought, I suppose, that I might be stretching my good fortune, by drawing attention to myself amongst all the formalities a marriage would entail. Or maybe that was always an excuse? I can't deny that I enjoyed the freedom of my single status ... I was happy to watch the years come and go, like the children in my care, and mostly I was content. Just now and then I would wonder what might have been - and what had become of Teddy.

And then today Lucy's son came to see me, bringing chocolates and glorious sweet peas – my favourites. He took my hand and whispered.

'Mother asked me – she made me promise – to tell you, if she was no longer here to do it herself.'

And then, as if he couldn't trust himself with the words, he pulled a small piece of paper from his pocket. It was a newspaper cutting and I had to find my magnifying glass to be able to read the minute print.

"Edward William St John Hathaway – passed away peacefully on 27th May 2001. Husband of the late Alice Margaret, and friend to many, he will be missed by all those who knew him."

The date of the funeral service had of course passed, but I re-read the detail behind the words.

I had never been convinced that Christopher - Jack - would stand by him. Life would have quickly taken him

328

elsewhere, to something, or someone, more glamorous and exclusive than Teddy. I was sure I had seen him some years ago, standing at the shoulder of some minor politician who was being interviewed on the television. It could have been someone else of course - we all change so much over the years - but there was something in the man's stance, in that smirking expression, which had Christopher's stamp on it.

The cutting set me thinking – about my life, and all the people in it; the parts with Teddy, and the parts without. The people I knew, and the people I only thought I knew...

But enough – I'm sure that's more than enough, and I'm becoming maudlin.

Suffice it to say I had a life – perhaps a better one than most; I was given a second chance, and I hope that some at least would think that I made good use of it. I hope it has done justice to the "unknown woman" whose title I have gazed upon so many times on the roll-call of the dead of Rushcombe, and to whom I owe so much. She will never know me ... and perhaps none of us know who we really are, until we are asked to face up to the darker corners of our lives.

POSTSCRIPT

As an eight year-old I was taken to Lynmouth, and was so engaged by what I saw there and the story I was told, that I went home and painted pictures of the boulder-strewn river. There will be many others who know the West Country – or who were born in the fifties or earlier – who will also be familiar with the story of the Lynmouth floods which devastated that small town.

This book owes much to those dreadful events, and although Rushcombe isn't strictly Lynmouth I have 'borrowed' parts of the town, and of course the events of 15th August 1952. None of the characters (with the exception of Alan Turing) are based on the real people of the town, or elsewhere – and are strictly products of my imagination.

The story of 'cloudseeding' remains controversial. It appears that such techniques were in use in the 1940s and 50s – and have been used in other parts of the world more recently – but the MOD have always strictly denied that such experiments were being carried out in the West Country – or at the time of the Lynmouth floods. Although I have done some research, this part of the story is speculation on my part, but the weather conditions prior to and during the fictional flood are based on the conditions on Exmoor and in Lynmouth during those few days in August 1952.

I am grateful to the Met Office for the information they have provided, and to the BBC Radio 4 article 'The Day They Made It Rain'. I found the books 'The Lynmouth Flood Disaster' by Eric R Delderfield and 'The Lynmouth Flood Disaster' by Tim Prosser of great help, as was the information provided at the Lynmouth Flood Memorial Hall. I am also grateful to Andrew Hodges for details regarding Alan Turing, and for providing a copy of the relevant article from the Alderley Edge and Wilmslow Advertiser. Invaluable also was an article on the "Weatheronline" site regarding cloudseeding, and the BBC archive which provided a variety of information about life in the 1950s.

Huge thanks are due to the many people who read or listened to all or part of this book and provided valuable feedback to improve the story, and particularly to Karen Mahony and Margaret Ingall. Thanks also to Terence Sackett for his help in producing the cover. Finally, and most importantly, I would like to acknowledge the people of Lynmouth – to those 34 who lost their lives, to those who lost their homes and loved ones, and particularly to the 'Unknown Woman' listed in the toll of the dead, who inspired this story in the first place, and whose life I have imagined here.

Printed by Amazon Italia Logistica S.r.l.
Torrazza Piemonte (TO), Italy

13358058R00194